*For David,
my cemetery stommpin' buddy.
Here's to tomato soup and Cheez-Its!*

CASEY DANIELS

DON of the DEAD

A PEPPER MARTIN MYSTERY

AVON BOOKS
*An Imprint of HarperCollins**Publishers***

This is a work of fiction. Names, characters, places, and incidents are products of the author's imagination or are used fictitiously and are not to be construed as real. Any resemblance to actual events, locales, organizations, or persons, living or dead, is entirely coincidental.

AVON BOOKS
An Imprint of HarperCollins*Publishers*
10 East 53rd Street
New York, New York 10022-5299

Copyright © 2006 by Connie Laux
ISBN-13: 978-0-06-082146-3
ISBN-10: 0-06-082146-9
www.avonmystery.com

First Avon Books paperback printing: June 2006
First Avon Books special printing: March 2006

Avon Trademark Reg. U.S. Pat. Off. and in Other Countries,
Marca Registrada, Hecho en U.S.A.
HarperCollins® is a registered trademark of HarperCollins Publishers Inc.

Printed in the U.S.A.

10 9 8 7 6 5 4 3 2 1

I have to admit, the first time Gus Scarpetti spoke to me, I didn't pay a whole lot of attention. After all, the guy had been dead for thirty years. How much could he possibly have to say?

DON of the DEAD

"'Spirited' Pepper Martin brings a delightful new dimension to sleuthing. There's not a ghost of a chance you'll be able to put this book down. Write faster, Casey Daniels."
USA Today bestselling author Emilie Richards

"Casey Daniels's *Don of the Dead* is a humorous and highly entertaining expedition into mystery and the supernatural . . . well seasoned with ghostly delights . . . A charming, imaginative mystery that transcends the boundaries of time, death and predictability, peppered with some delightful romantic twists."
Linda O. Johnston,
author of *Nothing to Fear but Ferrets*

"A spooky mystery, a spunky heroine, and sparkling wit! Give us more!"
Kerrelyn Sparks, author of *How to Marry a Millionaire Vampire* and *Vamps and the City*

DON
of the
DEAD

Chapter 1

I have to admit, the first time Gus Scarpetti spoke to me, I didn't pay a whole lot of attention.

After all, the guy had been dead for thirty years. How much could he possibly have to say?

"Hey, doll baby!" He called out from the back of the crowd that was gathered around me, and though I'm usually pretty quick on my feet, I was so freaked when I saw him that I was speechless.

I glanced over my shoulder at the black marble mausoleum that contained the worldly remains of Gus Scarpetti. I looked back toward where this Gus Scarpetti wound his way in and out of the clumps of tourists waiting for me to begin the day's talk: "Cleveland's Famous Dead."

Dead being the operative word.

I reminded myself of that fact while I watched Scarpetti sidestep between two blue-haired ladies. "Doll baby. Hey!" He gave me the once-over. Like I'd been hearing since I was thirteen, I was too tall for a girl. Five eleven. Just about the same height as this guy. I also happened to have a size 38C bust.

Guys always noticed. Even guys who were pretending to be dead guys.

Scarpetti stared at my chest for a while and he smiled when he looked me in the eye. "You got no manners? I'm talking to you. The least you could do is say hello."

"Hello." I answered automatically. I was still trying to figure out who concocted a joke this lame. Whoever it was, I had to give him (or her) credit. Where they found a Gus Scarpetti who looked exactly like the Gus Scarpetti I had seen in the pictures in the cemetery's research archives was a mystery to me.

The guy was shaped like a bull, compact and big-boned, with a nose that sat on his face at an angle, a souvenir of his early years working as mob muscle. He had a football player's neck, as beefy as a porterhouse. Like the photos I'd seen, this Gus Scarpetti was dressed in a perfectly tailored dark suit, a fat tie, and a diamond ring on the pinky finger of his left hand. A white handkerchief peeked out of his breast pocket.

It was probably what he'd been buried in.

The thought sent a shiver up my spine, and I shook it away. Good thing. My too-curly carrot-colored hair was wound into a braid and it twitched against the back of my white polo shirt, snapping me back to reality.

It had taken me a solid week to get the script for this tour down pat. Now this guy shows up and throws me off my game? He deserved to be put on the spot. I made a sweeping gesture toward our guest. "Ladies and gentlemen, I'd like you all to meet Mr. Augustino Scarpetti."

You'd think it would have had a little more effect on the crowd. A little more than none, anyway.

Two dozen pairs of eyes stared at me. As empty as my checkbook. Two dozen people whose sticky tags said their names were things like Gladys and Rose and Henry, waited for me to say more.

No one at Garden View Cemetery had ever bothered to tell me how to handle a cemetery-tour heckler. I knew I had to punt.

"Mr. Augustino Scarpetti is buried here." I pointed toward the mausoleum with its Egyptian columns at the front corners and a door that had been imported all the way from Italy. It was brass with a glass insert, and according to what I'd been told by the folks who knew about these things, the door cost more than I paid in rent for an entire year. I guess that was only right since the mausoleum was bigger than my apartment.

Pretty classy digs for someone who was too dead to appreciate it.

From the other side of the door, I could see the glow of the stained-glass window at the far end of the mausoleum, the oriental rug that covered the marble floor, and the dozen red roses that were delivered every week like clockwork. Always on Thursday, the day Gus Scarpetti had been gunned down.

When I turned back around, I half expected that the Gus clone would be gone. But he was still there, looking as interested in what I had to say as everyone else in the group. Which was pretty much the reminder I needed to get my head back into the game.

"I'll bet most of you have heard stories about Gus," I said, and everybody but Gus nodded enthusiastically. "His mob nickname was the Pope, and he was the head of one of the largest crime families in—"

"One of the largest?" Scarpetti looked me over like I was a salami hanging in a deli window. His eyes glinted. Just like the diamonds in his ring. "What idiot told you to say that? One of the largest? That's what they get for letting a girl talk about something as important as this. The Scarpetti Family was *the* largest. *The* largest family. Go ahead, you tell them that."

"I don't have to. You just did."

"Did what?" The question came from a woman named Betty in the front row. I looked her way.

"What he said," I told her.

Betty turned toward where I pointed. "He who?"

"He. Him." For a second, I wondered how the practical joker (whoever he—or she—was) had convinced the Heights Lutheran Senior Citizens League to go along with the gag. Just as quickly, I decided there was no way. They couldn't be bullshitting me. Not all of them. Not Lutherans.

"Gus Scarpetti. The mobster." This time I didn't just point, I stabbed, the gesture broad enough so that even Chester, the guy with the thick glasses who stood at Betty's side, could see it. "Gus Scarpetti is—"

My stomach hit bottom, then bounced up again and lodged in my throat.

Because that's when I realized that nobody else saw the guy.

"Crazy." The word escaped me on the end of a gasp of 100 percent pure panic.

Didn't it figure, the Scarpetti figment of my imagination noticed. Smiling, he stepped back and settled his weight against one foot. "You know what to do, doll baby," he said, his voice smooth and satisfied. "Tell them all about me."

It's not like I had a lot of options. Being a tour guide at Garden View might not be the most ideal job in the world, but it paid better than the barista job at Starbucks that I'd tried and hated. It also didn't involve typing and filing (at least not much), like the phone company job I'd been told I didn't have enough experience for. So it wasn't Saks. Or even Nordstrom. I'd applied at both those places, too, but until I heard back from them (if...when) or figured out some other way to handle the monumental screwup that was my life, this was all I had.

Besides, I had to get the tour over with and get out. Fast. Before I convinced myself that the crackup I'd been waiting for had arrived, not only in living color but wearing a two-thousand-dollar suit.

"Gus Scarpetti. Born in 1921. Got his start with the New York mob. Tried to take over somebody else's territory. Forced to leave town. Came here to Cleveland. Died."

Even before the last word was out of my mouth, I turned and walked away from the mausoleum. "Follow me and we'll see the grave of famous entrepreneur—"

"But isn't there more to the story?" Betty's question stopped me dead in my tracks. "Aren't you going to tell us all that interesting stuff? You know, about how he was killed?"

With a sigh of surrender, I turned back to the group. And to Gus Scarpetti, who looked pretty satisfied. Like he'd just won the first round and I was the down-for-the-count loser.

I sucked it up and scrambled to remember my tour script. "One summer night thirty years ago, Gus walked out of his favorite restaurant."

"And that's when he was killed, right?" A man in the front row asked the question. "He was shot to death by a mob hit man."

No way could that guy know how grateful I was. Now that everyone knew the not-so-happy ending to the story, I didn't have to tell them. That meant we could get out of Dodge. I backstepped my way toward the street where the tour bus waited for us. "No one was ever arrested," I said. "But the cops are sure that's what happened."

"You were doing fine right up until then, sweetheart." Like I was some kind of big ol' disappointment, Scarpetti shook his head. "You bought into that same line of bullsh——*Madonn*'!" He pressed a hand to his heart. "I beg your pardon. I forgot myself. When there are ladies present—"

I couldn't help it. I started to laugh.

"Did I miss something?" Betty tapped her hearing aid. "Did I miss a joke?"

"No!" I tried my best to explain away my sudden fit of the giggles, but my panic got the best of me and sent me into a serious laughing jag. How could I be serious when I felt myself on the brink of the mother of all nervous breakdowns?

Not only was I hallucinating, now I was getting apologies from the hallucination.

I wiped away the tears I knew were smudging my mascara and so I could try to get a grip, I waved the group back toward the bus.

At the last minute, I remembered the advice that had been drilled into me during my training. "Be careful," I told them. "The ground at a cemetery is pretty uneven. It's easy to trip. Just a couple days ago—"

The truth hit me like a whiff of knock-off perfume. Just three days earlier, I was giving this very same tour when I stepped in a hole and twisted my ankle. The heel of my right shoe snapped off and I went down in a heap and smacked my head on the front step of Scarpetti's mausoleum. When I came to, I was in the ER. The doc there told me I was just fine and at the time, I believed her.

Apparently, neither one of us figured leftover delusions into the mix.

The tour group walked ahead of me and now that I had finally figured out what was going on, when Scarpetti walked past, I was ready for him. "I'm just seeing you because I hit my head," I told him. "You're not really here."

He kept right on walking. "You think?"

I didn't just think it, I knew it, and it made me feel a whole lot better. I wasn't a whack job. I wasn't cracking up. My walking, talking dead guy was nothing more than a figment of an imagination that got scrambled like an egg when I thwacked my head.

Of course that didn't explain why I was wasting a perfectly good hallucination on something as weird as a dead-and-gone mobster. You'd think if I was going to fantasize, it would be about something really worthwhile.

Like my ex-fiancé Joel Panhorst.

Wearing nothing but a Speedo that was two sizes too small.

Swimming in a lake full of piranha.

Wishful thinking, and I snapped out of it just in time to see my Scarpetti fantasy disappear behind a nearby marble column with a statue of a sad-looking lady at the top of it.

I breathed a long sigh of relief. As hallucinations went, I was glad this one was over.

That probably explained why I was in such a good mood when I got back on the bus.

It didn't explain why when we got to the chapel, the next stop on our tour, Scarpetti was leaning against the front door.

This time, I wasn't just upset, I was pissed. At my own brain for letting this happen. At myself for letting it get to me. When I gathered my clipboard, my hands shook. When I climbed down off the bus, my knees buckled like they were made out of peanut butter. But I had to give myself a lot of credit. The first thing I did was face my own warped fantasy. I marched over to where Scarpetti waited.

"You're not here," I told him and big points for me, I sounded like I meant it. I guess I figured if I could convince him, I could convince myself. "That means you can go away. Right now."

"But we're not done."

I didn't realize that Chester was standing behind me.

"She wants us to go away, Mother." He handed Betty off the bus. "But we're not done yet, are we? We're supposed to see the grave of that Supreme Court justice. And the former mayor. And that woman. You remember. The one who wrote that cookbook."

Chester was right, and that meant only one thing. As the cemetery's one and only full-time tour guide, I was trapped like the proverbial dirty rat. As the afternoon ticked by and we visited one grave after another, Gus Scarpetti was always there. Lounging against the headstone of the Supreme Court justice. Sitting next to the angel that topped a long-dead mayor's final resting place. Walking alongside the bus as it wound its way through the two hundred and seventy-five scenic acres of Garden View.

By the time we were done, I wasn't just tired of my Gus hallucination, I was more convinced than ever that I was teetering on the brink. My stomach was tied in knots. My breathing was shallow. I was shaking and, let's face it, sweat is not an attractive thing.

As soon as I could, I said goodbye to my tour group and hurried into the ladies' room near the cemetery's main office.

"Cold water," I mumbled to myself. "Lots of cold water."

I splattered it on my face. I soaked a paper towel with it and held it to the back of my neck. I tried the face again, leaning over the sink and splashing so much of it on me that the front of my polo shirt got damp and there were drops all over the PEPPER MARTIN printed on my plastic name tag.

It wasn't until an icy cold drop trickled between my breasts that I realized I was finally breathing a little easier. I stood and looked at myself in the mirror above the sink.

It wasn't a pretty picture.

My mascara was a mess. My bangs were soaked. I had long since chewed off my lipstick and without the help of the Pretty in Pink that I made sure I put on when I so much as ducked into the hallway for my morning newspaper, I was as pale as a coed on the first day of spring break. I had never been fond of the freckles that coated my cheeks and nose. They looked worse than ever against the background of washed-out, wrung-out, stressed-out me.

It's not like I needed a reminder of what was making me feel like a full-blown nutcase. Still, it took me a minute before I dared a look over my shoulder.

For the first time in what seemed like forever, there was no sign of Gus Scarpetti.

I let go a long sigh of relief and, as calm as I was going to get and finally back in control, I headed out of the ladies' room.

The first person I saw outside was Gus.

I must have turned green because he took one look at me and shrugged. "What? You didn't think I was going to follow you into the ladies' room, did you? Just because I'm a wiseguy doesn't mean I'm some kind of pervert."

"Are you having headaches? Do your eyes hurt? Is your stomach upset?"

Each time I shook my head *no,* Dr. Cecilia Cho checked off another item on her list. When she was done, she looked at me over the rims of her glasses. "You don't have any symptoms. You say you have no pain. Why did you come back here to the ER to see me, Pepper?"

"I just thought..." I glanced toward the wall. It was backlit, and hanging from it were a series of head X-rays and CT scans. I knew I was looking at my own brain. "I just wondered..."

Dr. Cho's dark hair was shot through with gray. She wore scrubs and a lab coat decorated with pastel butterflies. She patted my hand. "It's common to feel a little shaky after a mishap like the one you had. Once the world slips out from under your feet, you expect it to happen again. But you've got to remember, you went through..." She checked the patient information sheet on the desk in front of her. "You went through the first twenty-five years of your life without an accident. Relax! Chances are, you aren't going to have another one any time soon."

"I know that. It's just that last night when I was lying awake—"

"You have trouble sleeping?"

"No. I mean, not usually. I mean..."

Actually, I didn't know what I meant. I had never had trouble sleeping until the night before. I tossed and turned all night long, thinking about the Gus Scarpetti I had met in the cemetery. Wondering what was wrong with me and what they did to people who were so crazy that they talked to people nobody else saw. And the people nobody else saw talked back.

I shrugged before I could stop it. "I just wondered if, you know, a hit on the head might cause a person to...I don't know...Maybe see things?"

Dr. Cho laughed. One of the nurses outside the office where we were sitting called to her and she popped out of her chair and headed into the hallway. "You've been watching too much TV. The brain doesn't work that way. Your X-rays and scans don't show anything abnormal and your EEG is fine, too. If you're not having any real symptoms..."

Before I could ask what, exactly, made a symptom real, Dr. Cho was gone.

I gathered up my Louis Vuitton bag, my sweater, and all that was left of my hopes that I'd find out that Gus Scarpetti was nothing more than residual brain scramble. Just as I turned to leave, a guy walked in. I stopped just short of slamming into his chest.

Too bad. I saw right away that this was one chest I wouldn't mind getting up close and personal with. Toned. Just like the rest of him.

Hey, I might have had my heart mashed, smashed, and bashed by Joel the Jerk, but I wasn't dead. No use letting an opportunity like that pass me by. I took a moment to check the guy out.

He had brown hair a couple weeks past needing a cut. Blue eyes behind wire-rimmed glasses. And one of those boy-next-door faces. Cute. Way cute. In an oh-boy-wouldn't-I-like-to-find-out-what's-under-those-clothes sort of way.

Speaking of clothes, he was dressed in a green lab coat and underneath it, a blue shirt with a button-down collar over rumpled brown pants and black loafers. There was a hospital ID around his neck. It said he was DAN CALLAHAN, PHD.

Okay, so Dan Callahan wasn't much when it came to color coordination. That didn't keep him from being the most delicious thing I'd seen in as long as I could remember. Even if he did have a plastic pocket protector.

Geek god.

Like I was giving off some sort of electrical charge and he didn't want to get zapped, Dan backed off and backed away. "Sorry," he said, but even though he might have been, it didn't keep him from glancing at my chest.

Like I said, guys always noticed.

Ever since Joel dumped me like a cup of cold

coffee, I hadn't been noticing back. This time, though, my hormones sat up and paid attention. A tingle zipped through my bloodstream. It was nice to remember how good sexual attraction felt.

Not so nice to realize that I was the only one feeling it. Done checking out my chest, Dan gave the rest of me the quickest once-over ever. He pushed his glasses from the tip of his nose to the bridge. "I thought Dr. Cho was done in here. I just wanted to…" He sidled his way between me and the examining table, heading for the X-rays and scans on the wall.

"That's my brain, you know."

Not exactly a subtle way to get his attention, but it worked. Dan stopped and turned to me. "Really?" He poked his thumb over his shoulder. "This is you?"

I pulled back my shoulders. "Well, it's just a little part of me."

"Remarkable."

I thought maybe he was looking at my chest again. But Dan was apparently more of a brain man. He turned right around and went straight for the pictures. "Has Dr. Cho seen these?"

"Sure." I gave up on the pulled-back shoulders. Dan wasn't paying attention and besides, my back muscles were cramped. "She said my brain is as good as the rest of me."

"Yes." He plucked the first X-ray off the wall and held it up to the overhead fluorescent lights. "I can see that. Except…" He looked at the X-ray so intently, I was convinced he forgot I was there.

"Except what? You don't see anything wrong, do you?"

He *had* forgotten I was there. I could tell when he looked at me through the picture of my brain. Like he'd never seen me before. "Wrong? No. I mean, there is a slight deviation in the occipital lobe." He squinted and took a closer look. At the X-ray, not at me. "And Dr. Cho ordered an electro-encephalogram, didn't she?" He ruffled through the papers on the desk, and when he didn't find what he was looking for, he tapped a finger against his top lip. "Of course if we had old scans to compare with these new scans..." He glanced my way. "You weren't lucky enough to have a brain injury before this one, were you?"

"Lucky? You mean the part about me smacking my head against a slab of marble was the lucky part?"

Apparently, Dan wasn't big on irony. He chewed his lower lip. "Too bad." He plucked one of the scans off the wall and held it side by side with the X-ray. "Of course Dr. Cho is the doctor and if she's convinced..." He drifted off again.

I wasn't about to give up. Not easily, anyway. While Dan studied my brain, I took a closer look at his nametag.

"You're a doctor, too, right? Your nametag says—"

"Not a medical doctor." He lowered the pictures. "I've got a PhD in psychology. And another one in biochemistry. And one in associated neurosciences. And one—" He gave me a quick grin. "All that doesn't matter."

"What matters is that you study brains."

Dan looked at the pictures again. "Yours is very interesting."

As compliments went, it wasn't much, but it was more than I'd gotten from any other guy in as long as I could remember. I perked right up. "We could talk about it."

"Really?" Dan perked up, too. The smile he gave me was toothpaste-white. He checked his watch. "I've got a meeting in ten minutes but if you're going to be around the hospital later, maybe we could—"

"Hospitals are for sick people!" He didn't get the joke. I gave up trying to be cute. I was too old for it and it wasn't working anyway. "How about a drink sometime?"

Like I'd suddenly started speaking a language Dan didn't understand, he gave me a blank look. The next second, he blinked, surprised. "You're not asking me out on a date, are you?"

"You're gay." I knew it. The good-looking ones always are.

"No!" A smile came and went over his expression. "I'm just really busy."

I knew a brush-off when I got one and let's face it, I wasn't exactly feeling like my usual I-am-woman-hear-me-roar self. I spun around and headed out of the office.

"Can we talk about your brain?"

Dan's question stopped me cold. I tried not to look too eager when I stopped and turned back to him. Kind of hard considering my sneakers left skid marks on the linoleum.

For the first time since I plucked the two-carat diamond from my finger and chucked it at Joel Panhorst, I was actually going out on a date. And so what if the guy just happened to be interested only in what was happening inside my skull.

It was pitiful. But it didn't stop me from telling Dan I'd meet him the next evening at Mangia Mania, a new bistro over in Cleveland's Little Italy neighborhood that was getting a lot of press and packing in a crowd of the young, the chic, and the trendy. It was right around the corner from my apartment and just a couple minutes from the cemetery.

By the time I left the hospital, I'd convinced myself that things were looking up. I had Dan to look forward to and maybe I could distract him enough to get him to notice the body that went along with my brain. With any luck at all, he also might be able to explain the static in my head. And why it had decided to morph itself into a wisecracking wiseguy.

Chapter 2

I was in a pretty good mood when I got to the office the next morning. Who could blame me? Six o'clock was only ten hours away and in ten short hours, I'd have Dan the Brain Man all to myself. Minus the distraction of X-rays, CT scans, and the hubbub of the hospital ER.

It was enough to make any girl smile.

Unfortunately, even my good mood wasn't enough to get rid of Gus Scarpetti. He was waiting in my office when I got there.

"No. No. No." I closed the door and stood with my back against it, my hands on the knob behind me. Just so my own personal I'm-not-really-here-but-you're-talking-to-me-anyway couldn't see that they were shaking. "You can't be here. You're not real."

"Not as real as I used to be." Gus was lounging in my one and only guest chair, one leg crossed over the other. He glanced around. Garden View Cemetery was established in the middle of the nineteenth century and the office was located in what used to be the caretaker's house. It was one of those big, rambling buildings with high ceilings and wooden floors. Somebody, sometime, had decided to chop up the rooms to make lots of small offices.

Mine was the smallest.

Desk. Chair. Guest chair. Bookcases that doubled as file storage and were filled to the brim. That was about it. That was all there was room for. As the tour guide and newest member of the cemetery's administrative staff, I was low man on the totem pole; I didn't even rate a window.

If I did have one, I'd be looking out at the high stone wall that surrounded the cemetery and on the other side of it, Cleveland's Little Italy. Cute shops I couldn't afford to buy anything in. Great restaurants that were way too pricey for me. Oh, and cheap apartments. That was one good thing. It was where I'd been living since the day three months earlier when Dad headed to the federal penitentiary and Mom left town for Florida, where she hoped folks would know her simply as *Barb* and not as *Barb whose husband the doctor was convicted of Medicare fraud.*

"The first thing I'd do is get somebody in here to clean up this place." Gus's comment snapped me back to reality. "Or maybe I'd just have it torched and put it out of its misery. You always this sloppy?"

"It's inherited slop." True. Sort of. The woman who had the job before me left most of the stuff there. The books about the history of Cleveland. The old magazines she swore, the one and only time I'd met her, contained "oodles of useful information." I wasn't so sure about the *useful* but I think the *oodles* part was right. There sure were a lot of them, and organization skills had never been my strong suit. In the month I'd been there, things had gotten a little out of hand.

There were old copies of *Life* on the floor and issues of *National Geographic* tucked between the file folders in the bookcase. There were more magazines on my desk along with the latest Abercrombie catalogue, a sale flyer from Victoria's Secret, and what was left of the taco salad that was the previous day's lunch. After my run-in with Gus, I'd left so fast the day before, I never went back to the office to clean up.

I crossed the room and flopped down in my desk chair. I didn't bother to open the Styrofoam container to see how the salad had fared. An overnight on top of my desk couldn't have done it any good. I jammed the container into the bag it came in and tossed the whole thing into my trash can.

It wasn't until I was done that something Gus had said hit me.

"What do you mean, as real as you used to be?"

He sounded just about as disgusted as anyone I'd ever heard. "You might be pretty, sweetheart, but you're sure not very smart. Don't you get it yet? I used to be real, all right. Now I'm a ghost."

My heart stopped right then and there. I swear it did. It started back up again with a sort of thump that made my ribs hurt and my breath catch. There was only one logical comeback to the announcement.

"You're shitting me."

Gus winced like he was in pain. "In my day," he said, "girls didn't talk like that."

"In your day—" I realized that I was falling into the trap. Just the way my brain wanted me to. I was so desperate to convince myself I wasn't a certified nutcase that I was willing to buy into this whole ghost theory. Almost.

I shook away the very thought with a motion that made my breasts jiggle inside my standard-issue Garden View polo shirt.

Gus grinned.

"There. See." I pointed an accusing finger at him. "That proves it. No way you're a ghost. Ghosts don't look at women's boobs."

"Who says? I may be dead but that doesn't mean I've lost my appreciation for the finer things in life. And your things, honey..." He gave a long, low whistle. "Those are really fine!"

I scraped my hands through my hair. "No way am I sitting here talking to a ghost."

"You'd rather think you're crazy?"

"I'd rather think—"

I never had a chance to finish the sentence. Which was probably just as well because at that point, I didn't know *what* I was thinking.

The door popped open and Ella Silverman, the cemetery's community-relations manager and my boss, poked her head into the room. Ella was round and middle-aged. She must have had a hippie moment somewhere in her past because she always wore dresses that were loose and flowing and hung down around her ankles. Her hair was cut short and spiked at the top and she liked jewelry. As usual, she was decked out in lots of beads and plenty of chunky bracelets.

"Sorry!" she whispered. "I just have to tell you that—" She looked around my office and her apologetic smile wilted. She knew she didn't have to whisper anymore. "I just wanted to tell you that we've got a staff meeting in a half hour. Jim's orders. I thought you were in here with someone. I could have sworn I heard you talking."

"Phone." I pointed.

Ella squinched up her nose. "Except that you're not on the phone."

"Speaker phone."

"We don't have speaker phones."

"Just thinking out loud."

"Uh huh." She came into my office and closed the door behind her. That day's choice of flowy dress was a little teal number with a matching jacket. Like she always did when she was slipping out of Ella-everybody's-friend mode into Ella-the-boss mode, she tugged on her right earlobe. Her turquoise and silver earring swayed. "Do we need to talk?" she asked.

"Talk? No." I slid the magazines on the desk together and tapped them into a neat pile. "I was just pulling your leg. What you heard was me practicing. For that talk I'm scheduled to give to the Junior League ladies next week. You know, the one at the chapel." For once my less-than-stellar filing system came in handy. The tour script I had been given two weeks before and hadn't even read yet was lying on the desk, and just to prove my point, I picked it up and waved it at Ella.

"I'm so glad!" She walked over to the chair in front of my desk and for a moment, I was afraid that she was going to plop down right in my guest chair. I don't know why the thought bothered me so much. Logic dictated that the chair was empty. But my eyes told me otherwise. When Ella stepped in front of the chair, Gus wiggled his eyebrows and patted his lap. She perched herself on the arm of the chair, and I let go the breath I was holding.

"I don't want you to get too hyper about it but remember, that's an important group, Pepper. There are a couple members who are married to cemetery trustees."

I tried not to notice that while we were talking, Gus gave Ella's backside a careful examination. When he was done, he nodded in appreciation and gave me the thumbs-up.

"That is so sexist!"

"Excuse me?" Ella's blank stare was familiar. It was just like the ones I'd seen so often on the previous day's tour. "Did you say—"

"I said..." I had no choice but to come up with an excuse. Half-baked or not. It was that or have her think I'd flipped my lid. "I said it was sexist. Yeah, that's what I said. I said that it's not right to define the women in the group by the men they're married to. Isn't that what you were telling me?

When we talked about what it was like back in the days when feminism got started?"

We had talked about the whole Stone Age feminism movement just a couple of days before. More precisely, over salads at a nearby cheap-food place, Ella had talked and I had pretended to listen. She looked pleased to realize that some of what she'd said had actually sunk in.

She beamed. "Exactly! I did mention that women need to be defined by who they are personally, not by the men in their lives. But when I mentioned the Junior League, I didn't mean—"

"Of course you didn't. I know exactly what you meant. See, I was paying attention."

"Better attention than my kids ever pay." Ella sighed. She was the mother of three teenaged girls so she had earned the right. "I try to tell the girls, Pepper. I try to explain what the world was like back in the sixties and seventies. But they don't listen. They think it doesn't apply to them."

Just like I was pretty sure it didn't apply to me.

Not that I was going to mention it. Number one, because of all the people I'd met since my comfortable upper-middle-class world fell apart, Ella was one of the nicest. Number two, because she was my boss. Number three...

Well, Gus was making like he was about to pinch Ella's ass, so I suppose my third reason was that I just wanted to get this whole thing over and done with. "A meeting with Jim, did you say?" I got out of my chair and opened the door that led into the outer hallway. "We'd better get going."

"You don't have to. Not yet." Ella checked the watch that was on her wrist along with a half-dozen beaded bracelets. "I do. He's going to want facts and figures and I'd better pull them together. From you, I think he'll want a list of the tours that are scheduled for the rest of the month. If you could just..." She motioned toward the mess on my desk.

And because she knew she didn't have to explain herself, Ella left.

As soon as she was gone, I closed the door.

I made sure to keep my voice down this time. "That was really rude."

"You think?" Gus sat back and stretched. "Back in my day—"

"Yeah. Back in your day. That's what we were talking about before Ella came in here."

"I take it that means you don't believe me when I tell you that I'm a ghost." Gus uncrossed his legs. He ran a hand over his big-as-a-dinner-plate tie. "You calling me a liar?"

"I'm not calling you a liar. But I'm not calling you a ghost, either. Ghosts are spooky. You know, woo woo!" I waved my hands around and hummed the theme music from *The Twilight Zone*. "I can't see through you. You don't glow. You're not misty around the edges. Besides, I don't believe in ghosts."

"I never did, either."

"Then how—"

"Listen, kid." Gus got up and tugged his suit jacket into place. "I can't explain how the whole thing works 'cause I don't understand it myself. I only know that I died and I got buried over in that mausoleum out there. At least my body did. But the rest of me..." He poked a finger at his chest. "I never left. I'm still here."

"And I'm supposed to believe this because..."

"Because I'm telling you it's the truth. My word of honor. And if you can't believe that, then believe your eyes. And your ears. And if you can't believe them..." Gus undid the buckle on his belt. He unzipped his pants.

I held my breath and my eyes went wide.

Flashed by a ghost?

Things had just gone from bizarre to way-too-kinky for words.

Lucky for me, what I had in mind wasn't what Gus had in mind. He untucked his shirt and tugged down the right side of his pants and his underwear just enough for me to see that he had a vivid red mark on his right hip. It was about the size of a quarter and it was shaped like a rose.

"There. See that?" Once he knew I did, Gus yanked his pants back in place. He tucked in his shirt, zipped his pants, and buckled his belt. "That there is a birthmark."

"Great." I smiled like it was. "Thanks for sharing."

Gus threw his hands in the air. "Are you some kind of *mortadella*? Don't you see what I'm getting at here? You think I'm a...what do you call it...a figment of your imagination."

"You got that right."

"But I'm proving to you that I'm not. By showing you this here birthmark."

I still didn't get it. I guess the spacey look on my face spoke volumes.

Gus made a sound like a growl. "Once you check into it, you'll find out that birthmark is real and then you'll know I'm not one of them there figments because your mind couldn't make up something that you don't know nothing about. *Capisce?*"

I did. I think. "You mean that when I know the birthmark is real, I'll know that you're really a—"

"A ghost. Yeah."

The fact that it all made so much sense only made me feel shakier than ever. I dropped back into my chair. I propped my elbows on my desk and cradled my chin in my hands. I tried to work through the whole thing logically but I couldn't get from Point A to Point B because I couldn't get past Point A. "What's up with that, anyway?" I asked Gus. "How come I'm the only one who can see you?"

He looked up at the ceiling. Like he was praying for patience. "Don't you get it? You fell. And hit your head on—"

"On your mausoleum." The blood drained from my face. It left me feeling chilled. "You mean because I smacked my head on your grave—"

"You're the only one lucky enough to be able to see me."

"It's weird."

"I don't make the rules. And let me tell you, I don't like it. Used to be better in the old days when I had final say."

"Then who does?" It wasn't like I thought I could talk whoever was in charge into changing anything. But somehow, I hoped I might be able to get a better handle on how it all worked. "If somebody can make me see you, then somebody can make you go away. Right?"

Gus laughed. Not like it was funny. More like he'd never heard anything so stupid. "Let me tell you the way I understand things." He sat back down and leaned forward, pinning me with the sort of look I imagined had intimidated more than one mobster in its day.

"Most of the dead are just that. Dead. They're here. They're gone. Over and done with. You know what I mean?" He didn't wait for me to say that I pretty much did. "But then there's me," he said, "and I've got what you might call some unfinished business."

"And the unfinished business is why you've been hanging around for thirty years?"

He pointed his index finger at me and brought his thumb down on it. Like he was shooting a gun. He winked. "You got it, baby. The way I understand this thing, I can't leave until all the unfinished business in my life is settled. And let me tell you something, I'm sick to death—you'll excuse the expression—of hanging around this place. Nothing but a bunch of stiffs and not one of them interesting."

"And you're looking to pass on. Or pass over. Or go to the light or whatever they call it."

"The light?" He waved like the suggestion was

an annoying insect. "That whole bright white light thing? It's for *babbos*. You know, dopes. The kind who believe in all that sappy stuff. Not me. When I go out, honey, I'm going to go out in style." He tipped his head back and smiled. "I'm going to make my exit to the strains of Sinatra singing 'My Way.'"

"So finish your unfinished business and leave!"

"You don't think I would have done that before now if I could?" Anger flared in Gus's eyes. He rose to his feet and when he reached across my desk, I thought he was going to slap me. Instead, he grabbed for the stack of magazines I'd just gathered up.

His hand went right through them.

"See?" He plunked back down in his chair. "How can I take care of things for myself when I can't do a thing? And when nobody can see me? Or hear me? Nobody but you."

There was some unspoken message in what Gus said. I wasn't sure what it was, I was only sure I didn't like it.

The next second, the truth dawned. I shook my head and sat back in my chair, distancing myself from the whole thing. "Oh, no. Whatever it is, I'm not going to help. I wouldn't know how if I wanted to and besides, I don't want to. You're the great criminal mastermind. Why don't you just—"

"Like I said, I can't." Gus's voice was as low and just about as friendly as the purr of a hungry lion. "You think I like asking for help? You think I wouldn't rather go to my friends? Or my son? A good *consigliere,* that's what I need right about now. Instead, I get a little girl with no brains and a big chest."

"Hold on there, pal. I might be young, but I'm not a little girl and I'm not dumb. I'll have you know, I'm a college graduate."

"College is wasted on girls. They should stay home, get married, and have babies. Besides, if I had to guess, I'd say you majored in something like home ec. Or was it art history?"

It was art history.

I wasn't about to admit that to Gus. Just like I wasn't going to tell him that at the time I declared my major, I never thought that I might actually have to use my overpriced education as a springboard to making a living. After all, my life had been laid out before me like my mother's had been before her. I had a tradition to uphold, and generations of Livingston (her maiden name) women who served as my role models.

First, college.

After all, it was expected, and besides, it gave me a place to make just the right contacts and Mom something to talk about when her friends at the tennis club asked about her only child.

Then, an engagement. But only, of course, if it was what Grandmother Livingston liked to call "the right match."

Three cheers for me, mine was as right as they came. It arrived in the form of Joel Panhorst, who just happened to be on the brink of being named a partner in one of the most prestigious financial firms in the area. Was Joel the man of my dreams? I hate to admit it, but yeah, I was nuts about him.

What was not to like?

Joel was good-looking. Joel was charming. Joel was going to make my dream of being a full-time CCW come true. That's Country Club Wife, and I was all for it. It would have been my parents' life, only kicked up a notch. A little more exciting. A little more interesting. A lot more stylish.

I was ready, willing, and able, and would have gone along for the happy ride if my life hadn't gone down the dumper when my dad's status officially changed from renowned plastic surgeon to just-another felon.

That pretty much explained it all, didn't it? With Dad up the proverbial river, my social contacts had withered, my engagement had crumbled, and, suddenly, my resumé actually mattered. Unless tennis and suntans counted, I had no job experience to speak of. I had few usable skills. *Presto*...here I was in the deadest of all dead-end jobs.

I got rid of the thought before it got the best of me, and got myself back on track.

"A degree is a degree," I told Gus, firmly ignoring all thoughts of my country club aspirations. "And women don't just get married and have babies anymore. Haven't you been paying any attention these last thirty years? We have careers. And real lives. And although I can't speak for other women, I can speak for myself. I'm smart enough to—"

"To take care of what I need you to take care of." Gus's smile was predatory.

And I knew I'd fallen for the oldest trick in the book. "Great, get me to admit that I'm smart just so—"

"So you can help me out." He nodded and smiled. "I always knew you would. Even if I had to—"

"Make me an offer I couldn't refuse?" I couldn't help myself, the opening was too good to pass up. It wasn't until the words were out of my mouth that I wondered if I'd said something I shouldn't have.

I was pretty sure of it when fire flared in Gus's eyes. "That was my line, you know. Way before that movie came along. That was my line and they stole it."

"Yeah. Right." I looked at the clock on the wall and got up. "I've got a meeting to get to. With Jim. He's my boss's boss."

"Bosses." Gus nodded. "Yeah, I understand that."

"Then you'll understand that if I'm late, he'll have my head."

"Heads? Nah! We never would have taken any heads. Too messy."

"It's just a figure of speech." I grabbed for the file where I kept a calendar of all the upcoming tours. I held it to my chest like a shield. "Look," I said, "I'd like to help you but I can't, so I think you'd better just go away."

Gus shrugged. "Wish I could, baby doll. But I can't. Not until this thing is resolved."

"But I wouldn't know where to begin."

"It's not like I wouldn't help you out."

"But—"

He held up one hand. "It is time for me to impose my will and just so you know, I don't take no for an answer."

"But—"

"I don't take no buts, neither. You don't like it. I don't like it. But you're the only one who can do this thing."

I could stand there and argue with this brain blip. Or I could try to move on. My sigh was a sure sign of surrender. "What do you want me to do for you?"

Gus stood and went to the door. He couldn't open it so I did that. He stepped back so I could walk out. "Honey," he said, "you're going to find out who really murdered me."

Chapter 3

Did I want to stick with the tried and true and stay with Pretty in Pink? Or was I looking to shake things up? Maybe I needed something a little more dramatic for my date with Dan the Brain Man.

I was deep in thought while I glanced through the selection of lipstick tubes in my top desk drawer.

Paris Nights? I twisted the tube and checked out the color.

Pink Passion? I held the two side by side.

Red Hot—

"So what kind of name is Pepper, anyway? Sounds like a schnauzer."

Gus's question snapped me out of my thoughts. I'd been hoping he'd get bored and go wherever it was he went when he wasn't hanging around my office. No such luck. He'd been sitting in my guest chair ever since I got back from my meeting with Jim, Ella, and the rest of the cemetery administrative staff, and I glanced at him over the stacks of newspapers piled between us. If he noticed I was irritated by the canine reference, he didn't let on.

"It's a nickname," I said. "Short for Penelope."

"Pen-el-op-e." He drew out each of the syllables, and I couldn't tell if he liked the sound or if he was making fun of a name that was too long and way too old-fashioned. "To give you a name like that, your parents, they must think they're pretty high-falutin.'"

Against my better judgment and certainly against all reason, he'd already talked me into raiding the cemetery archives for all the info I could find about him. He wasn't about to Dr. Phil me into a heart-to-heart about my family.

I refused to answer, hoped he got the message, and decided on Paris Nights. I put the tube within easy reach so I could toss it into my purse when the time came to close up shop and head out for the evening. According to the clock on the wall opposite from where I sat, that was in exactly sixteen minutes.

Sixteen minutes…a drive home, where I could leave my car in my reserved space so I didn't have to fight for a parking place near the restaurant…a quick walk to Mangia Mania…

And then I'd have Dan Callahan all to myself. And Dan Callahan was the yummiest guy I'd met since—

"You're not listening to me. You need to get down to work here, honey. You're supposed to be thinking about me, not about how soon you can go home."

I forced my gaze away from the clock and my thoughts from Dan back to the not-so-dearly departed don. I wasn't about to correct him and tell him that I wasn't going home. At least not to stay. It wasn't any of his business and besides, I didn't think I needed to run my social calendar by a guy who'd been too busy being dead to worry about dating.

"I have been trying to get some work done," I said, my words cut in half because my teeth were gritted. "I've been at this all afternoon. In case you haven't noticed, we're getting nowhere."

To emphasize my point, I slapped a hand against the stack of yellow and brittle newspapers closest to me. A little puff of dust and who-knows-what-else rose up and tickled my nose. Just in case I needed it, I plucked a tissue from the box I swiped from Ella's office while she and Jim still had their heads together after our meeting.

The tissue box was decorated with teddy bears dressed in picture hats and strings of pearls. As much as critters in clothing offended my fashion sensibilities, the tissues had come in handy plenty of times in the hours since I started researching Gus's life. And his death. I sneezed.

"There's nothing in any of these newspapers that's new." Considering that the news and the papers were thirty years old, it was an understatement. I touched the tissue to my nose and wondered how red it was and how bad I was going to look by the time I got to Mangia Mania.

For the third time in as many minutes, I snapped open my compact and checked out the damage. Not bad considering. Nothing a touch of moisturizer and a dusting of powder wouldn't help. If I ran to the ladies' room now—

"How do you know?" Over the wall of newspapers, Gus pinned me with a look. "How do you know we won't find anything? You've barely scratched the surface."

At the moment, the surface in question was the copy of the *Cleveland Plain Dealer* on top of the pile. I snapped the compact shut, but rather than look at the grainy black-and-white photo that showed Gus flat on his face in the middle of the street, a dark liquidy pool all around him, I shuffled the newspaper to my left and glanced at the next one on the pile. This one was the *Cleveland Press*, and the picture on the front page was just about the same. Cops. Street. Gus. Blood.

Plenty of blood.

I guess I must have made a face.

"What?" Gus stood and cocked his head, the better to see what I was looking at. "That bothers you? All that blood?"

"I'm surprised it doesn't bother you. I can't believe you're not upset by the fact that you're—"

"Dead?"

I still wasn't ready to say the word out loud. I slid back in my chair. "Aren't you mad?"

"At whoever did that to me?" He pursed his lips, thinking. "I was," he finally said, tipping his head back and studying the mottled ceiling panels. "When I first sort of...you know...When I woke up and realized...well, I suppose I realized I was never really going to wake up."

"And that's when you knew you were…" It wasn't exactly a question but then, I wasn't exactly sure I wanted an answer.

Gus grunted. "I didn't think dead. Not right away. After all, in my family, we'd been raised to think that dead meant heaven. Or hell." He looked away. Just long enough for me to wonder if the thought bothered him.

Not that I was going to ask. It was one thing having a conversation with a dead guy. It was another to question his religious beliefs. Or to ask if he thought he deserved eternal fire and brimstone because of his life of crime.

"And once you realized you were de—" I caught myself before the word slipped all the way out. Gus didn't miss a trick. He grinned.

"Glad you're finally getting the picture, chicky." He winked. "Now if we could just get back to business…" He glanced at the newspapers we hadn't looked through yet.

My gaze automatically traveled to the clock. Twelve minutes and counting.

"I'd love to." So I lied. I had to believe that Gus had told a lie or two himself in his lifetime. I figured it was payback. I checked the calendar hanging on the wall to my left. The following afternoon, the Sacred Heart of Jesus Ladies' Guild was coming for our angel tour. Which meant that the next morning, I'd have to dig the angel tour script from one of the piles on my desk and actually read it. In the time I'd been here at Garden View, I hadn't conducted the angel tour yet. I didn't know anything about angels.

And something told me that the Sacred Heart of Jesus Ladies' Guild did.

"I really don't have the time tonight," I told Gus. "And tomorrow isn't looking much better. Maybe next week or—"

"I am not a man who likes to be jerked around." Gus leaned across my desk, his eyes narrowed and fire burning in them. "Next week is too damned late. You're wasting my time, little girl. Get busy. Now."

Call me diplomatic. Or maybe I'm just a weenie. I didn't think it was smart to piss off a guy who, according to what I'd been reading in the newspapers, was a combination Tasmanian Devil and Hannibal Lecter.

I sighed and my shoulders slumped, and Gus knew he'd won this round.

"A couple minutes more," I told him, checking the clock one more time. "That's as long as I can stay. And it's not like we're going to find anything new. There's nothing in any of these news reports that we haven't seen already. It's all the same story. You went to dinner at..." I should have remembered but I'll confess, after hours of rummaging through news that was older than me, it was hard to keep all the facts straight.

"Lucia's Trattoria." Gus supplied the information and a smile touched his lips. "Ah, Lucia's! Best veal parmigiana in the world! And the wine cellar..." He kissed the tips of his fingers. "Magnificent!"

"So you ate dinner and drank wine. Who were

you with?" I thought I knew the answer to the question but I wanted to see if Gus's memory agreed with the newspaper reports. Besides, if I could get the few facts we knew for certain covered— quickly—maybe I'd have time to slap on a coat of lipstick, check my makeup, and get to Mangia Mania before it was too late.

"Johnny the Rat. Benny No Shoes. Mike the Dumper. And Pauly." Gus listed his dinner companions. "That would be Pauly Ramone. When he was a kid we called him Pudgy Pauly but then Pauly got bigger than everybody else and we couldn't get away with it no more. We knew him as Pounder. Just Pounder. And when you said Pounder, everybody on the street, they knew who you were talking about."

I glanced down at the cheat sheet I'd started on a yellow legal pad, a list of the facts I'd been able to glean from the newspaper articles. Johnny, I supposed, was the John Vitale who was said to have been seen leaving the scene of the crime. Benny No Shoes must have been the Ben Marzano who was wounded in the attack that killed Gus. Mike was Michael Cardorella. He was identified as one of the onlookers at the scene pictured on the front page. Pounder I didn't need to guess about. As Gus had pointed out, he was Paul Ramone.

All present and accounted for.

"No one else was there?"

"You second-guessing me?"

I didn't like the tone of Gus's voice. Or the fact that he shot daggers at me across my desk. It was getting to be a habit but I couldn't help myself. I sighed. Right before I sneezed again. "I'm not second-guessing anyone, just trying to get the story straight. And wondering if the newspapers got it right. Nobody else was there?"

"Sure. There were a lot of people there. Lucia's was a popular place."

"But there was nobody else there with you?"

Gus straightened his tie. "Nobody."

So much for that line of questioning. I felt my shoulders slump again and this time, the dust and eye-straining research had nothing to do with it. I had asked all the questions I could think to ask and, let's face it, I didn't have a clue what I was doing. The closest I'd ever come to any kind of criminal investigation was watching *Law & Order* reruns on cable. I wracked my brain, wondering what Detectives Lenny and Ed would do next.

Something clicked and I grinned, feeling pretty smart. "Who knew you were going to be there for dinner that night?"

Gus laughed. Not like it was funny. More like it was the dumbest thing he'd heard in a long time. "If you was paying attention, you'd know what everybody in town knew: I had dinner at Lucia's every Thursday night, kid. The whole freakin' world knew it."

Nothing like getting a hole a mile wide blown in your one-and-only theory to take the wind out of a girl. I propped my elbows on top of the stack of newspapers and cradled my head in my hands. "Which means anybody could have arranged the hit."

"Sure." He shrugged. Like it was no big deal that someone had planned and executed (pun intended) the hit that left Gus Scarpetti with no less than sixteen gunshot wounds. Of course, it only took one to kill a guy, but whether that one shot straight to his heart had come before or after the other fifteen, nobody could tell. At the time, the coroner hadn't even tried to guess. I suppose it didn't matter. Dead was dead. And one look at the photographs of Gus lying facedown in the middle of Mayfield Road, his left leg cocked at a funny angle, his right arm thrown over his head...

Well, even I could tell he was dead.

" 'Unnamed police sources speculate the hit was the work of the LaGanza crime family and its boss, Victor LaGanza.' " The words stared up at me from the front page of the newspaper and I read them out loud, dangling the tidbit in front of Gus like it was a choice morsel of Lucia's veal parmigiana.

He didn't bite. "Victor the Mosquito didn't have the balls. You should excuse the expression. He didn't have the muscle, neither. Besides, no way it's as easy as that. That's the story the cops put out and they probably wanted to believe it. It wrapped everything up neat and clean, you know? They didn't have to get off their butts and do any work. But like you'd remember if you were listening when I told you before, if it was that easy, I wouldn't be here right now. My unfinished business would be finished and then I'd be finished. *Capisce?*"

"I *capisce*. But if LaGanza didn't do it—"

"Pepper and Penelope. They're not really close,

are they? I mean like if someone's name is John and they call the guy Johnny. Or if somebody is Vittorio and his friends call him Vito. So how did they do it? How did your family get from Penelope to Pepper?"

The change of subject left me momentarily disoriented. At the same time I wondered why Gus didn't want to talk about Victor LaGanza, I scrambled to regain my hold on reality. It didn't take me long to realize there was no use even trying. I was talking to a dead man. And I was concerned about reality?

"I couldn't say Penelope. Not when I was little. Then when I was a bit older..." Heat touched my cheeks and I instantly regretted it. I didn't like dredging up the past. And I didn't like admitting that I had faults. Even when they were faults that I'd mostly outgrown.

Stalling for time I didn't have, I checked the clock again and realized it was almost five. I scooped up Paris Nights in one hand and my purse in the other. When I was done, Gus was still staring at me. Still waiting for an explanation.

"I had a temper," I said, even now reluctant to admit that I was the preschooler who refused to sit and listen, the one who talked back to teachers, not because I was disrespectful but because when they pushed me past my limit, I just couldn't keep my mouth shut. "My parents said I was fiery. Like pepper."

He nodded. "It's the red hair. True every time, and not one of them...what do you call them?...

stereotypes. Redheads." He clicked his tongue. "I knew better than to ever trust a redhead."

"Thanks." I stood, the better to get to the door the moment the big hand hit the twelve. "But we weren't talking about me," I reminded Gus. "We were talking about your—" I couldn't bring myself to say *murder*. It was one thing to read about homicides in books or newspapers. It was another to watch the crime shows on TV. But standing there, face to face with someone who was actually a victim of the ultimate in violent acts…

Rather than think about it, I turned to head to the door. How Gus got there before I did, I don't know. I couldn't make a grab for the doorknob. Not without reaching right through him.

Something I was definitely not prepared to do.

He knew it, too. Gus grinned. "What do you say, chicky? You could stay a while longer."

I wasn't about to be schmoozed. Not by a ghost with the chutzpah to block the door with his own body.

Or ectoplasm.

Or whatever it was.

I didn't have the time or the energy to even try to work through the thing. Instead, I propped my fists on my hips. "You could wait," I told Gus.

"I've been waiting thirty years."

"Then a couple more days won't matter."

"I'm damned tired of waiting."

"Then tell me about Victor LaGanza."

Gus wasn't used to being outsmarted. Especially not by a woman. His top lip curled and for a minute, he just stood there and stared at me, waiting for me to back down.

Maybe he forgot that redheads had a reputation for being stubborn, too.

"Me and Victor..." Gus rubbed a hand across his jaw. The diamonds in his pinky ring glinted in the overhead fluorescent lights. "We went back a long way. We came up in the organization together. He stood up for me at my wedding. He was my son, Rudy's, godfather."

"Friends. But not all that friendly. Not if the police think he was the one who ordered the hit."

"The police were wrong."

"How do you know? I'm all for this gut-instinct stuff but if we're going to work through this, we need facts. How do you know, Gus? How do you really know that LaGanza isn't the one who had you killed?"

Gus sniffed like he'd caught wind of a bad smell. "Shows what you know. No way Victor would have offed me. It would have been bad for business. You see, we were doing a deal."

"And he was the trustworthy sort."

"Yeah." With a twitch, Gus pulled back his shoulders. "There was a brand new state lottery back then and people being people, we knew that pretty soon, the suckers would be spending millions on it. We figured a way to get us a piece of the pie."

Logic had never been my strong suit. If it was, I would have reasoned my way to figuring out that Joel Panhorst was a dud long before he pulled the rug out from under our relationship and the fifty-thousand-dollar wedding I was in the middle of planning. But this time, even I could see the writing on this wall.

"That explains everything!" I told Gus. "Finished business or no unfinished business, it must have been LaGanza. He wanted the money for himself. Millions, right? That's what you said. Sounds like a motive for murder to me."

"No way." Gus shook his head. "It's all wrong. Just sit back down and—"

"Not a chance." I dared one more look at the clock and it confirmed my worst fears. By the time I drove down the hill to Little Italy…

By the time I parked in back of my apartment building…

By the time I raced over to Mangia Mania and ducked into the ladies' room to check my hair and my makeup…

I'd be lucky if Dan didn't give up on me and go home.

And there was no way I was going to take a chance on that.

I shooed Gus out of the way and maybe because he wasn't used to being bossed around, he was too stunned to argue. He stepped aside, and before he had a chance to change his mind, I raced out the door.

My head down, I flew by Ella's office, and even though the door was open and I could hear her on the phone, I refused to make eye contact. She'd wave me inside. Like she always did. She'd want to chat. I said a hurried goodbye to Jennine, who answered the phones in the main office, and I was out the door and into my car in record time.

But it wasn't until I drove through the impressive iron gates at the main entrance to Garden View and out onto Mayfield Road that I breathed a little easier.

No more work for the day.

No more cemetery.

No more Gus.

At least for tonight.

I flicked on the radio and sang along with "Old Time Rock and Roll," my mood improving with each block I put between myself and the cemetery.

For the first time since Gus Scarpetti showed up outside his mausoleum, I could finally concentrate on having a good time.

I could keep my mind on Dan Callahan.

And off murder.

Chapter 4

He was wearing black pants with a brown shirt and one of those blue windbreakers I was used to seeing on the old men who hung around Corbo's Bakery. Fashion sense aside, it was easy for me to keep my mind on Dan from the moment he walked into Mangia Mania, spotted me, and waved. He was cute. Scruffy hair, worn sneakers, and all.

That was the good news.

And the bad?

It was apparently not going to be so easy for Dan to keep his mind on me.

He brought my brain scans with him.

He slipped into the chair across from mine and slid the large manila file folder marked MARTIN, PENELOPE onto the table right next to the list of drink specials. He scooped a lock of hair off his forehead. "Sorry I'm late."

"Not a problem." Really, it wasn't. Except for the file folder and a niggling worry that Dan was thinking more *professional* than *personal* when it came to me, I was feeling magnanimous. Especially since I was a little late myself. And since when I got there and Dan was nowhere to be found, I had time to add a quick coat of Paris Nights to my lips and run a comb through my hair.

I felt like a new woman. A new woman who wasn't going to let anything spoil the evening.

Not even that file folder.

As if he was reading my mind, Dan's smile was apologetic. It was also as adorable as a basket of puppies. In the dim light that was supposed to pass for ambiance, I saw his eyes spark with excitement.

Some guys get that look when they talk about money. Or sports. Or sex.

Dan's hot button was bound to be a little different. Just like Dan himself.

He shrugged out of his windbreaker and leaned his elbows on the table. "The time got away from me," he confessed. "That happens a lot. I was getting ready to leave the hospital when I ran into Dr. Cho. I told her how I'd talked to you in the ER the other day and she mentioned why you were there. That's when it hit me. You see, I've been searching for just the right topic for a new study. Not that I don't have enough on my plate to keep me busy what with working with the patients in the psych unit, but..." His words trailed away. I guess he figured he'd said enough for me to understand the workings of a mind that was obviously way above mine.

"There's always room for more research," Dan said, and because he had no idea how much I didn't agree with him, he went right on. "I had this really great idea about the possibilities of comparing the aberrant behavior of patients who had sustained head injuries and showed damage to their occipital lobes to the behavior of patients who—"

"Aberrant behavior?"

I admit, it was a touchy subject. I guess that's why I jumped on it, my voice sharp, my insides suddenly bunched, as if a hand had reached down my throat and tied my stomach into a couple hundred tight, painful knots.

Dan was talking about aberrant behavior. He was talking about me. All in the same sentence.

It pissed me off, especially since it was impossible to even begin to come up with any sort of argument to counter his. At that point, I suspected my behavior was a little aberrant, too.

Not that I was about to admit it.

To him or to myself.

I took a deep breath and offered him a smile that was tight around the edges. "Just so we can set the record straight, I want you to know that when I talked to Dr. Cho about hallucinations, it was a hypothetical sort of thing. I'm not a nutcase. I wasn't talking about me."

The twinkle in Dan's eyes melted into an expression so close to disappointment, I almost felt guilty for not being crazy.

My guilt lasted about as long as his disappointment did. Not one to be put off, he cocked his head and studied me with a sort of laser intensity, the way I remembered him looking at my X-rays back in the ER. "That's exactly how I thought you'd respond," he said. He tapped a finger against my file folder. "But remember, brain scans speak louder than words."

"I thought that was actions."

He either didn't get it or he didn't want to. He ignored me and went right on. "Even though Dr. Cho didn't find any physical problems as a result of your fall, your brain scans are unusual, Pepper. When I thought about that, it made the whole thing click. I suppose I owe you a great big thank you."

What he really owed me was some kind of explanation about what the hell he was talking about.

My blank expression pretty much said it all, but Dan didn't let that stop him. His eyes lit with that weird spark that told me that, occipital lobes notwithstanding, his brain functioned in a different dimension from mine. "You've heard the old saying: Publish or Perish. Well, I haven't published anything recently. Not for at least six months. I've been on a sort of hiatus and let me tell you, for a researcher, that's not a good thing. Then I met you and it all came together in a flash of inspiration. That's when I realized how lucky I was that we were meeting here tonight."

Okay, so it wasn't exactly the most romantic thing a guy had ever said to me.

It was, however—pathetically enough—the most romantic thing a guy had said to me in a long time. It was also the perfect opportunity for me to change the subject.

I grinned and leaned forward, fingering the edge

of the file folder and walking the fine line between flirting and sounding too cutsie.

"I think we're pretty lucky, too," I said. "I mean, tripping over each other like that in the ER. It was as if fate—"

He pushed his glasses up the bridge of his nose. "Fate? Do you believe in it? In something you can't see and can't touch and can't feel?"

I was a practical woman. At least I always had been before I'd started hanging around with a guy who'd been dead since before I was born. Before I met Gus, I would have told Dan that I didn't believe in anything that wasn't as real as the table between us.

Now I wasn't so sure.

I got rid of the thought with a twitch of my shoulders and reminded myself that Mangia Mania was a Gus-free zone. That night, I wasn't supposed to be thinking about the ether. Or the ozone. Or wherever it was that ghosts came from. I was thinking Pepper. Pepper and Dan. I was thinking a couple drinks, a few laughs, a little fun.

If any of that good stuff was going to happen, I knew I had to toe the line between sounding philosophical and coming across as a whack job. "I believe things exist that none of us have ever imagined. But that doesn't mean I hallucinate," I added, so he didn't get the wrong idea.

Dan gave me that laser look for another couple seconds. "You're awfully defensive and you really don't need to be. You see, I believe in stuff like that, too. Most people are surprised when I tell them. They think that scientists don't have any imagination. But I do. After all, I'm a researcher. If I only believed in what I can see and touch and feel, I'd never discover anything."

It made sense. It also provided me with the perfect opportunity to bare my soul and share my secret.

I didn't.

Dan was just waiting for me to prove his aberrant-behavior theory and no way was I going to fall for that. It was too early in our relationship to admit that I had my very own thing that went bump in the night.

Something told me that even if we ended up living happily ever after with two-and-a-half kids, a house with a picket fence, and a golden retriever romping in the backyard, it would still be too early in our relationship.

"I believe in opportunity as well as in fate," Dan said, his voice whisking me out of my daydream and back to the reality of the Mangia Mania bar and the manila file folder that sat on the table like the reminder I didn't need that I was there because of Dan, and Dan was there because of my occipital lobe.

"That's the thing I wanted to talk to you about tonight," he continued. "This study could be monumental. Groundbreaking. If I can get approval from the hospital board and the right funding, I'd like you to—"

Whatever he was going to say, he was interrupted by a burst of applause and a chorus of "For He's a Jolly Good Fellow" coming from the next room. Like most of the art galleries, restaurants, and bars in the area, Mangia Mania was located in a building that was as old as Little Italy. From my work at the cemetery, I knew that the neighborhood was established when the cemetery was—back in the middle of the nineteenth century. A cemetery needed stonemasons to sculpt statues and carve headstones, and Garden View imported artisans all the way from Italy for the task. The stonecutters brought their families. Their families brought their culture and their Old World traditions.

The bar at Mangia Mania was long and skinny with a window that looked out at the pizza place across the street, and walls that were covered in sepia-toned photographs of women holding steaming bowls of pasta, men playing bocci ball, and kids in Catholic school uniforms. There was a doorway on my left and through that, the main restaurant, a room that was just as long but not as skinny. It was filled with tables, people, and the beginnings of what sounded like one kick-ass celebration.

Another explosion of laughter broke through my thoughts.

"Some party." I made the off-hand comment at the same time the waitress finally arrived to take our orders.

She glanced over her shoulder toward the restaurant. "Retirement," she said, turning and aiming a thousand mega-watt smile on Dan as if he was the one who had made the comment. "The party is for Nick, our cook. Been here like forever and is finally calling it quits. Heading to Arizona."

Personally, I didn't much care, and if she expected a reaction from Dan…well, she didn't know him nearly as well as I did, and though I didn't know him well, I knew that social niceties weren't his bag. He nodded in a distracted sort of way and ordered a German beer. I opted for a sour-apple martini.

Dan's mind was clearly on brains, and it was going to take a lot more than small talk about retirement and Arizona to sidetrack him. He was back at it even before the waitress walked away.

"I suspected all along that there was an unusual reason for your second visit to the ER. Dr. Cho confirmed that for me. If you would consider—" Dan's gaze drifted to the front of my shirt and he lost his train of thought. I had to admit, I breathed a little sigh of relief. Finally, he wasn't thinking brains.

I sat up a little straighter.

As though he was waking up from a deep sleep, he shook himself and forced his eyes back to mine. "What I mean, of course, is that if I set up a study and if you'd agree—"

His gaze drifted back to my white cotton shirt, and a tingle of heat shot through me. It had been a long time since I experienced that kind of thrill. I liked it.

But not the way he wrinkled his nose. "What did you say you did for a living?"

It wasn't the question I expected, which was more in the ballpark of "your place or mine?"

"I'm a tour guide," I said. "At the cemetery at the top of the hill."

"It must be a pretty messy job."

I dared a look down to where he was looking and the nice warmth he'd kindled inside me froze beneath an icy layer of social faux pas. There was a smudge of dirt across the front of my shirt that went from breast to breast and was a couple of inches wide. After a day of breathing it in and washing it off my hands, I'd recognize it anywhere. Dust. Old newspaper. Mold.

I brushed at the smear. "Sorry. I spent part of the day in the cemetery archives. Doing research. I didn't realize—"

I didn't realize that by brushing at the smudge, I would only make it worse.

No doubt Dan would say my knee-jerk reaction was a result of years of behavioral programming. To me, it sounded more like my mother's voice echoing through my head, reminding me that cleanliness was next to godliness. And that right about now, I was about as far from the Maker as it was possible to get.

I popped out of my chair, all set to head to the ladies' room in search of a wet paper towel.

It wasn't until it was too late that I saw the couple walking by, headed to a nearby table. Luckily, I stopped just short of ramming right into a woman with bad hair and worse makeup. Then I lost my footing.

First it was aberrant behavior. Then it was dirt. All I needed to make myself look like a complete fool in front of Dan was to end up flat on my face on the floor.

Scrambling to regain my balance, I grabbed for the back of my chair, untangled my feet, and pivoted.

I found myself nose to frame with the picture that hung over our table. I'd been too keyed up about meeting Dan to pay any attention to it when I sat down. But as my heartrate slowed and my eyes focused, I had a chance to give the photograph a long look.

From the age of the cars parked along the street, I guessed that the picture was taken back in the sixties. It showed a dark-haired woman in a Jackie Kennedy dress and hat. She was posed outside a building that, in spite of time and various renovations, I recognized as Mangia Mania. She had an ear-to-ear grin on her face and she was pointing up at the sign above her head. A sign that said—

"Lucia's?" The word squeaked out of me. Chalk it up to aberrant behavior. I knew I was talking to myself, but I couldn't help it. I looked over at the bar and the woman who was mixing my martini. "This says Lucia's," I said, raising my voice so she could hear me above the party noises. "This place didn't use to be—"

"Lucia's Trattoria. Yeah." The woman finished with my drink and brought it over herself. She probably figured it was easier than yelling to me across the room. "That was a while ago, of course," she said, nodding toward the photograph. "The place has changed hands a couple of times since then. But my mother, she grew up in this neighborhood. I remember coming here for dinner as a kid. That's when it was Lucia's. Best spaghetti in town."

"And one hell of a veal parmigiana," I said. I had it on good authority. I glanced over my shoulder to the party going on in the other room. "How long has your cook worked here?" I asked the bartender.

She shrugged and looked at our waitress, who just happened to be passing by.

The waitress shrugged back. "Like I said, forever."

"Forever like thirty years?"

"At least thirty years." It was the bartender who answered, clearly confused by the fact that I seemed to care. "Nick, he told me once that he started here right out of high school and he's got to be like sixty-five or so. You gonna try your drink?"

It wasn't until she asked that I realized I'd already taken a couple of steps away from the table. I didn't stop to taste the drink. I didn't give Dan a chance to remind me that I was acting aberrantly. I didn't even listen to the voice of reason that told me in no uncertain terms that by doing what I knew I was doing, I might be blowing any chance I had with Dan.

I excused myself with a not-so-untrue story about needing paper towels and the ladies' room.

Then I headed for the party.

It wasn't hard to find Nick.

He was the guy wearing a spanking-new T-shirt that proclaimed RETIRED, IT'S WHAT I DO in blue block letters.

I sized up where he stood in the center of the large and noisy crowd, a collection of fellow workers, relatives, and customers who were familiar enough with the place and with its cook to get up from their tables and their plates of pasta, thump Nick on the back, and wish him well. I considered my options.

When a waiter walked by carrying a tray filled with glasses and an open bottle of red wine, I saw my golden opportunity. While he shot the shit with one of the busboys, I grabbed a glass and the bottle. The waiter didn't object; he probably figured I had every right to be there. Before he realized he was wrong, I poured a glass and sidestepped through the crowd, closing in on my target.

"Hey, Nick. Happy retirement!" I wedged myself between Nick and a woman in a red dress and offered him the wine along with my biggest, brightest smile.

Nick was a short, skinny guy with a shock of white hair that was in stark contrast to his dark and bushy brows. I could tell from the slightly glazed smile on his face that he'd already downed a couple glasses of wine but, hey, who was I to criticize? The guy was celebrating! And he was obviously good at it. He eyed the glass I held out to him with real appreciation. But when his gaze slid from the wine to me, his brows dropped low and his face clouded with confusion.

"Do I know you?"

I was about to make up some story about how often I ate there and how much I adored his rigatoni when a smile like sunshine broke over his expression.

When I realized he was staring at my chest, I knew I was in trouble.

"I get it!" Nick gave me a wink and a nod. "The fellas arranged this, didn't they? Like they did for my fiftieth birthday. It's kind of early in the evening but come on..." He grabbed my arm and tugged me toward the kitchen. "We can do it fast and get back before anyone misses me."

I stood my ground, my legs locked, my eyes wide. When Nick looked at me over his shoulder, I untangled his hand from around my arm and tried for a smile that was friendly. But not as friendly as Nick would have liked.

"Your friends didn't send me to—" Just thinking about it made me queasy. "What I mean is...well...I heard you were retiring and I wondered...that is, I was just having a drink over in the bar with a friend and I thought this was a perfect opportunity to..." I dragged in a breath. "I wanted to ask you a couple questions."

"Questions? Not—" The look Nick aimed at the kitchen door said it all.

I hated to disappoint him but there was only so much I was willing to sacrifice. With any luck, a little anticipation would be enough to cheer him. "Maybe your friends have something planned for later," I told him. "I just wanted to talk to you. About Gus Scarpetti."

I was still holding the glass of wine, and as it turned out, Nick was a good sport. When I saw him glance at the wine again, I handed it to him. That was enough to seal our deal. He tipped his head toward the swinging door that led into the kitchen.

Once the door was closed behind us, he gave me a careful once-over. "Why?" he asked. "All these years later, why is somebody like you interested in Mr. Scarpetti?"

I suppose I should have anticipated the question, but chalk one up for aberrant behavior. I was operating on instinct, not reason. Because I didn't have time to concoct a story, I settled for the truth.

"I work at the cemetery," I said, pointing in roughly the direction of Garden View. "I'm the one who gives the tours. We stop at Scarpetti's mausoleum and I thought if I knew more about him—"

"You could tell better stories. Yeah, I get that."

I breathed a little easier. "I know that Lucia's was his favorite restaurant and since you've been here so long…"

Nick shrugged. "Ain't nothing I can tell you that hasn't been said before."

"Maybe not, but it would mean so much to the people who come to the cemetery to hear about Gus from a—" I wrestled with my memory, struggling to recall the things Ella tried to drill into my head about research.

"Primary source!" I said, prouder than I had any right to be. "It would mean a lot to get information from a primary source."

Nick pursed his lips and stood a little straighter. "And that's me? That what you call it? Primary source?"

"That's you, all right. And because you're a primary source, I'm thinking that maybe you can confirm some of the things I've only read. Gus...er...Mr. Scarpetti, did he really come here every Thursday night for dinner?"

"Like clockwork."

"And the night he—"

It was hard to say *died* in connection to a guy I'd spent the afternoon with.

I swallowed down the thought with a gulp. "The night he was shot, he was here?"

"Yeah, with all his usual crowd."

By now, I knew the names as if I had dinner with them every Thursday night. "John Vitale, Ben Marzano, Michael Cardorella, Paul Ramone." I rattled off the list. "The same people he was always with."

"Hey, you done your homework!" Nick poked me on the arm. I guess it was supposed to be a compliment.

"And..." I pinned Nick with a look.

"And nothing." He looked away. "Except for the fact that Mr. Scarpetti ended up dead outside, nothing happened here that night that you could talk about to those people at the cemetery." Nick downed the rest of the glass of wine in one gulp. "End of story."

Someone called out to Nick from the restaurant, and he moved toward the door.

Maybe Nick was right and nothing out of the ordinary happened that night. Maybe he was Boy-Scout honest and as truthful as anyone could be about something that had happened so long before.

That didn't explain why I had the sneaking suspicion that he wasn't telling me everything.

If I was going to find out what that everything was, I knew I had to act fast. I was about to lose him and my only connection—aside from Gus himself—to the night of the murder.

"I'm writing a book." Where the lie came from, I didn't know, but when Nick's eyes lit, I knew I was going to grab on and run with it. "Well, maybe I'm writing a book. If I can find out enough to make it interesting. If there's nothing else you can tell me about that night, I suppose I won't be able to acknowledge you as one of my sources. Too bad. I'll bet the people in Arizona would love it if you showed them your name in print."

I let the words float between us like the smell of garlic that permeated Nick's clothing.

It worked. I could tell when he glanced over his shoulder to make sure the door was still closed.

"Anyone tell you about Carmella?" he asked.

I had the distinct feeling I was supposed to know who he was talking about.

"They've mentioned her, of course," I said, hoping that he wouldn't pin me down as to who the woman was and how she figured into the whole thing. "But no one ever told me—"

"Nah. They wouldn't. And I wouldn't say nothin' now because I don't think it's something you should be talking about over at the cemetery. But if you're writing a book, that's a whole different thing."

It wasn't like I had a lot of choice. I confirmed the lie and waited for more.

"I never mentioned it to the cops when they came around," Nick said. "And I don't think anyone else who was here that night talked about it, either. We figured it wasn't important and besides, why dishonor Mr. Scarpetti's memory with something like that." Nick briefly rested a hand over the big blue w on his shirt, and his heart. "He was a fine man, Mr. Scarpetti."

"He was a mobster."

"He was a credit to this city. Built the neighborhood community center. And that playground behind the school. Always remembered me at Christmas time, too."

"And Carmella was..."

He looked at me as if I had a screw loose. "His wife, of course. Carmella Scarpetti. If you're writing a book—"

"Oh, that Carmella!" I waved away the information as if it were incidental. "Of course I know about her. I thought you were talking about—"

"Did you know she was here that night? And that she was rip-roarin' mad?"

This was something Gus had neglected to mention, and it was that more than anything that told me it might be important.

"Mad? At Gus?"

Nick snorted. "Mad at Mr. Scarpetti. Mad at the world." He leaned in close and for a moment, I wondered if I needed to worry about Nick's fiftieth birthday and what had apparently happened in the kitchen that night. Lucky for me, Nick had other things on his mind. Like getting his name in the book I wasn't writing.

"She was a drinker, you know. Tanked up most of the time and when she was, she was as nasty as they came."

"And she was drinking that night?"

"Hotter than a firecracker. Stumbled in here toward the end of the evening and started cursing a blue streak before the door was closed behind her. There she was, yellin' at Mr. Scarpetti so that everyone could hear. Disrespectin' a man of his stature." He shook his head, as disturbed by the whole thing as he had been when it happened. "She didn't mince no words, neither. She laid it on the line, told Mr. Scarpetti that he had a lot of nerve spending every night of the week out with his associates. She demanded, right then and there, that he come home with her, where she belonged."

Somehow, the notion of Gus as henpecked didn't fit with his mob boss image. "That must really have pissed Gus off."

Nick shrugged. "Mr. Scarpetti, he didn't show emotion like that, you know? He listened for maybe fifteen seconds, decided Carmella wasn't sayin' anything he hadn't already heard and didn't want to hear again, and let one of his boys take care of her. Last I saw, Pounder was escortin' her out the back door. Right there." He pointed toward the far wall, and the door just beyond the industrial stove. "And Carmella, even while she was being half pushed, half carried out, she was still cursin' like a sailor, sayin' that she wouldn't be treated this way. That Mr. Scarpetti was goin' get his."

"And you never told the police about this?"

Nick laughed. "If Carmella was the one who ended up dead that night, it might have been important. The way it was—"

Again someone called Nick's name and this time, he wasn't about to miss out on any more of the fun. He pushed the kitchen door open and the sounds of the party washed over us.

"If you have any more questions, they'll have my new address and phone number here at the restaurant. Give me a call sometime." He grinned. "It's been a pleasure talking to you, honey. Too bad you weren't what my friends sent over for the night."

The door swished closed before I had a chance to even try to come up with a polite response.

I don't know how long I stood there in the kitchen, thinking about everything Nick had told me. Long enough to picture the scene at Lucia's all those years before. Gus busy with his veal parmigiana and his criminal empire.

While the Little Woman sat home and drank herself silly.

One of the waiters bustled in and I shook myself back to the present and gave myself a mental high five. A couple little white lies and a too-close call with Nick's libido had resulted in me knowing more than I knew when I got there. I knew about Carmella and I knew she threatened Gus. It was a not-so-little detail he'd forgotten to mention.

The night wasn't a total bust.

I punched open the door and headed back into the restaurant. The first person I saw was Dan. He was standing in the doorway that led from the bar into the restaurant. He was wearing his blue windbreaker and he had a beer in one hand and a sour-apple martini in the other.

I'd forgotten all about him.

I swallowed down the guilt that mingled with the what-are-you-nuts-how-could-you-forget-such-a-hotty, waved, and headed over to him, an apology ready on my lips. It wasn't until the last second that I realized my story about the ladies' room was never going to hold water; I hadn't even tried to clean the smudge of dirt off my shirt.

Maybe I was lucky. Or maybe Dan had had his fill of looking at my chest. He didn't notice the dirt was still there. Instead, as soon as I was within range, he handed me my drink along with a half-smile I'd seen before.

I braced for the letdown and reminded myself to look on the bright side. At least this time, I hadn't ordered the invitations and bought the gown.

Dan raised his voice to be heard over the noise. "I got a call. From one of my research assistants at the hospital. She's in a bind about some computations. It can't wait until morning. She needs the data for a paper she has to turn in to a professor tomorrow. I'm going to head back to the hospital to help her out."

I managed an anemic smile that told him I understood. And I did. Honest. Dan was dumping me and I knew it really had nothing to do with his research assistant. I'd left him sitting in the bar all by himself for who-knows how long. I couldn't blame him for giving up.

I set down my martini and followed Dan out the door.

It was dark out and sometime while we were inside, it had started to drizzle. The neon signs from nearby restaurants, coffeehouses, and bars were reflected in the wet sidewalks. It was a film noir sort of way to end what we had of a relationship, and I was about to tell Dan exactly that when he tapped the manila folder that he had tucked inside his windbreaker.

"I looked at the address in your file," he said. "I know you live close by. Your car is probably parked close by—"

"I left it at home." I answered automatically, not sure where we were headed and afraid of saying the wrong thing.

"Then you walked here?" Dan asked.

I nodded and he smiled. "I did, too," he said. "From the hospital. And you're kind of on my way back. Would it be okay if I walked you home?"

He didn't mind being abandoned in the bar? I wasn't being dumped?

Even as I smiled my agreement, my spirits rose. They might have stayed right up there in the stratosphere if I hadn't followed Dan's lead and started across Mayfield Road when the light changed.

I hadn't gone three steps when it hit me. That was exactly where Gus died.

Traffic was stopped and I took the opportunity to look up and down Mayfield, trying to imagine what he had seen that night when he walked out of Lucia's and straight into a hail of gunfire. Did he get a look at the car that careened around the corner and came at him full speed? Did he hear the first shots?

I guess I was in a unique position of sorts. The next time I saw Gus, I could ask. But at the same time, I wondered how much he'd leave out, just like he'd left out any mention of his wife the drunk. If I asked, would he tell me what the last thing he thought about was? Was it the taste of Nick's veal parmigiana? Or was Carmella's tirade still ringing in his ears?

Did he feel the first bullet tear into him and know the end was near? Did he regret his life of crime? Or did he look over at the school and picture the playground he built behind it?

The sound of Dan's voice calling to me from the other side of the street snapped me back to reality and I found myself staring at the blacktop and thinking one thing: It was a lousy place to die.

Aberrant behavior.

There was no other explanation for it.

Because as I hurried out of the way of oncoming traffic and over to where Dan was waiting for me, a single tear slipped down my cheek.

Chapter 5

Dan never questioned what I was doing with Nick. It would have been nice to think he was giving me space, but I had a sneaking suspicion that until he happened to see me walk out of the kitchen, he never really noticed I was gone. The good news is that he was true to his word; he escorted me all the way to the door of my apartment. I might have been feeling better about the whole date-that-wasn't-a-date thing if while we walked he hadn't spent the whole time talking about brains and scans and something called synapses. He asked if he could call me again, too, but the warm-and-fuzzy moment was dampened by the fact that he said something about his research study in the same breath.

I actually might have taken the time to be pissed at Dan.

If I wasn't so busy being pissed at Gus.

How did Gus expect me to get to the bottom of his murder if he didn't tell me the whole truth and nothing but? He'd failed to mention Carmella or her threats. How much else hadn't he told me?

As much as I tried, I couldn't keep the questions from bouncing through my head all night. I couldn't sleep. And it was all Gus's fault. By the next day, I was keyed up, wrung out, and dragged down. I was also ready to have it out with him.

I would have done it, too. If I knew where to find him.

It wasn't like he had a busy to-do list. The least he could have done is made an appearance so that I could read him the riot act.

Instead, I spent the morning taking care of the little details that were all part of my job. I accompanied our head groundskeeper on a golf-cart circuit around the cemetery while he pointed out the various unusual trees and plants he thought should be included on a new horticultural tour. I scheduled a visit for a third grade class from a local school and even though the little darlings wouldn't be arriving for another month, I spent some time planning how I would call in sick that day. Against my better judgment and no doubt to the horror of my college English professors should they ever catch wind of it, I gave in when Ella pressured me to write an article on tombstone symbolism for the next issue of the Garden View monthly newsletter.

But I never saw Gus. Not even once.

I actually would have been happy about the turn of events and thrilled to consider the possibility that he might be gone forever if I wasn't seething inside and so hot to let my anger out, I could barely sit still. Let's face it, I couldn't exactly take it out on anyone else. That wouldn't be right. I couldn't explain my sour mood, either. What would I say?

Sorry I'm so cranky today. No, it's not PMS. It's GSS. Gus Scarpetti syndrome. You see, there's this ghost...

I snapped out of the thought just as the Garden View visitors' bus rolled up to our first stop. As if they'd choreographed the move, the members of the Sacred Heart Ladies' Guild got up from their seats en masse, and I knew I had to get moving, too. Time to introduce them to the first angel on our tour.

Like I always did, I got off the bus before anyone else and stepped aside so that Bill, our driver, could stand next to me and help if he was needed. I reminded the ladies to watch their steps at the same time I waved them over to where I would start into the script I hadn't even read until right before they showed up.

Naturally, the slowest movers were the last in line. I offered my assistance to a lady in blue pants and a green sweater who was having trouble walking. Once she was safely settled, I climbed back onto the bus to grab on to another woman who was wearing orthopedic shoes and mumbling something about how steps were hard for her. I helped her, too, and handed her to Bill. He had been doing this for a long time and two hard-to-maneuver old ladies were nothing to him. One on each arm, Bill started toward the angel. Without looking, I automatically reached for the next person in line.

Turns out it wasn't a person at all.

I stopped just short of poking my hand right into Gus's stomach.

"What the hell are you doing here?"

He shushed me, one finger to his lips. "You want these nice ladies to think you're crazy?"

I didn't.

I glanced over my shoulder, and it wasn't until I was sure they were out of range that I dared to say another word.

"Where the hell have you been?" I was forced to whisper and it made my words sound like exactly what they were, the hiss coming off a boiling teakettle. "We need to talk."

Gus straightened his suit coat and when he got off the bus, I was forced to back down the steps. Once we were both outside, we were eye to eye. "We need to talk," he said, "when I say we need to talk."

He walked away and headed for the angel statue.

"No." I dared to raise my voice. The members of the Sacred Heart Ladies' Guild were busy chatting and I didn't think any of them would realize I was talking to not-so-thin air. And so what if they did? By this time, I was way too mad to care. "If you want my help with this, Gus, we talk when *I* say we talk."

Not surprisingly, Gus wasn't used to this kind of sass. He stopped and I saw his shoulders stiffen. When he turned back to me, his eyes were narrowed and his lips were pressed in a thin line. "What did you say?"

I grew up in an upper-middle-class family with every privilege in the world. Public schools in a stellar system. A college that was better than some and pricier than most. What I wanted when I wanted it. And a circle of friends and acquaintances whose lives were carbon copies of mine.

I had never had to stand up for myself against a mob boss.

I gulped down a sudden, icy fear but just as quickly reminded myself that mob boss or not, Gus couldn't lay a hand on me. Funny how much courage a realization like that can give a girl.

I straightened my shoulders, too, and when I looked Gus in the eye, I made sure mine were just as narrowed and just as steely as his. "I said we need to talk."

"We've said everything we have to say."

I let him think he'd won. I let him turn and walk away. When I threw my next comment at him, I made sure my voice was as breezy as the one I'd use in a minute or two when I talked about the marble angel that stood nearby.

"We haven't talked about Carmella."

Big points for Gus. He winced but he didn't stop or turn to look at me. He kept right on walking. He skirted the crowd of ladies gathered around the angel statue and walked straight into an obelisk that was carved out of a single block of granite and stood more than seven feet high.

When he didn't come out on the other side, I knew I'd hit a nerve.

It didn't make up for my sleepless night, but at least it was something. Cheered, I joined my tour group.

Once I had everyone's attention, I told them all about angels, or at least as much as I could remember from the script that had been written by the woman who held my job before me. I mentioned how some people believe that angels are messengers between heaven and earth. I faked my way through a field guide to angels: seraphim and cherubim, archangels and the rest of the heavenly crowd.

I guess I must have held my own pretty well. The women of the Sacred Heart Ladies' Guild didn't argue.

I was just about to launch into the statistics— how many angel statues there were at Garden View, how much marble it took to make them, which stood the highest and which was the smallest—when a voice whispered in my ear.

"Carmella, she didn't have nothing to do with it."

I refused to acknowledge Gus. We weren't going to discuss this on his terms, and the sooner he realized it, the better. As if the only sounds around us were the birds in the trees, I went right on.

"As you can see from the name carved into the pedestal, this particular angel marks the burial place of—"

"And who told you about Carmella anyway?"

"The burial place of the Smith family." I pronounced each word carefully, sending the message (I hoped) that Gus was going to have to wait his turn. "Now if you'll get back to the bus, we'll head to our next stop and another angel."

I don't know how he got over there so quickly,

but by the time I made my way over to where the bus was waiting, Gus was already there. He was leaning on a tall headstone carved with shamrocks and a Celtic harp. "Who told you?"

The ladies were talking and laughing as they waited to climb onto the bus, and I turned my back on them, pretending to look through the papers on my clipboard at the same time I made sure to keep my voice down. "You're not paying attention," I told Gus. "*You're* not asking the questions anymore. From now on, I ask the questions. And if you don't want to answer them…"

It wasn't exactly a threat but I tried to make it sound like one. I turned back around, and because I knew there was a ladies' room near the next angel and that those ladies would visit it just as every group of women tourists did, I knew I'd have time to kill once we arrived there. I signaled to Bill that I would walk to our next stop, and I waited until the bus pulled away.

"If you don't want to answer my questions—"

I was wasting my breath. Gus was gone.

I grumbled a word that would have made the Sacred Heart women blanch and started off in the direction of our next stop. Unfortunately, that was the first time I'd conducted the angel tour and though in theory I knew exactly where I was going, in reality it was a little harder to get my bearings. I watched as the bus glided around a corner up ahead and followed, but after a couple minutes and an endless landscape of headstones, statues, obelisks, and mausoleums, I was pretty much lost.

"Shit." I plunked down onto the nearest flat surface, which happened to be a stone bench tucked between the surrounding branches of two ancient evergreens. I carried a map of Garden View with me and I fished it out from the bottom of the pile of papers on my clipboard and looked around for one of the section marker signs posted near the road. I was in Section 45 and if I was headed to Section 53...

"Girls shouldn't talk like that."

At the sound of Gus's voice, I just about jumped out of my skin. All the more reason to do what I could to annoy him. I slanted him a look. "Shit. Shit. Shit," I said.

He clicked his tongue. "If you were my daughter, I'd wash your mouth out with soap."

"And if I were your son, Rudy, you wouldn't even think to criticize the way I talk."

He sat down on the bench next to me. "Of course not. Men talk like men and women—"

"Should stay home and have babies. Yeah, I've heard all about that." Disgusted, I rose to my feet. "It's the twenty-first century, Gus. Get with the program."

"And the program is what? Going out with a boy who is interested only in your body?"

"The only part of my body he's interested in is my brain and—" Gus's words sank in and I stopped, startled. "How do you know about Dan?"

He shrugged. It was an elegant little movement, out of character for a man as beefy as Gus. "I pay attention," he said. "And besides, I was in your office when he left a message. On your answering machine."

"And you're waiting for me to ask what the message was about."

"You're not going to?"

"I'll listen to it when I get back to the office."

"And if I erased it?"

He wasn't about to catch me on that one, and I let him know it with a little I'm-alive-and-you're-not smirk. "Can't," I reminded him. "Pressing the erase button would require a corporeal body."

Gus actually smiled. "It never hurts to try a bargaining chip. Even if it's not a good one. Remember that, kid. It might come in handy someday. So…" He got up and straightened his suit coat. "Who you looking for?"

It took me a second to figure out what he was talking about. I checked my script for the next monument on our tour. "Anderson, Louis and Matilda."

"And you don't know where they are."

"You wouldn't know where they were, either, if you had something to do all day other than whatever it is you do all day. And what do you do all day, anyway?"

"Is that one of those questions you said you'd be asking from now on?"

I should have known he wouldn't forget our little tiff at the first angel monument. All well and good. Because I wasn't about to forget it, either.

I raised my chin. "I haven't really thought about it but now that you mention it, yeah. That is one of my questions. What do you do all day, Gus?"

"I keep busy. Plenty busy. I watch. I listen. Like to that boy on your answering machine. I walk around. Hell, I've been walking around this place for thirty years. I'm familiar with every inch of it. Which means one of us knows exactly where Anderson, Louis and Matilda are located."

I guess he figured I was smart enough to catch his drift. This time, he didn't even bother to use the words "bargaining chip."

I gave in with as much good grace as I could. "Nick told me about Carmella."

"Nick? The cook from—"

"Lucia's. Yeah. Only it's not Lucia's anymore. It's—"

"Did you try the veal parmigiana?"

I sighed my annoyance. "I'm thinking murder and you're thinking veal parmigiana?"

"Are you thinking about my murder?"

"Are you going to tell me where to find Anderson, Louis and Matilda?"

A smile touched Gus's lips. "You're a quick learner, kid. Come on."

He started off across the section, and because I didn't have any choice, I followed along. This was one of the oldest parts of the cemetery and back in the day, only the wealthiest of Cleveland's citizens could afford to be buried here. Unlike the newer sections where common folks spent their eternal rest side by side and in neat rows marked by flat-to-the-ground stones, the older sections were a maze of sculptures, standing headstones, and mausoleums.

We walked a staggered path through it all and though he didn't say a word, I knew Gus was waiting for the rest of my story. We had made a bargain of sorts. I was honor bound to keep my end of it.

"Nick says Carmella was drunk."

"Nick is wrong."

"Nick says Carmella was drunk a lot."

"Nick doesn't know from nothing."

"Nick says Carmella threatened you."

Gus stopped midstride and glared at me. "I told you, Carmella didn't have nothing to do with it."

"And you know this how?"

Instead of answering, he glanced up at the tree over my left shoulder. He studied it for so long, I might have thought he was a candidate for the new horticultural tour. If I didn't know better.

Gus was stalling.

I knew it.

He knew I knew it.

Before I could call him on it, he twitched his broad shoulders and looked me in the eye. "After Carmella left Lucia's, she was busy for the rest of the night."

"You're sure about that?"

"Yeah."

"How do you know?"

He smoothed a hand over his fat tie. "She told me."

I rolled my eyes. "Right. And it's not like I don't believe you, but I should talk to her."

"You can't."

"Because you say so."

"Because she ain't around." Gus started up again. He walked right into the closed front door of a rose granite mausoleum and a second later, stepped out of a stained-glass window at the back.

I was forced to take a more conventional route. I ducked under the branches of the tree growing near the door, and sidestepped between the mausoleum and the one that stood nearby.

Gus was waiting for me. "She spends the winter in Florida," he said. "It's only what, the second week of April? She's not back yet."

"Then I'll talk to her when she gets back."

"You'll leave Carmella out of this."

I stood my ground and I'll admit it, I stamped my foot. It was a pretty juvenile way to make a statement, but it was exactly what Gus expected from a girl. It got his attention and that was the whole point. "Why? Why can't I talk to Carmella? Because she's family? Seems to me that's exactly why you should suspect her. Which brings up another whole subject. What about your son?"

When he looked my way, anger flared in Gus's eyes. "Rudy?"

"Yeah. Rudy. You haven't said much about him. But according to what I read in those newspapers, he inherited your criminal empire."

"I didn't have no criminal empire."

"Don't give me that bullshit. That's what you said in every interview you ever gave the press. You might have fooled them but you're not fooling me. If it wasn't a criminal empire, what was it?"

Gus sniffed. "It was business."

"Okay then, did Rudy take over your business interests?"

"Yeah."

"Then maybe he's the one who—"

"No! You—" Gus stabbed a finger at me. "You are getting on my nerves, little girl."

"Then we're even."

"We're only even if I'm pissing you off big-time. Because that's exactly what you are doing to me, honey. But even that...that's not keeping you from thinking about my murder."

My own words came back to haunt me. Which didn't mean I was going to let Gus have the upper hand. "How can I think about your murder when you're not telling me the whole story? You've been holding out on me, Gus, and that's not fair. And it's not going to do you any good, either. If you want this thing solved, you're going to have to help me out. I'm not exactly Columbo."

Gus's eyes lit. "I always liked that guy. He still on TV?"

I didn't explain about cable or syndication. What good would it have done me? Besides, as we got to the top of a sloping rise crowned with a series of free-standing statues depicting the twelve apostles, I saw the tour bus across the winding road. Now that I'd wasted all this time talking to Gus, I knew I'd better get over there before the crowd got antsy.

"The point is, I'm not a detective," I told Gus, sidestepping a standing headstone that was as tall as me. "I can't investigate because I don't know how to investigate."

"You start at the beginning."

My sigh rippled the spring air. "I thought we already did. You'll excuse the pun but as far as I can see, we're at a dead end."

Rather than admit that I was right, Gus made a face. "What happened, it had to have something to do with me, with my past."

"No shit, Sherlock. You want to come up with any other lame theories?"

He was good at ignoring sarcasm. Or maybe my sarcasm just wasn't that good. "What I'm telling you is that you should start with me. With everything that ever happened to me."

"You're not going to tell me your life story, are you?" The prospect didn't cheer me. I took off walking again, making my way toward where I saw Bill craning his neck, hoping for a glimpse of me. I had already taken stock of the lay of the land and I knew there was nothing between me and the street but a strip of grass. I turned back to Gus but I kept on walking. "Just thinking about it gives me the willies," I told him. "Hour after hour of you telling me how you weren't a criminal. No, thanks."

"There is the police museum down at the Justice Center."

I pursed my lips, considering the suggestion. "They've got documentation?"

Gus puffed out his chest. "I hear they've got a whole display. All about me."

It was a good idea. I wasn't about to let him know it.

"Whatever," I told him instead. I felt the ground beneath my feet change from springy lawn to street and knew I was almost all the way over to where my group was waiting. "We'll talk about it after—"

After that, I'm not exactly sure what happened.

I heard Gus scream my name. At the same time, I felt a weird sort of tingle. Like an icy hand had gone right through me.

It was enough to make me snap to attention and when I did, I saw a funeral procession led by a big black hearse. It was just a couple feet away. Coming right at me.

I jumped back onto the lawn just as the hearse zoomed past. Gus was standing by my side.

I pressed a hand to my heart, hoping to stop it racing. "Thank you."

He waved away my words as if they were nothing. "Nothing to thank me for."

"If you hadn't warned me those cars were there—" Reality hit like I hear it always does after that kind of near-death experience. My eyes filled with tears and I dashed them away with the back of one hand. I was still shivering with that funny sort of icy cold, and when I saw Gus pull his arm back to his side, I knew why. "You tried to grab me. And your hand went right through me, just like it went through the magazines on my desk. And now I feel…"

I hugged my arms around myself, hoping to get

rid of the chill that went all the way through to my bones.

"You all right, kid?"

I glanced over to find Gus watching me carefully. "I'm fine." I was, thanks to—

"You warned me, Gus. You saved my life."

He glanced away. "Big deal."

"It's a very big deal. I could have been hit. Or killed. I could have traded in my employee ID card for a headstone."

"Nah!" He stuffed his hands into his pockets and maybe it was a trick of the spring sunshine. I could have sworn I saw him blush.

That's when the truth hit me and a sudden warm flush melted the ice in my veins. I grinned.

"You know what, Gus? You're full of it."

"Full of—"

"You love the big, bad mob boss image. But something tells me that deep down inside, you're a pretty nice guy."

His eyes lit, but that didn't erase the sting of his words as he walked away. "What are you, some kind of jamoke? Don't fool yourself, sweetheart. I didn't save you because I care. I saved you because you're the only one who can help me."

Chapter 6

Three days later, I was still frozen to the bone.

Always an optimist, I did my best to look on the bright side. The spine-tingling cold was a result of Gus trying to grab me, but as weird (not to mention disturbing) as it was to think of his hand going right through me, the resulting chill had its advantages. Even though the spring day was warm and heading for the humid side, I bundled up. I pulled out the pink Abercrombie sweater I'd stashed away with my winter clothes and paired it with coffee-colored pants and brown heels that added a full two inches to my height. My hair was down around my shoulders in a tumble of curls.

I looked good, and it was a good thing I did. I needed every advantage I could get when I arrived at the Justice Center.

"Closed?" In case I hadn't read the sign right the first time, I checked it out again, looking over my shoulder toward the door of the Cleveland Police Historical Society Museum, just a couple feet inside the lobby and to the right of the main doors. "What do they mean, closed?"

The guy sitting behind the security desk wore a plastic badge that said his name was Frank. He was middle-aged and heavyset. Frank had a phone book open on the counter in front of him and he was running a finger down a long column of names. He barely gave me a glance. "That's what the sign says, lady. And that's what it means. It's Saturday. The museum is always closed on Saturday."

"But I didn't know that."

Frank answered with an unconcerned shrug.

"But I came all the way down here and paid four bucks to park."

He yawned.

"But it's my only day off and—"

I was getting nowhere, and I gave up with a sigh. Fortunately, Frank was at the end of a column and looked up at just the right moment. The gleam that brightened his dark eyes told me that sighing did great things for my sweater. He stood, the better to give me a not-so-subtle once-over. It was especially easy for him to get a good look at my boobs since I was a full five inches taller than him.

"I might have seen one of the cops go in there a little while ago," Frank said. "I could check."

I leaned forward just a bit. "I'd be grateful."

"Phone number grateful?"

"Can I get inside the museum?"

He hurried over to find out.

When he returned a couple minutes later, Frank had a piece of paper in one hand. Call me shallow. Or maybe I'd been hanging around with Gus too long and was starting my slide toward the Dark

Side. When he handed me a Bic, I didn't hesitate to write down a phony name and number. Right before I told Frank to give me a call and scampered toward the museum.

The door was still closed, but when I gave it a push, it swung open.

"Hello?" I stepped inside and closed the door behind me. "Anybody here?"

There was no answer. Not that I cared. Once I was in, I had a perfect chance to look around, and I took it.

It didn't take long. The museum was one big nondescript room painted institutional white. It had a high ceiling and a tile floor, scuffed squares of blue and white. On my left was a cubbyhole that featured a display of illegal drugs. In front of me was a glass case full of old police uniforms. I hurried past both. A motorcycle took up one wall, a jail cell filled another. According to the sign above it, it had been lifted whole from an old police station. The graffiti on the walls inside the cell was testimony to that. A crash course in ballistics—complete with guns and bullets—was featured in an exhibit case in the center of the room. Along the wall to my right...

I gave the black-and-white photos displayed there a quick look and grinned as if I'd found treasure.

With any luck, I had.

One of the photos was familiar, the picture of Gus lying facedown in the middle of Mayfield Road. AUGUSTINO SCARPETTI, the sign above the display said. THE LIFE AND TIMES OF CLEVELAND'S MOST NOTORIOUS MOB BOSS.

My heart beat double time and before I could remind myself that there was probably nothing there that I didn't already know and that what I already knew didn't shed any light on Gus's murder, I zipped over and took a look at the rest of the photos displayed on the board. One showed Gus at his First Communion, fresh-faced and angelic. In another, he was older, but not much. He was standing against a wall, holding a sign in front of his chest that had his name written on it along with a bunch of numbers. His first arrest, and he didn't even look scared.

I refused to get suckered in by the whole emotional quagmire that had swamped me as I stood outside Mangia Mania. Who cared how Gus had turned from choir-boy cute to a life of crime? Maybe he was just bad, and maybe bad was the reason he'd ended his days bleeding out into the gutters of Little Italy. Or maybe the real reason, as Gus had suggested, could be found there in the photographs and memorabilia that—except for his pain-in-the-ass ectoplasm—were all that was left of his life.

There was only one way to find out. I'd brought a notepad with me, and I pulled it out of my purse and fished around for a pen, ready to get to work.

"You don't look like a history buff."

What with Gus materializing at the drop of a hat, you'd think I'd be used to people sneaking up on me by now. I wasn't. At the sound of the voice right behind me, I gasped and whirled around.

Whoever I expected to find, it wasn't a drop-dead gorgeous guy in black pants and a cashmere sweater that fit a chest as solid as if it had been chipped from granite. He had a lean and stubborn chin and hair that was as inky as his sweater. It had enough of a wave to make me itch to run my fingers through it.

In between the chin and the hair was a face that would tempt an angel to mortal sin.

"Sorry." He went through the motions, but he didn't look sorry and I knew why. Like hunks always did, this hunk figured he owned the world and was entitled to do whatever he wanted. No apologies necessary. "I didn't mean to startle you. I thought Frank told you there was somebody here."

"Frank told me—" Was that my voice? The one that sounded as if I was trying to zip myself into jeans that were two sizes too small?

I told myself to get a grip. Guys—even ones as gorgeous as this—had never gotten the upper hand with me. Just so he'd know it, I stepped back and gave this gorgeous guy a long, leisurely look. "Frank said there was a cop in here. No way you're a cop."

He looked me over, too, and when he was done, his dark brows inched up. His voice was as hot as sin. "You want to see my badge?"

Oh yeah, I wanted to see his badge, all right. Along with the rest of him. But I knew it was bad form to admit it. At least this early in the game.

"Cops are old and gray," I told him, wrinkling

my nose so he'd understand right off the bat that "old and gray" wasn't something I was interested in. "They're overweight from eating too many donuts and crabby from all that sugar."

"Hey, we've all got to start somewhere."

"Cops wear uniforms."

"Not when they're in the Detective Bureau."

"Cops don't work in museums."

"You got me there." He kept his tone light and his words casual, but he winced, and that made me think that working in a museum was not something he was proud of. "Cops don't work in museums. Which is why I'm not working. I'm volunteering."

"Out of the kindness of your heart?"

"Kindness my ass." His eyes sparkled even though his expression didn't. "I've got a lieutenant who's got a soft spot for this place."

"And you're trying to get on his good side."

"*Her* good side, and believe me, it isn't easy." He stuck out his right hand. "Quinn Harrison."

"Pepper Martin." We shook hands. His was large and well shaped. He had long fingers and a firm grip. And if he noticed that at the contact, my hand started trembling just the slightest bit? At least he didn't point it out.

Just like I didn't point out the obvious fact that he was staring at my chest.

There was no use wasting an appreciative audience. I pulled back my shoulders and Quinn grinned his approval.

"So…" He rocked back on his heels. "You come here often?"

"That's a lousy pick-up line. Even in a bar."

"Then it's a good thing we're not in a bar."

"And if you really are a detective like you claim to be, you'd realize that if I came here often, I'd know the museum isn't open on Saturdays."

"But I only come in on Saturdays. That means if you came here often and you knew the museum was closed on Saturdays, we never would have had a chance to meet and then you wouldn't be about to give me your phone number."

"The same one I gave Frank at the security desk?"

Quinn laughed. It was a deep, rich sound, and it sent a little tremor up my spine and across my shoulders. Like champagne bubbles.

"Frank's a moron," he said. "He's sitting out there as happy as a clam, thinking about how he's going to romance you with a shot and a beer and get you in the sack right after. It will take him forever and a day before he figures out he's been conned. I, on the other hand, can smell a dodge a mile away. Just so you know…" His smile inched up a bit. Dazzling enough to blind even a level-headed woman.

And no one had ever accused me of being level-headed.

Quinn moved in close enough for me to smell his aftershave. It was Flavio, the same fragrance Joel always wore.

I tried not to hold it against him.

"Just so you know what a good judge of character I am, I can tell that a shot and a beer isn't your style," he said and Flavio notwithstanding, Quinn's voice, deep and resonant, made me forget that Joel Panhorst had ever existed. "So I'm thinking Pietro's. You know, that new place in the Warehouse District. I hear they've got a reservation list a mile long but...well..." Just like he didn't do apologies, he didn't do modest, either. He tried for sheepish and only ended up looking hotter than ever. "I've got a few connections. I'm pretty sure we could get a window table some night soon. So what do you think? Candlelight. Wine. White tablecloths and flowers. And did I mention the candlelight?"

He did, and just thinking about studying the planes and ridges of Quinn's face in the light of a flickering candle made me weak in the knees.

I stayed strong. "I'll check my social calendar," I told him.

Quinn chuckled. "Don't check. Just say yes."

"Yes."

Okay, so I crumbled. Who could blame me? As hunks went, this one was on top of the food chain. Plus he hadn't said one word about my brain.

What woman could resist?

"So tell me, Pepper Martin, what brings you to our little depository of things nobody cares about?"

"One of the things nobody cares about." I pointed to the pictures of Gus. "Him."

Quinn pursed his lips, considering. "Scarpetti? I've heard stories about him around the station. Some of the older cops remember him."

"And what do they say about—" I sounded too

anxious, and I knew it. I reined myself in and tried for the cool composure that always worked better than too fast, too hot, and too heavy.

Except in the bedroom.

"I work at the cemetery where Scarpetti is buried. I give the tours and the more I can find out about our residents—"

This time when Quinn's eyebrows slid up, it was in surprise. "Residents?"

Heat shot through my cheeks. "I've been hanging around Ella too long. She's my boss. That's what she calls them. Anyway, the more I know, the more I can tell our visitors. I heard there was an exhibit here about Gus...er...Scarpetti. I thought if I stopped down, I might be able to find out some things that other people don't know."

Quinn scraped a hand through his hair. One strand refused to be corralled, and it hung over his forehead like an inky question mark. It took more self-control than I knew I had not to reach up and smooth it into place. "Can't help you there," he said, and he sounded honestly disappointed. "From what I've heard, Scarpetti was an ornery son of a bitch and my buddies over in Organized Crime say his son has continued the family tradition in grand style. But personally, I don't know anything about these old mobbed-up types. I have heard Larry, the collections manager, say he's got a stash of stuff about Scarpetti in the storage room. He claims that if the museum ever gets enough funding for more space, he could double the size of this display."

I didn't care much about the museum doubling in size. Not as much as I did about that one word: stash.

Though I suspected he encountered it so much he was immune, I batted my eyelashes at Quinn. "I don't suppose you'd consider—"

"Maybe if you ask really nice."

He was taller than me—always a big plus—and I scooted close enough so that I had to look up into his eyes. They were as green as spring oak leaves, shot through with a color that reminded me of amber. When I asked really nice, it wasn't hard to sound head over heels. Heck, I already was.

"Please."

I knew he'd cave. Guys always did. "Let me lock the door so Frank doesn't send any more pretty women in here," Quinn said and he did just that. "The storage room is out the back door of the museum and down the hall and I think I know where Larry keeps the key."

On his way from the front door, he grabbed my hand and tugged me along with him.

Suddenly, I wasn't so cold anymore.

It's not easy to own up to my weaknesses. But hey, I've already admitted that I talk to a dead guy. I shouldn't be embarrassed (at least not too much) to confess that I know exactly what would have happened with Quinn in that cramped storage room if we hadn't found two middle-aged volunteers in there sorting through mountains of stuff.

Damn it.

The good news is that Quinn looked just as disappointed to see that we had company as I felt. A spark in his eyes that mirrored the fire that threatened me with self-combustion, he shrugged his regret, gave me a grin that promised *another time,* and let go of my hand. The last I saw of him, he was headed down a long aisle where cardboard boxes were stacked one on top of the other in a precarious version of organization.

Every inch of me tingling as if I'd touched electricity, I waited for Quinn to return, nodding hello when the volunteer couple sidled by with piles of newspapers in their arms. They staked out the only desk in the room and got down to work, which meant that when Quinn finally came back carrying a roll of paper towels and a battered box labeled SCARPETTI, we had no choice but to drag two wobbly metal chairs over to one corner and set the box on the floor between us.

Not much room to move much less work, but the tight quarters had advantages. Quinn ripped a paper towel from the roll and leaned over to wipe an inch-thick layer of dust off the top of the box. His knees touched mine.

It wasn't much, but the contact sent a shiver of anticipation through me.

Maybe that's why my breath was tight in my chest as I watched him open the box. Or maybe it was because now that I found myself so close to information that might explain so much about Gus, my heartbeat sped up a couple dozen beats and my palms itched. I scraped them against my pant legs, craned my neck, and bent over the box. "What's inside?"

"Newspaper articles." Quinn reached in and pulled out a stack of old newspapers that matched the ones in the cemetery archives. Down to the coating of mold.

I sneezed and reached into my purse for a tissue.

Quinn dug deeper into the cardboard box. "More photographs like the ones in the museum display." He took them out and set them on the floor, and once again, I found myself face-to-face with the young Gus Scarpetti. Dead Gus wasn't a handsome man, but even when he was young and alive, he was nothing to write home about. Beefy neck. Prominent nose. Piercing eyes that glared at the camera as if he was daring it and anyone brave enough to look at his picture to come and get a piece of him.

"What?" The sound of Quinn's voice snapped me out of my thoughts, and I looked up to find him studying me, his head cocked to one side. "You're looking at the guy like you know him."

"Me? Scarpetti was dead before I was born." I laughed and wondered if Quinn noticed that I relayed the fact and sidestepped his comment at the same time. "I was just thinking. That's all. About looking at the face of a guy who has a mausoleum over at the cemetery."

And about how one bright and sunny afternoon, Gus Scarpetti stepped out of that mausoleum and into my life.

The now-familiar chill came back in spades and before I even realized I was doing it, I found myself with my arms crossed over my chest.

"Cold?"

Quinn's question was innocent enough. His expression was anything but. I could practically see the wheels turning inside his head. I didn't need him to figure out that I had more than just a professional interest in Gus's life.

"Just a chill." To prove my point, I sniffed into my tissue. "I've been a little under the weather."

He grinned. "Glad you warned me before we exchanged any germs."

"I'll let you know when it's safe to get close again," I promised, and he got back to work, bending over the cardboard box and fishing around inside.

He came up holding a stack of yellowed papers that he set on his lap so he could riffle through them. "Arrest records. Witness statements." He laid them aside and reached into the box again. This time, he pulled out a folder. It was once manila-colored but by then, it was a shade that reminded me of the caramel they used as the not-so-secret ingredient in the tiramisu at the coffee shop downstairs from my apartment. "There's even a copy of Scarpetti's autopsy report in here."

For reasons I can't explain and are probably way too close to deranged to even think about, there was something about reading the cold, hard facts of Gus's death that fascinated me. Before Quinn could offer it, I snatched the autopsy report out of his hand.

"Cold hard facts" doesn't begin to describe what I found inside the folder. At the top of the first page was a case number, along with Gus's name and the date and time of his death.

No big news there.

I also found out how tall he was, how much he weighed, and that when he went to Lucia's for veal parmigiana and ended up kicking the bucket, he was suitably attired in a gray suit, white shirt, black and red silk tie, white jockey shorts, black socks, and alligator shoes. All custom made, I was sure, and as flashy as what he'd been buried in.

I didn't care how much Gus's brain, his heart, and the rest of his internal organs weighed so I zipped past that info and on to a section titled EVIDENCE OF INJURY. The information here confirmed what I'd read in the newspaper articles. All told, Gus had sustained sixteen bullet wounds. The autopsy report described each and every one in its own paragraph, complete with long medical words I didn't know and didn't really want to understand. None of that mattered. What was important was the last line of a couple of the descriptions: "This is a fatal wound."

It wasn't like I didn't know that Gus was dead, but just reading the words, detached and clinical, made my insides bunch. Before my gag reflex could get the best of me, I leafed past the anatomical data.

A good plan.

If I hadn't found myself staring at the autopsy photos.

Looking at the pictures of Gus cut open and laid out on a surgical table made my stomach do a flip-flop. I shuffled through the pictures as quickly as I could, and I would have kept right on shuffling if one photo in particular hadn't caught my eye.

One of the wounds listed as "unfatal" was to Gus's right thigh and the photo showed it in detail. But it wasn't the bruised flesh around the bullet hole that caught my eye and held me spellbound.

It was the red mark on Gus's right hip. The one that was about the size of a quarter and shaped like a rose.

"Hey, you look a little green." Quinn plucked the folder out of my hand. "Not everybody's cut out to look at this stuff and not get queasy. You okay?"

Was I? Not if okay involved finding the irrefutable evidence Gus had displayed the first day I met him.

A birthmark.

One I couldn't have dreamed up, no matter how warped my imagination might be.

I promised myself that when I got home, I'd scream. Or cry. Or whatever you were supposed to do when you discovered that something you knew couldn't possibly be true really was.

For now, I had a handsome detective to deal with.

I cringed, looking at the autopsy folder he still held in one hand. A shiver snaked up my spine. "How can anybody get used to looking at dead bodies?"

He shrugged. "You get used to it."

"You? Does that mean—"

"I'm in Homicide," he said. "All it takes is a couple weeks on the job and a couple of shootings. After that, all the bodies, they pretty much look alike."

His assessment was just as clinical as that of Gus's autopsy report. But I didn't hold it against him. Something told me it was the only way professionals were able to deal with a daily dose of death and not lose their marbles.

An idea popped into my head. "Homicide, huh? So tell me, if this was your case, how would you investigate?"

"If this was my case, I'd still be sitting here doing nothing." There was no mistaking the sudden sting of bitterness in Quinn's words or that he regretted it instantly.

"Sorry." This time, I knew he was. Not for getting angry. For letting it show. He was sorry he'd lost control and let me get a glimpse of his vulnerability. Just as sorry as he was that now that he'd mentioned it, he had to explain himself.

"I'm not exactly on the job at the moment," he said. "Administrative leave."

"You did something you shouldn't have done."

"Oh no!" Quinn's eyes sparked with defiance. "I did something I *should have* done. I just shouldn't have gotten caught."

"Which explains why you're trying to get back into your lieutenant's good graces."

"You got that right."

"Is it working?"

"God, I hope so." He got up from his chair, and if there had been a little more room than none, I think he would have paced like a caged lion. "I'm as bored as hell."

It wasn't fair but, hey, how often did I have the advantage of professional input? I used Quinn's confession to my advantage. "So indulge me," I said. "Pretend it all just happened and that it's your case. How would you investigate Scarpetti's death?"

Quinn was still hanging on to the autopsy report. He tossed it into the box. "Nothing to investigate. Never is when it comes to these sorts of organized crime killings."

"But wouldn't you wonder? About who was behind the shooting? And why? How would you find out what really happened?"

"I'd do exactly what I'm sure the cops did back then. Talk to all the usual suspects. And I guarantee I'd find out exactly what they found out—nothing. They never could prove who ordered the hit. As to why..." Quinn dropped back into his chair. He tucked the rest of the papers into the box and folded the top closed. "Back then, they probably figured it didn't matter who issued the orders. One dead mob boss was as good as another. And I bet that's exactly what happened. One bad guy whacked another bad guy. End of story."

I knew it wasn't but there was no way I could tell

Quinn. Not without looking like a certified nut-case.

I stuck to the facts. Always a better choice than dabbling in possibilities. Especially when one of those possibilities was that the dead guy was definitely dead but not gone. And that this same dead guy was convinced that there was more to his murder than a simple mob hit.

"So you think there's a possibility that Gus's death wasn't investigated as carefully as it could have been?" I asked Quinn.

He held out one hand, palm out, the gesture so authoritative I wondered if at one time he'd been a traffic cop. "I never said that. I said—"

"That one dead mob boss is as good as another. That it doesn't matter who killed Scarpetti. Doesn't justice figure into this anywhere?"

"Hold on!" Quinn studied me, his eyes narrowed. "Are you a reporter or something?"

"No."

"Then a relative? Do you know the Scarpetti family?"

I sighed. It was a genuine enough reaction to my frustration, and I hoped the rise and fall of my breasts might distract Quinn long enough to make him notice my body. And forget his accusations.

It didn't work.

Apparently, a cop could be as single-minded as a research scientist.

I sighed again.

"Look, I might as well tell you the truth," I said,

even as I prepared for another lie. "I got interested in Scarpetti because of my work at the cemetery. And now I'm thinking I might want to write a book about him. That's why I'm doing this extra research. I thought I could make the story more interesting if I could find out—"

"Something juicy that no one else knows."

"Yeah. Something like that. I thought if I looked through the records, I might come up with something that wasn't mentioned in the newspapers. You know, something that will make my manuscript stand out. Maybe even get it turned into a movie."

"I hate to burst your bubble, but I don't think it's going to happen. You saw the reports. Gunshot wounds, blood and guts, blah, blah, blah. There's nothing new here."

"Then I guess I'll have to look somewhere else."

Quinn jumped out of his chair, reached for my hand, and dragged me up alongside him.

"I want you to make me a promise," he said.

The comment came out of left field and I hesitated.

Quinn's eyes glittered. "I don't like the way you're talking, Pepper. I want you to tell me that you don't have any crazy ideas about poking around in Scarpetti Family business."

"But—"

"These are dangerous people. If I didn't have an appointment with my union attorney in..." He checked his watch. "...exactly twenty minutes, I'd

give you chapter and verse about just how dangerous they are. You understand that these aren't ordinary, everyday folks, don't you?"

"Sure, but—"

"And they're not going to like somebody asking
questions. Even when that somebody is as innocent-
looking as you."

"Am I?" I stepped closer. "Innocent-looking, I
mean?"

The spark in Quinn's eyes told me that he got my
message. Even if he wasn't about to be distracted by
it. He tightened his hold on my hand. "I'm serious,
Pepper. You may think it's a sort of scavenger hunt
and that you'll find information you can use on
your cemetery tour or in your book, but Rudy
Scarpetti is as much of a scumbag as his father
ever was. That's why they call him the Cootie. If
he hears that you've been poking your pretty little
nose—"

"Is my nose pretty?"

It was Quinn's turn to sigh. "You're trying to
change the subject and it's not going to work. Yes,
your nose is pretty. So is the rest of you. But—"
His compliments were completely ruined by that
one word. "You have to believe me when I say I
know what I'm talking about. I've had some deal-
ings with these people and it hasn't been pretty. I
want you to promise. Right here. Right now."

"Promise that—"

"That you won't pry. That you won't ask questions. That you'll stay out of Scarpetti business."

I promised.

And if Quinn didn't happen to notice that behind my back, my fingers were crossed?

It was just as well. There was no use trying to explain that staying out of Scarpetti Family business... well, it was way too late for that.

Chapter 7

Things were finally looking up.

And it wasn't just because of my close-but-not-quite-close-enough encounter with Quinn, either. All right, sure, right before he hurried out to meet with his attorney, we talked about seeing each other again and every time I thought about it, my heart pumped hot and hard, like I'd drained an entire pot of the high-octane coffee Jennine made at the office. But like they say on those hokey TV commercials...wait! There was even more.

There were three messages on my answering machine when I got back to Garden View on Monday morning. One was from the aforementioned Quinn, who didn't ask if I had the evening free or even if I wanted to go; he'd called in a favor, he told me, and he got us a table. His message was short and sweet: I was to meet him at Pietro's the next Thursday night at eight o'clock sharp.

If I listened to half of the female-empowerment speeches Ella spouted, I would have known enough to be insulted by his high-handed tactics.

Guess I'm not much of a listener. I wrote Pietro's

on my calendar for eight o'clock on Thursday and underlined it. In red.

The second message was from Dan. In spite of how it probably sounds, I hadn't forgotten about him. At least not completely. As opposed to Quinn who, cashmere aside, struck me as the take-no-prisoners type, Dan was one of those guys who held doors for women. Heck, he'd even asked my permission before he walked me home.

There were times a girl needed to feed off the kind of raw energy that shivered around Quinn like the halo of a flame. But there were times she was looking for warm and fuzzy, too.

Until I decided which I wanted—and needed—more, I'd be a dope to let either Quinn or Dan get away.

Especially since when Dan called and asked me if I could please meet him for coffee, he never once mentioned my cerebellum.

The third message...

Well, as soon as I heard it, my spirits soared and the reason was simple. The third message—finally and hallelujah—was from Saks.

"Saks. Saks. Saks." It was Monday evening and I chanted the single, wonderful word in a happy sing-song as I drove up Cedar Road toward Beechwood Mall, the city's premier shopping area.

Saks, where I used to shop with wild abandon and my dad's credit card.

Saks, where long before I ended up leading old people around the graves of dead people, I'd applied for a job, number one, because I had to pay my rent and number two (and far more important), because I loved everything from the ambiance to the merchandise to the pricey smell of the place. I'd filled out the application so long before, I figured they'd lost it in the shuffle. But then...

A call. From Saks. About a job.

Saks.

Where I'd bought my wedding gown.

The ugly thought struck out of nowhere, and I got rid of it with a twitch of my shoulders. There was no room in my head for negative energy. Not that evening. That evening was about positive vibes, a confident attitude, and—with a spot of luck and the skilled application of a little of my legendary chutzpah—a favorable outcome.

I eased my car into a parking place, checked my lipstick in the rearview mirror, and headed inside. I hoped that by the time I walked out again, I'd have an offer for a new job.

Yeah, I know. It would mean leaving Garden View. That, of course, was the whole point. Not only did the Saks job pay two dollars more an hour than my job at the cemetery, but getting away from the mausoleums and headstones would also mean that I could put a whole lot of distance between myself and Gus.

So what if I hadn't solved his little mystery?

What were the chances of that happening, anyway?

And who ever said that I cared enough to really try?

*   *   *

The woman in Human Resources said I was "ideal." The shift manager in Women's Wear used the word "perfect." After an hour and a half of filling out papers, smiling my way through interviews, and completing not one but two personality profiles, I had only one more hurdle to cross: the manager of the shoe department.

It was a good thing I'd used my head as well as my fashion sense and slipped on my Ferragamos before I left the apartment.

I arrived at Shoes wearing a hopeful smile, my newly created personnel file under my arm, waiting for this crucial and final stamp of approval. The department manager's name was Charles. He was young and black and he was dressed in a navy suit that fit his tall, thin frame to perfection. He moved with elegance and efficiency, and after only a couple of minutes watching him in action, I knew I'd like working with him.

He had a real knack for knowing when to smother a customer with attention and when to back off. He also had a wonderful sense of style. He paired shoes and purses as if it were a talent he'd been born with and I, for one, had no doubt he had been. The fact that I had been, too, made us soul-mates of sorts, and by the time he was un-busy enough to spend ten minutes sitting and chatting with me, I was so giddy from the smell of expensive leather and the promise of a life after the after-life of Garden View, I was tempted to ask Charles if along with every other Sunday off, he could guarantee me a ghost-free work environment.

I might actually have done it. Except that in the middle of a serious discussion of the advantages of Miu Miu versus Kate Spade, I looked toward a chichi display of even more chichi summer sandals and straw bags—and saw Gus.

My heart stopped, the astonishment so complete and so unexpected, it solidified inside me until every inch of my body was flash frozen. I'd been describing my idea of the perfect spring outfit to Charles and my arm went numb in the middle of a Vanna-like gesture toward a pair of silk and lizard T-strap pumps. I swear, if I hadn't been a) in public, b) in the middle of a job interview, and c) wondering if, finally, I hadn't completely lost my mind, I would have screamed.

Instead, before I could stop myself, I popped out of my chair, my arm still extended, my body language now more accusatory than it was graceful. "You can't be here," I said.

"Excuse me?"

I realized my mistake the moment I heard Charles's befuddled voice. I yanked my gaze away from Gus and back to Charles, who was eyeing me as if . . . well, as if I'd seen a ghost.

"All the time," I blurted out along with a smile that was tight around the edges and too wide to be genuine. "You can't be here all the time, is what I meant to say. That's why you need reliable people to work for you."

"Absolutely." My recovery was so smooth, Charles never lost the gleam in his dark eyes. Seeing that we shared the same concerns about work ethics, he just about sparkled. He stood. "I'll let you in on a little secret, darling. That's exactly why it's taking me so long to hire a new associate. I can't entrust this department to just anyone. I need to find some-one with fashion sense. Someone with common sense, too. I think that you might be that person."

"Oh, I am." I swallowed hard and kept on smil-ing and when Charles moved back and motioned me toward the cash register desk, I dared another look at the sandals and straw bags.

Gus was nowhere in sight.

The tension drained out of me, and since we were standing so close, Charles must have felt it. He smiled. Being a reasonable person, he assumed I was feeling good because our interview was pro-gressing so well.

I wondered how long that smile would have lasted if he knew this was a totally different kind of relief. I had been imagining things.

Thing.

One thing.

Gus.

My nerves were on edge from the stress of the interviewing process and I'd let it get to me. Of course Gus wasn't there at Saks among the Pradas and the Jimmy Choos. Gus was back at the ceme-tery. Right where he belonged.

"Let me show you around," Charles offered, but before he could, a woman walked into the depart-ment and eyed up the Dolce & Gabbanas. He ex-cused himself, promised he'd be right back, and left me on my own.

Now that I was calmer, I allowed myself the extravagance of indulging in a little visualization. Me in summer white, assisting pleasant and polite customers, enjoying the atmosphere—the wonderful civility—of Saks. Me, making more money than I was making at the cemetery, free of worry. No more watching every step as I maneuvered my way through the sometimes-treacherous Garden View landscape. No more digging through dusty files to find the solution to a mystery that probably wasn't much of a mystery, anyway.

A warm wave of peacefulness rippled through me, and I cradled an adorable Moschino Cheap & Chic pink polka dot slingback in one hand.

I spent a few minutes picturing the outfit I'd buy to go along with the shoes and how I would wear it to spend an evening with Quinn. I imagined wearing the same shoes for a date with Dan and wondered if he'd notice them. I smiled, deciding right then and there that after I gave Ella my two weeks' notice and served out the remainder of my sentence, I'd never again set foot inside the gates of Garden View. Which meant I'd never again have to deal with—

"Gus?"

He was waiting just inside the doorway of the room where the extra shoes were kept and when I walked by, he stepped out in front of me. Though I hadn't noticed it before, I sure noticed now. He was not a happy camper.

The fire in Gus's eyes just about fried me. "What the hell do you think you're doing?" he asked.

I glanced over my shoulder to make sure Charles

was still busy. "What I'm doing," I told him, "is completing a job interview. Which you shouldn't even know about. How do you know about it? And how can you be here? We're outside the cemetery. How can you be—"

"I've always been able to leave."

Just thinking of the possibilities made my stomach pitch. "Always? Anywhere?"

Gus was indignant. "Anywhere I want. Only it ain't as great as it sounds, you know? Where should I go? Home? To watch Rudy running things? Or maybe I should pop over to Italy. See the sights. Enjoy the food and wine." He made a noise from deep in his throat that reminded me of a growl. "Never wanted to leave before," he said. "Never had to. Until today."

As if he was taking aim over the barrel of a gun, Gus narrowed his eyes at me.

"I heard that message from this store, here, and I swear on my mother's grave—bless her soul—that I thought I must have been imagining things. You couldn't possibly be walking out on me. But then I come here and..." He threw his hands in the air. "I can't believe you would do this to me. That you of all people would stab me in the back. Especially when we had a deal."

"First of all, coming here to talk about a job doesn't qualify as stabbing you in the back. And second—"

He opened his mouth to say something but I didn't let him.

"Second, we never had a deal."

"And what about your job over at the cemetery?"

"My job is exactly that. A job. Nothing more. It's something I can walk away from. Whenever I decide I want to."

"And your investigation?"

It was my turn to growl. "I don't have an investigation. I told you from the start that I didn't want to investigate, Gus. I told you I didn't know how. I haven't found out anything new. I'm not going to find out anything new."

"So you're going to give up?"

"Hell, yes." I didn't realize how loud my voice was until I heard my own words echo back at me. I cringed, checked again to make sure Charles was still busy, and turned my anger back on Gus where it belonged. "This is the job I want."

He grunted. "Selling ugly shoes to spoiled women? You're better than that."

"And you're only saying that because you need me to do your dirty work for you."

"No. I'm saying it because it's—"

"Oh please!" I rolled my eyes. "You don't care. Remember? You told me as much back at the cemetery. You only saved me from ending up like a pancake under the wheels of that hearse because I'm the only one who can help you."

"And you're going to hold that against me? That I saved your life?" Gus shook his head in wonder. "The world is a different place than it was thirty years ago. There was a time when obligations meant something to people."

"We're not talking obligations. And besides, I don't have any. Not to my job at the cemetery and certainly not to you."

"Then to who, that cop who's sniffing around?"

He was trying to catch me off guard, and it wasn't going to happen again. I knew he listened to my phone messages. "Quinn is none of your business," I told Gus.

"You're a jamoke." He shook his head with disappointment. "A cop? I would have thought you had better taste than that. And that other boy? The one who wants your brain?"

"Oh, like it matters!" I screeched my frustration. "And like it's any of your business, anyway. Who I see is no concern of yours. Just like where I work. I'll go where I want, with whoever I want, and I'm not going to check in or run it by you, got that?"

"Yeah, I do, except I'm the one who makes out the schedule."

Damn, Charles was right behind me.

This time, no matter how hard I tried, I couldn't manage a smile. My stomach hit bottom, then bounced into my throat, blocking my breathing. I squeezed my eyes shut, braced myself, and turned to him. When I opened my eyes, I found Charles looking just a little concerned and more than just a little frightened.

"This isn't nearly as crazy as it looks," I said.

"I hope not," Charles said. "Because I'll tell you what, it's looking pretty crazy."

"Pretty crazy as in—"

"Thanks for stopping by, Pepper." Charles slipped the personnel file out of my hands and clutched it to his Emilio Pucci tie like a protective shield. "We've got a couple more candidates to interview and if you're the one we choose, we'll give you a call."

"But I—" I tried, honest, but I couldn't come up with an excuse. Not one that didn't sound psychotic, anyway.

Maybe I am psychotic. Because I don't remember saying goodbye to Charles or leaving the mall. The next thing I knew, I was in my car, staring at the keys in my hand, too numb to even stick them in the ignition.

"Someday you'll thank me for this."

Was I surprised to find Gus in my passenger seat?

I barely spared him a look. "How do you figure?"

"You don't want to work with them snooty types." He made himself comfortable. "You're too much of a free spirit."

"No, that would be you."

I wasn't trying to be funny but Gus chuckled. "That's a good one. Me, a free spirit. Yeah, I guess I am."

"And I..." I poked the keys into the ignition, started the car, and pulled out of the parking lot. "I just crashed and burned."

"Who needs them." He aimed a look of disgust at the mall. "You've got better things to do."

We were out on the street and stopped at a red

light before the enormity of my humiliation finally sank in. A tear streaked down my cheek and I wiped it away with the back of one hand.

"What?" Gus looked at me in wonder. "Don't tell me you're crying because of those people. They aren't worth it."

"Two dollars more an hour is."

He cocked his head to one side. "This is about money?"

I snorted my outrage but try as I might, I couldn't get the oomph of anger into my voice. It wavered on the tears that threatened to erupt full force. "You're the one who says that everything is business. Then you should realize that I've got business, too. I have bills to pay. Rent and utilities and—"

"Why didn't you say something?"

"Oh, yeah." I sniffed and gave a watery laugh. "I forgot. When I need money, all I have to do is ask my friendly neighborhood dead guy."

Gus shook his head. "You disappoint me. I thought you understood, about the way things work. You are doing this thing for me, this investigation, and you think I'm not going to show my appreciation?"

"By going away?"

This he didn't think was funny. And I knew all along it wasn't open to discussion.

Gus steepled his fingers and tapped his upper lip with his index finger, and though I was concentrating on traffic and couldn't take the time to watch him, I could sense that he was making a decision about something important.

We had already left the upper-middle-class vicinity

of the mall and were headed into the blue-collar neighborhood I called home when he finally cleared his throat. "You'll excuse me. For not saying something sooner. You have to remember..." He glanced out the passenger window, watching as the everyday world slipped past us. "It's been a long time since I've had to deal with the living. A man, he forgets."

"What a pain in the ass he can be?"

"Exactly how business is done. Turn. Here," he said when we came to the street that would lead back to Garden View.

"No way you need a ride home. Not with the way you pop in and out of places."

"I'm not looking for a ride. I'm looking for money."

"What, we're going to knock over the local convenience store?"

His smile was wry. "Not a robbery," he said. "A payment. Your payment. After all, you are working for me."

"And you're going to pay me how?"

"Don't ask questions." We were near a little-used side entrance to Garden View, the one that was kept open on those nights when staff worked late. Tonight, I knew the groundskeeping guys were there repairing damage done to a bridge by the spring thaw. Gus pointed me inside. "Just keep driving," he said. "And don't stop until we get to my mausoleum."

* * *

In the summer, there were evening angel tours on the schedule, morning garden walks, and even a couple sunrise services that I would be obliged to attend. In the winter, the Friends of Garden View volunteers always sponsored an afterdark wildlife hike. But I hadn't been in my job long enough to participate in any of those things.

That was the first time I'd been in the cemetery after hours.

I pulled up to the section where Gus's mausoleum was located and cut my engine. The sounds of traffic out on Mayfield Road were muffled and distant. From even farther off, I heard the low-pitched groan of the heavy equipment the groundskeepers were using for their repairs. In the place where the branches of tall trees arched over the road like skeleton fingers, not even a bird chirped. The place was as quiet as a...

The usual metaphor came right to me and I cringed.

"As quiet as a tomb," I told Gus.

Except that when I turned to see if he got the joke, he wasn't in my car.

"Gus?" I didn't really expect to find him there, but I peered into the backseat and when I saw that it was empty, I opened my door and got out of the car. "Gus?"

"Over here."

His voice came from somewhere near the mausoleum, though in the dark and shadows, it was impossible to see from where. Remembering to watch my step (not to mention my Ferragamos), I crossed the swath of lawn that led to the impressive little building that housed Gus's earthly remains.

Right about then, though, it was his unearthly self that I was more concerned with.

"Gus? Where are you?"

"Over here." Through the brass door with its decorative glass inserts, I saw Gus look out at me from the inside of the mausoleum. "Get in here."

I stopped dead at the place where three wide, shallow steps led up to the door. "In? There? No thanks."

"Don't be ridiculous." Suddenly, Gus was right beside me, and because I figured it was too dark for him to see me do it, I pressed a hand to my heart, startled. "Get inside. I can't get the money myself. You know that."

I eyed Gus, then turned and looked skeptically at the mausoleum. "You have money in your tomb?"

"It's not a tomb. A tomb is—"

"A tomb is a burial half out in the open and half underground, like a mausoleum built into a hillside. Yeah, I know. I've done my homework."

"Then you shouldn't be afraid to come inside. It's not a tomb."

"I'm not afraid."

"And I'm not dead." He walked toward the door.

I held back. It was one thing walking around the grounds of Garden View, pointing out what Ella liked to call its architectural treasures. But actually going inside one of the mausoleums? To a place where a body was closed into a coffin and slid into an opening in the wall?

I swallowed the sudden sour taste in my mouth and scrambled. "Why would you have money in your—" I wasn't about to launch into another debate of proper cemetery vocabulary. "Why would you have money in there, anyway?" I asked Gus.

He let go a sigh of impatience. "This here mausoleum was built long before I got clipped. I helped design it. And I watched it being built. Because I wanted to make sure it was done right. When it was finished...well, let's put it this way. A man in my position, he never knows when he might need some cash. Fast. When this here mausoleum was finished, I made sure I stashed some cash away. Just in case."

It sounded plausible. But even the promise of money wasn't going to get me inside. Not until I had some more answers. "Just in case of what? Like in case you needed to leave town?"

Gus pursed his lips, considering. "It's been known to happen."

"Or in case you needed to arrange a hit on someone?"

He snorted. "I told you, this was private money. Not business funds."

Another thought occurred to me and I looked at him hard, as if that might help me figure out if he was lying. "Money you got how? Robbing banks?"

"Your questions are out of line."

"Then answer them and I'll stop asking."

He scratched a finger behind his right ear. "The money is mine. Won fair and square. Poker."

"And you tucked it away here, where nobody could find it."

"Here. Other places. Like I said, a man never knows—"

"When he's going to have to skip out on his business associates and not leave a forwarding address."

"My murder proves as much, wouldn't you say?"

He had me there. Which didn't mean I walked up to the door of that mausoleum with a light heart. Gus pointed to one of the rocks tucked into the landscaping and I realized it was one of those phony, hide-a-key thingees. I retrieved the key and unlocked the door, and the second I touched the brass knob, ice filled my veins. I pulled the door open and stepped into the place where thirty years earlier, Gus Scarpetti had been laid to his not-so-eternal rest.

Chapter 8

A deal was a deal.

From a booth in the corner by the window, I watched Dan up at the counter, ordering my double latte (skim milk, no whipped cream), and thought about the nine thousand dollars in cold, hard cash that I'd deposited in my checking account that morning.

Like it or not, I knew exactly what it meant.

Sure, the money from Gus's mausoleum would go a long way toward supplementing what I made at Garden View. Sure, I wouldn't have to worry about paying my rent. Not for a long time, anyway. Sure, I was grateful. More than grateful. I was relieved. Overjoyed. Flat out happy. For the first time in what felt like forever, I didn't have to wonder how I would stretch my paycheck to cover my bills. (That pair of Moschino Cheap & Chic pink polka dot slingbacks had my name on them, too.)

But the money meant more than that. I knew it. More importantly, so did Gus.

The moment I took that fateful last step out of the real world and into the marble, brass, and glass extravaganza that was a fitting place for a guy nicknamed the Pope to call his home for all eternity, Gus had all the proof he needed that I was hooked. And the second I followed his directions, twitched back the Persian rug that covered the floor, and found the sliding panel and the pile of tens and twenties stashed under it, I knew I'd passed the ol' point of no return.

We had a deal, me and Gus.

I was now working for the mob.

Dan set my latte down in front of me, effectively drawing me out of my thoughts. The teddy bear smile he gave me didn't hurt, either. He slid into the seat across from mine. "So, what have you been up to?"

It was an innocent question. Dan wouldn't ask any other kind. Still, it made me uncomfortable enough to shift against the vinyl seat. I couldn't tell him what I'd really been up to so I didn't even try.

"Working mostly," I said instead, leaving out the part about how I was now employed by the most notorious bad guy this side of Al Capone.

"It must be fascinating to work at that cemetery."

I'd almost forgotten. "Oh, the cemetery! Fascinating isn't exactly the word for it. It's more like—"

"Interesting?"

No lie there, especially since I found myself officially in the private-investigation business.

"Speaking of interesting…" Dan took a sip of his coffee. House blend. No sugar. Black. "I have news. I got approval. For the study."

Suddenly, the invitation for coffee made a whole lot of sense.

"That's not why I wanted to see you tonight." Dan jumped in with the explanation so quickly, he must have been reading my mind. Or maybe he just noticed the flash of anger in my eyes. "I mean, I wanted to see you. Just to...you know...to see you." He blushed to the roots of his shaggy hair.

"But I wanted to tell you about the study, too," he added, his eyes glittering with excitement behind his wire-rimmed glasses. "It starts immediately and I'm authorized to recruit a dozen subjects. I can even pay. Well, a little, anyway. Enough to cover parking over at the hospital and dinner in the cafeteria on the nights we meet. I wanted to ask you—"

"To be one of your guinea pigs."

Dan's expectant smile faded. "It's all in the name of science."

Science.

I guess private investigation is something of a science, too. And it didn't take a peek at my college transcripts for me to remember that I'd never been very good at science. Which made me think that Dan might be good for something other than coffee and pissing me off.

I ripped open a little bag of sweetener, dumped it into my cup, and stirred. "How do you investigate?" I asked, "I mean, how do you know where to begin?"

He took my questions at face value. "I start with the basics," he said, and I checked it off on my mental clipboard. I'd started with the basics about Gus, too. Maybe I knew what I was doing after all. "And then I get into the nitty-gritty."

"Like?"

"Like details. You know, go one layer under the basics. Dig around. Then one layer under that. For instance, in this study..."

Dan had found a subject he knew more than a little something about, and he glommed onto it with gusto. While he rhapsodized about monosynaptic reflex pathways and nonmyelinated neurons, I zoned out. It was the perfect opportunity to think about my investigation.

It would have helped, of course, if I had even an inkling about what to do next.

"...and then there's receptors." Poor Dan was talking and I wasn't listening. He raced right on, adorably oblivious. "In layman's terms, receptors encode information into electrochemical messages. Things like light and sound and touch. That's one of the things I'd like to focus on in my study. The relationship between my subjects' occipital lobes and how their electrochemical messages are transmitted by their sensory neurons. You don't have any siblings, do you? Because as an adjunct, I'd love to look at how any anomalies I might discover could be analogous to genetics and relationships within a family."

Family.

Even though Dan added another dozen tendollar words to the sentence, my receptors latched on to that one and wouldn't let go. I guess those electrochemical messages kicked in because a light-bulb went off over my head.

I was so grateful, I leaned over the table and kissed Dan on the cheek. That got his attention.

"What's that for?" he asked.

"For the quarter you're going to loan me." He continued to stare. I suppose he was waiting for an explanation. Or maybe he was wondering what sort of brain anomaly was making me act like a crazy person. I was too jazzed by the sudden insight to care. There was no use getting into it, the whole, ugly thing about how my cell-phone service was suspended because my carrier was a little touchy about bills being paid on time. Or at all. Thanks to Gus and my newfound fortune, I'd be back in the wireless age in a matter of days but until then, I needed a pay phone, a phone book, and a little bit of luck.

"Quarter," I reminded Dan, and when I snapped my fingers, he dutifully reached into his pocket, retrieved the coin, and handed it over. I was out of the booth and across the coffee shop in a flash. I staked out a place outside the restrooms and thumbed through the beat-up White Pages that hung from the wall next to the pay phone.

Honestly, I didn't really expect to find the phone number that I was looking for. But there it was, and my heart skipped a beat as I skimmed my finger across the name and held it there under the numbers so I wouldn't dial wrong. When I dropped Dan's quarter into the phone, my hands were shaking. I listened to it ring on the other end and held my breath.

He didn't answer his own phone. I didn't expect him to.

The man who did answer didn't bother to identify himself but he didn't blow me off, either. Another surprise. He listened while I went through my song and dance about how I was writing a book about Gus and how I needed all the primary-source information I could find.

I expected him to hang up on me. When he told me to hold on instead, I was so stunned, I could have been knocked over with a spritz of Eternity. After a wait that seemed like next to forever, I heard another phone receiver being lifted. A gravelly voice said, "So you're writing a book, huh? And I suppose you want to interview me. I'm a busy man. I don't have a lot of what do you call them...windows of opportunity."

I swallowed down the little voice of common sense that told me lying was wrong and that lying to the wrong people was dangerous. It didn't stop me from going through the writing-the-book story again. I ended it with a hopeful, "You'll see me, right?" My voice wavered over the question. My hand was so tight around the phone receiver that my knuckles were white. What I didn't expect was—

"Thursday? This Thursday?" No quavering in my voice this time. This was out-and-out I-can't-believe-this-is-happening. Thursday was the day I was supposed to have dinner with Quinn. And suddenly—

"Thursday." The single word rumbled from the

other end of the phone like thunder. "Seven o'clock. It's a one-time offer. Take it or leave it."

I took it.

By the time I walked back to the booth, I didn't know if I should have been happy or scared to death. I did know that I owed Dan big time. For the quarter and for getting me started in what I hoped was the right direction. I knew two other things, too: it was hell having a conscience. And paybacks were a bitch.

I plunked down in the seat across from Dan. "I'll do it," I told him.

"Do—?"

"I'll be in your study."

At the same time I got the details and told him I'd show up at his lab the following week for our first session, I wondered how Dan would feel if he knew I'd only agreed to help him because I felt obligated. I wondered how Quinn would take the news that I was canceling out on him and, more importantly, if he'd ever give me a second chance for dinner. Just like I wondered what the sexy cop would say if he knew I was standing him up to spend my Thursday night with Rudy the Cootie Scarpetti.

Whoever said that crime doesn't pay?

Rudy Scarpetti had an address in one of those out-in-the-country suburbs that made even the most social-climbing blue bloods green with envy. This wasn't the status-conscious, winter-home-in-Florida, Rolex-for-Christmas universe that, before Dad got greedy, I had always thought of as my comfortable little corner of the world. This was serious-money territory. The kind of place where residents never had to worry about status because they *were* status, the top of the upper crust that the rest of us could only dream about. When they weren't skiing in the Alps or tossing the dice in Monte Carlo, these folks spent their days thinking about which of their Rolls-Royces to take out for a drive.

Like most of the properties I had seen on my trip from the city, the Scarpetti household came complete with an iron gate at the mouth of a winding drive, grounds that were landscaped to perfection, and a house that was so spectacular I cut my engine and spent a couple minutes staring out my windshield, wide-eyed, at what must have been at least twelve thousand square feet of architectural achievement.

Sharp angles and clean, modern lines. Gleaming chrome. Glass. Lots of glass. Sweeping vistas. Slate walks. Patios and balconies and just a glimpse of an Olympic-size pool.

Oh, and two goons in black suits and Ray-Bans, one stationed on either side of the front door. They had automatic weapons in their hands.

I was pretty sure they weren't the standard neighborhood welcoming committee.

It was all the reminder I needed that this was no ordinary social call, and while I gathered the leather portfolio I'd bought specifically because it made me look like an author, and my tape recorder, I gulped down the lump of panic that suddenly blocked my throat.

"What? You're not gonna let those chumps scare you away, are you?"

At the same time I let out a little squeal, I gave myself a mental kick in the pants. I should have known that Gus was along for the ride. I plunked back against my seat. "Could you announce yourself, do you think? Maybe play some spooky music or something?"

"Music was never my thing." Gus sniffed and glanced at the extravaganza his son called home. "This was never my thing, either. Too showy."

"Let me guess, you lived a simple life."

"Simpler than this. I didn't need to keep up with them Joneses. All I ever wanted was to take care of my family."

"And so maybe your family took care of you."

It was a couple seconds before Gus got my meaning. "You think Rudy...?" He glared at me, then swiped a hand in the air, dismissing my theory as effectively as if it were nothing more than an annoying insect. I made sure I kept well out of range of his hand. I had finally warmed up after our last too-close encounter. I wasn't going to take that chance again.

Gus's growl reminded me of Rudy's voice on the phone. "First you fingered Carmella. Now you're thinking Rudy. Not a chance, sweetheart. He's my son."

"Looks like he's done pretty well for himself. Family business, do you think?"

"You think he wanted to take over my turf so he could have it all for himself? You're not funny."

"I'm not trying to be. But Gus..." I turned in my seat, the better to see my passenger. "If you really want your murder solved—"

"You must want it solved, too, or you wouldn't have called off your date with that cop."

He spit out the last word like it tasted bad.

And I refused to get sidetracked. Gus wasn't going to get me to say out loud what I'd only admitted to myself: that I was working for him now and that meant (not too often, I hoped), that I'd have to put my social life on hold. He also wasn't going to pull me into a conversation about Quinn. Quinn was my business. And my business was private. It was bad enough that I had to cancel out on Quinn. Worse, that I made up a lie to justify it and told him there was a special evening cemetery tour that night and that I had to conduct it. Way worse because—

I sighed, trying not to think about how much I wanted a second chance with Quinn. Better to concentrate on what I was doing than thinking about Quinn and that candlelit restaurant. Or what might have happened when I invited him back to my apartment after dinner.

"We have to consider all the possibilities," I told Gus at the same time I warned myself that for the rest of that evening, the possibility of all that might have happened with Quinn was something I wasn't allowed to think about. "That's got to include the possibility that Rudy was behind your murder."

"And what are you going to do, come right out

and ask if he's the one who put the contract out on me?"

"I'm not that dumb," I told Gus, and before I could convince myself that just being there pretty much proved I was, I got out of the car.

I had parked where a long walk led from the driveway to the house, and I had just gotten to where one part of it continued to the front door and another section swung around to the back of the property when an old lady rounded the corner.

I'm not kidding. Old. Really old.

The woman was half my height and skinny enough to be any fashionista's role model. She had a head of silvery hair that was pulled into a neat bun and she was dressed in an elegant pink pantsuit and wore a string of pearls every bit as flawless as her complexion. She was wearing white sneakers like the ones kids wear. The kind with Velcro instead of laces. They were the only sour note in an otherwise very-together presentation.

That, and her eyes.

"Did he come with you?" The woman plucked at my sleeve, and she didn't so much look at me as right through me. Her eyes were blank, like there was nothing going on behind them. They were also dark, like Gus's, and before I came to my senses and realized there was no way, I thought that might be who she was talking about.

"He...?" I glanced over my shoulder in the direction she was looking but there was no one there. Not even Gus. "I didn't bring anyone. Anyone but me. I'm—"

"He told me he's coming. Today." Her hand tightened on my arm. Her voice was frazzled around the edges. "He called and said he'd be here. He promised."

I've never been very good with old people. Maybe I have issues because of my dad's practice and the fact that it was the Medicare fraud that finally did him in. But issues aside, I always find myself at a loss for words when it comes to this kind of rambling desperation. I would like to say that I'm caring and know exactly how to handle things, but I'm not. I don't.

One by one, I plucked the old lady's bony fingers from my arm and took a step back, well out of reach.

"If he said he'd be here, I'm sure he will be," I told her, mostly because I figured it was what she wanted to hear. "Maybe you just need to wait a little longer."

"I've been waiting and waiting." Her voice trailed away and I could have sworn she forgot I was there. "He called about the tulips. And he said he'd be here. He promised."

Okay, so tell me, who was the crazy one here? The woman blabbering on and on about some no-show and tulips? Or the one who decided that heading over to the wiseguys with weapons was a better choice than standing there being uncomfortable?

Unfortunately, it was impossible for me to get up a whole head of steam. The old lady latched on to me again, and when it looked like she was never going to let go, I gave up even trying. I tried to keep up a good pace but she kept forgetting the whole process of putting one foot in front of the other. Together, we clomped our way toward the front door.

Did I mention that the house was as big as my old high school? Before we were anywhere near the imposing entrance and the guys in the sunglasses, another woman raced around from the back. She was tall and broad and middle-aged and she had a severe underbite that was accentuated by her red lipstick. Her hair was salt-and-pepper, her eyes were colorless, and she wore a nurse's uniform. It was white, which did little for her complexion. It was also short enough to expose a strip of skin between where her skirt ended and her white knee-high stockings began.

So not attractive.

At the spot where the two paths intersected, the nurse screeched to a stop fast enough that her thick-soled shoes squeaked. She glanced down the drive and into the woods that bordered us on every side, and the only way I can describe the look on her face is pure panic.

That is, until she spotted the old woman.

Then, the nurse's expression teetered between relief and anger. It wasn't until the anger won out and she came at the old lady, eyes flashing and teeth bared, that I stepped between them.

She hadn't noticed me until that moment, and when she did, she stopped dead in her tracks, no doubt trying to decide if I was *somebody*. Apparently, just the fact that I had made it past the front gate with its security system, video cameras, and motion detectors made it a very real possibility. She might be homely but she wasn't dumb. She wasn't about to take any chances.

She checked to make sure she hadn't attracted the attention of the two tough guys at the front door and, reassured, she slapped a smile on her face and reached out a hand to the old lady. "Marie, dear! There you are." She blinked really fast, the way people do when they're lying. "My goodness, you had me worried."

Call me a sucker, but it didn't seem fair to make pink, blubbering David face down that polyester-clad Goliath on her own. Marie ignored the nurse and clung to me like a limpet on a rock, her eyes round with terror. I guess that meant I was involved whether I wanted to be or not. "You didn't look worried," I told the nurse. "And Marie wasn't doing anything wrong. She was escorting me to the front door."

"And I just fell off a turnip truck." The nurse crossed her arms over a chest that would have done a linebacker proud. "You have no idea what it's like trying to keep an eye on her," she said, obviously building her case in the event that anyone called her on the carpet for her lapse. "All I did was go to the kitchen to get a cup of tea—"

"Tea for Marie? Or tea for yourself?"

"No one ever said I couldn't have a bit of a break." The nurse pulled back her shoulders and clutched her hands together in front of her. "I need one now and again. Four years she's been like this."

The nurse sniffed, and though she was talking about her like she wasn't there, Marie was still latched on to me. The nurse gave her a look that was nothing short of disgust. "Four years I've been putting up with her and her crazy talk. Let me guess, she said she was out here waiting for her son. She's always waiting for her son. But you know what, Marie?" The nurse leaned forward and caught Marie's eye. "You. Don't. Have. A. Son. How many times do I have to tell you? You're just a crazy old lady and one of these days, you're going to walk away from me and you're going to get lost. Then I'm going to lose my job."

"You'll be lucky if that's all you lose." Winding my arm through Marie's, I let the nurse chew over the gruesome possibilities and took the old lady along with me to the front door.

"She's wrong, you know."

It wasn't so much Marie's words as her voice that struck me as odd. It was as even and reasonable as it had been incoherent only a minute before. When I looked at the old lady, her eyes were bright and clear. She smiled up at me. "She's a bitch."

"You're not kidding." I decided I liked Marie. "Why do you put up with it?"

I suppose I'll never know. Because as quickly as the flash of awareness came, it was gone again. Marie's eyes went flat. Her expression was blank. "He's bringing tulips," she said. Her empty gaze roved all around. "He said he'd be here. He promised."

The conversation pretty much stayed one-sided like that all the way to the front door. Which was a good thing, I guess, because I didn't have to keep up my end. It was especially helpful when Gus popped up next to me.

He looked to his left and shook his head. "My little sister."

"She's a little out of it right now."

"She was always a little out of it." Though his assessment was hard-edged, Gus's eyes betrayed a sadness I hadn't seen in them before. "I haven't bothered to look in on her. On any of them. All this time. Now, to see her like this…"

"She's waiting for her son."

Gus shook his head. "Marie has daughters. Four of them. I ought to know, I paid for their weddings."

"He's coming today." Marie nodded, talking to herself. "He promised."

By that time, we were at the front door, and even though Gus stayed at my side, I refused to look his way or say another word to him. He knew better than to egg me on, too. We were passing into dangerous waters. If I needed any more proof, it came when Goon #1 stepped between me and the door.

It wasn't like I didn't expect some kind of challenge. In spite of the fact that I'd flashed my driver's license in front of the security camera at the gate and that I had an appointment, I knew these guys were paid to look after Rudy's welfare. That included making sure that not just anyone got in to see him.

I understood all that, and I actually might have

gritted my teeth and endured it if Goon #2 hadn't been staring at my chest. He was a huge guy with a long, black ponytail and, at exactly the spot where his Ray-Bans ended, a scar that cut across his left cheek. It was pink and glossy. Recent. Ugly.

He slipped off his sunglasses, winked at his sidekick and handed him his weapon. "Gonna have to pat you down." He did a slow inventory, from the tips of my pink slingbacks, up my legs, and across my hips. Apparently, he wasn't the type who concerned himself about looks because he never got as far as my face. He stopped at boob level. "Mr. Scarpetti's orders."

"Forget it, scumbag." Marie batted his hand away. "She's with me."

It was apparent that neither of these guys was used to resistance. Especially not from little Marie. While they hemmed and hawed and wondered how to handle the boss's aunt, Marie charged past them and to the door. Since she was still clinging to me like static to a linen skirt, I got dragged along and into the house.

Did I say house?

That place was spectacular enough to send the Queer Eye guys into waves of rapture.

I took a couple seconds to check out the three-story entryway with its floor-to-ceiling window and the winding staircase directly in front of us. I had just started in on the wall (lit from behind, of course) that featured a display of art-glass sculptures when a man in a gray suit appeared in a doorway to my right. He introduced himself as

Teo Conigliaro, and at the same time he gently but expertly plucked Marie's hand from my sleeve and led her away, he informed me that Mr. Scarpetti would see me now.

I was left alone outside a closed door.

Well, not precisely alone.

"You ready, kid?" Gus asked.

"I could ask you the same thing. You were surprised by how much Marie has changed. And you haven't seen your son in a long time."

"He's still my son."

"He collects art glass."

Gus looked back at the display and his top lip curled. "In my day—"

Before he could get started with a reminiscence, I raised my hand and rapped on the door, and when I was met with a gruff, "Come," I squared my shoulders and headed inside.

There were no windows in that room and after being outside, then in the flood of soft evening light that filled the entryway, it took a couple seconds for me to get my bearings. I don't suppose I made a good impression standing there staring like a lunatic but I couldn't help myself. When my eyes finally got used to the light of the single lamp that was lit on the huge mahogany desk in the corner, the first person I saw was Gus.

But of course, it wasn't.

The man seated behind the desk was the spitting image of his father. I should have expected it, but it caught me off guard, anyway. Rudy was just about the age then that Gus had been when he was murdered. They had the same pit bull body, the same bullet head. Even Rudy's nose was a duplicate of Gus's and the thought crossed my mind that somewhere along the way, he'd probably had it broken on purpose. Just so nobody could miss the resemblance and forget whose son he was.

Instead of an Italian silk suit like his father wore, though, Rudy was dressed country club casual, in khakis and a red sweater every bit as expensive as the furnishings in his office. He jumped out of his leather chair and headed over to me, his hand extended, his voice simmering with admiration.

"Hey, sweetheart. You told me you were writing a book. You didn't tell me you were gorgeous and writing a book."

"Can you believe the nerve of the boy?" Gus clicked his tongue. "Talking that way to a respectable woman. I never would have—"

I ignored him. So I'm shallow. It was nice to know that someone appreciated the just-above-the-knee black skirt and the hot-pink shirt I'd paired it with. Even if the someone in question was the local godfather.

I managed a smile and the oh-so-professional tone of voice that had gotten me my job at Garden View. "That's because the only thing that matters about this visit is that book I'm writing," I told Rudy. I let him hand me into a chair and when I sat down, he went back to his spot behind the desk. "I think I explained all that on the phone."

Rudy made himself comfortable. "I see you met Zia Marie."

I didn't ask how he knew. If Rudy didn't know everything that happened around there, I'd have been surprised. "She's a little..."

"Confused?"

Understatement of the year. I thought about Marie and Nurse Godzilla. "Your aunt doesn't like her caretaker," I told Rudy.

He steepled his fingers and looked at me over them. "And you know this how?"

"Marie is afraid of the woman. And the nurse... well, I've watched the Discovery Channel. I've seen more caring instincts in a jellyfish."

"I'll take care of her."

It was as simple as that. And it scared me to death. Not to mention what I thought it might do to the nurse. I know I went as white as a sheet because my face got cold. "I didn't mean for you to—"

Rudy's laugh cut me short. "What? You think I'm going to take a hit out on the woman? Honestly, Miss Martin. I'm not talking murder, I'm talking a severance package. A pretty hefty one, if I do say so myself." Still laughing, he took a cigar from a wooden case on the desk, trimmed it, and fired it up. It stank. In an expensive sort of way.

Rudy took a puff and blew out a ring of white smoke. "You're confusing me with my father."

"And you're not like him."

Another puff and I held my breath when the smoke headed my way. "This isn't the old days," he told me. "I'm a legitimate businessman. You must know that if you've started your research." He swept an arm toward the shelves of books behind him. "I have the annual reports here to prove it. I'll have my executive assistant put a packet of them together for you, if you like. You'll see. Things are different now. Don't let those Hollywood movies make you think any different. We aren't pieces of shit—you should excuse the expression—in three-thousand-dollar suits."

"And your father was."

It wasn't a question, but Rudy tipped his head back and thought about it. I didn't bother to look to see what Gus was doing. I didn't have to. The next thing I knew, he was standing right behind Rudy. It was a little disconcerting to see them together, one like the mirror image of the other. Rather than think about it, I kept my eyes on Rudy and my notepad clasped in my hands.

"Back in my father's day, we conducted business in a different manner," Rudy said. "The way my father died, well, that's pretty much all the proof you need to know that."

"The way he died…" I cleared my throat. It was the only way I could get the words out. "That's exactly what I came to talk to you about."

Rudy eyed me through the gloom. "Are you asking me if I had anything to do with it?"

"No. That is…I…Oh, what the hell!" I tapped my pen against the red leather cover of my portfolio. "Actually, that's exactly what I'd like to know. Not if you had anything to do with it!" I added, just so he didn't get the wrong idea and think that I was too nosey. Or that I was accusing him of anything. "Just what you know about it all. For the book, of course."

"Looks and nerve." Rudy shook his head in a way that said he admired both qualities. "I hate to disappoint you but at the time of my old man's untimely demise, I had a pretty ironclad alibi. I was a guest of the feds."

"Witness protection?"

"Prison."

"Oh. Federal prison. My father—" I stopped short of getting into it, then decided that it might actually help build some kind of rapport. "My father's in federal prison," I told Rudy. "Medicare fraud."

"Really." Another nod of admiration. "That takes brains. And guts. And how are you getting along on your own?"

"I never said I was alone." My smile was as sleek as the smoke that rose from the tip of Rudy's cigar. "And you never said if you know who had your father killed."

Rudy shrugged. "Could'a been anybody."

"Anybody but you."

"Damned straight." He stabbed his cigar into the Waterford ashtray on his desk. "He was my father."

"And that deal he was working on with Victor LaGanza? The one that would have gotten them a share of the lottery pie?"

At this, Rudy sat up straight. "How the hell do you know—"

"I told you. I've done plenty of research already.

I know there were millions of dollars at stake. My theory is that when your father was killed, those millions of dollars went to someone else."

For a long time, Rudy didn't say a word. He stared. Just stared. And I didn't dare look to see how Gus was reacting to all this. Something told me if I took my eyes off Rudy, it was the equivalent of holding up a white flag. Right now, I couldn't afford a show of weakness.

Just when I thought I couldn't stand the tension any longer, Rudy backed down. In an I'm-still-the-boss-and-don't-get-any-idea-I'm-not sort of way. "Yeah, well…if there was a deal, and we're talking in purely hypothetical terms here, if there was a deal and there were millions at stake, we would have lost the money when Pop got iced."

That was news and apparently, my blank expression said it all.

"It looks like you haven't done your homework very good, honey. You see, *if* there was such a deal, then when Pop was killed, the deal would have fallen through. Back in the day, that's how these things used to be structured. The Scarpetti Family wouldn't make the money. The LaGanza Family wouldn't make the money. So you see, if it was true—and believe me, I'm not saying it is—but if it was, thanks to my father's murder, me and Victor LaGanza, we would'a lost millions. Just about takes care of both our motives, don't you think?"

It did.

"Then who—"

"Look…" Rudy got up, went to the door, and

opened it. Not one to ignore messages when they're sent by mob bosses, I stood and followed him across the room.

"I agreed to see you," he said, "because I think it's about time the Scarpetti family got a little good press. I'm an honest businessman. I support a dozen different charities. I give to my church. Hell, I even sit on the board. I back a number of worthy causes. I even take care of the people who were once my father's business associates. You know, at a retirement home sort of place. That's the kind of thing you should be writing about, not who killed my old man. Because that's ancient history and it don't serve no useful purpose. If you decide to write my side of the story, give me a call some-time." When I got close enough, he looked down my cleavage. "Or maybe if you want to have din-ner and a few laughs. But this other stuff, this mafioso bullshit..."

Rudy put a hand on my back. He nudged me into the hallway at the same time he leaned in close and whispered, "If you're smart, you'll forget all about that."

Chapter 9

I was smart.

Smart enough to notice that when I snaked down the drive, pulled through the iron gate that whisked open in front of me like magic, and headed out of the Scarpetti compound, a car that was parked a hundred feet up the road turned on its lights and swung onto the street behind me.

But smart doesn't automatically mean suspicious and at that point, I had more important things to worry about than who besides me was out for a Thursday night drive.

Rudy the Cootie's last words still rang in my ears. Was it friendly advice? Or a threat?

I would have asked Gus for his take on the situation, but the last I'd seen of him was back in Rudy's office.

I wondered, too, what he'd have to say in regard to Rudy's explanation about the lottery scheme gone bad. If the Cootie was telling the truth and Gus's death canceled out the deal...well, th pretty much eliminated both Rudy and Vi LaGanza from my very short list of suspects.

Then again, if Rudy was lying…

With a single, grumbled, "Shit," I set the thought aside.

If Rudy was lying, I didn't know how to prove it. Or not prove it. So there I was. Nowhere. Again.

After a full day of work at the cemetery, not to mention the stress of meeting with Rudy, I was tired, and rather than waste any more brain cells trying to work through motives and clues and who was who in the world of bad guys, I deserved a break. I snapped on the radio and tapped my fingers against the steering wheel to the beat of a technodance tune that had been out a year earlier and already sounded dated. At the next intersection, I took a right.

For a couple seconds, my rearview mirror was dark. Then headlights glared in it.

The car behind me had turned, too.

Was I worried? Why should I be? I was doing the speed limit (almost) so even if it was a cop, I didn't care.

I negotiated a curve and a picturesque stone bridge that spanned the Chagrin River. The foothills of the Appalachian Mountains begin east of Cleveland and there, the countryside is scenic in a way that assures the folks lucky enough to own property in those parts of both privacy and priceyness. In the light, I knew I'd see steep hills, rocky outcrop-nd once in a while, a break in the trees that long driveway and a house set in pristine far from prying eyes.

It was just past sunset and the road in front of me twisted and turned in the light that was quickly changing from plum to midnight blue. I put both hands on the steering wheel. After all, it was spring and every driver who ventured off Northeast Ohio city streets and into the suburbs knew what that meant: deer. Not that I don't think they're adorable, but no way did I want to meet one up close and personal with my front bumper.

I topped a hill and coasted down the other side. The road smoothed out and I cranked my car stereo, and in the spirit of the season, opened the moon roof. The yellow line in the center of the road changed from solid to broken so if the driver behind me was so inclined, he could have passed. He didn't. He kept his distance and for a couple miles, I drove on in stereophonic oblivion. Another mile or so, no sign of deer, and ahead of me, a traffic light marked another intersection. It turned from green to yellow but I had clearance. Just as the light changed to red, I zipped through.

So did the car behind me.

It may have taken me a while, but I was starting to catch on. I glanced in my rearview mirror but since there were no streetlights, it was too dark to see who was driving the car or even what color it was.

I didn't lose my head. After all, I was a priva detective. Sort of. And I was smart.

Just to prove it, when I saw a street up ahea my left, I slowed, turned, and kept on drivin

My rearview mirror remained dark.

I admit it, in addition to relief, I felt pretty dumb. I had let my imagination (not to mention my love of *CSI* reruns) get the best of me and I swore I'd never let it happen again. If I was going to solve this case for Gus and earn my nine thousand bucks, I had to remain logical and rational. I had to stop being a drama queen. I had to—

A house the size of my apartment building loomed directly ahead of me and I punched my brakes, slowed, then stopped.

I was in a cul-de-sac.

Did I say *smart*? It didn't look that way. To me or, I'm sure, to the driver in that other car. The one that was pulled over to the side of the road waiting for me when I flipped around and came back out the dead-end street the way I'd come in.

Good thing it was dark. At least the other driver couldn't see how red my face was. But I couldn't see his face, either; the windows of the late-model black sedan were tinted.

I pulled out onto the main road, and I didn't look in my mirror. Why bother? Besides, I could just about feel the headlights of the sedan boring into the back of my two-year-old Mustang.

I was being followed.

Reality sank in and my brain froze. I forgot all ~~d~~ advice I'd read over the years in countless ~~about~~ what women should do to protect ~~situations~~ situations just like this. I never consid- ~~a~~ a police station. I didn't think about a fire station or a busy convenience store, either. All I could think was that I had to put as much distance as I could between me and the car behind me.

I sped up.

So did he.

We had been on the road nearly a half hour and then the countryside melted into plain ol' suburbia. Strip malls, gas stations, restaurants.

Did I think to stop at any of them?

I wasn't thinking anything at all. Anything except getting away from the car on my tail.

At the next intersection, the light was already changing when I barreled through. Yeah, it was dumb. But my timing was right. There was a pickup truck coming the other way and the car behind me had no choice but to stop. I raced on ahead and took the next corner on two wheels.

Another street, another turn. A fork in the road and I headed to the right. A couple hundred feet in front of me, there was a drive and a sign that said HOME OF THE INVADERS, an entrance to a school. I cut my lights and turned in, heading straight to the back of the two-story brick building. I tucked my car between the back door and a dumpster.

And I waited.

How long? I can't say. I only know that I sat and listened to my blood pump in my veins and my pulse pound inside my head. It wasn't until th pumping slowed and the pulsing settled that I w dead certain no one knew I was there. That's w' I headed home.

I parked in the spot in back of my apartment building that I paid an extra sixty bucks a month to reserve, and even though I was confident that the crisis was over, I wasn't about to take any chances. Finally, some crumb of what I'd read in all those self-defense articles rose to the surface. I yanked the keys from the ignition and poked them up between my fingers in case I needed to use them as a weapon. It wouldn't do much in the shock-and-awe category, but at least the feel of cold metal in my hot hand deluded me into thinking I had some control over my own destiny.

As prepared as I would ever be, I scrambled from the car into my building.

I took the steps two at a time all the way to the third floor and when I got to the landing, I didn't stop. I raced down the hallway and unlocked my door with shaking hands. Inside, I locked the door behind me and stood with my back against it, fighting for breath.

I was safe.

The tension drained out of me like the fat off Oprah. I didn't even realize my knees were quaking until they decided not to hold me. I collapsed on the couch. My bedroom window faced the side of the duplex next door, but both my living room win-dows looked out onto the street. Exhausted and overwhelmed, I stared at the streetlight directly across the way.

When I noticed a movement out in the

"Cat," I told myself. "Stray dog. Someone out for a jog."

But of course, it wasn't.

I inched closer to the window just in time to see a late-model black sedan cruise by nice and slow.

Did I say I was smart?

I was smart, all right. Smart enough to lead whoever was driving that car right back to my home sweet home.

The first person I ran into at the office the next morning was Ella. More precisely, Ella ran into me. The way her eyes sparkled with excitement, I knew there was nothing accidental about our meeting.

Ella's tie-dyed skirt rippled against her ankles. Her beaded earrings twitched. Sometime between that morning and the last time I'd seen her (which as far as I could remember was late in the afternoon of the day before), she'd had her hair highlighted. Spikes of gold—moussed, gelled, and sprayed into submission—rose like sunny rays from her nut-brown hair and framed her chubby face.

She darted into the hallway long enough to grab me and drag me into her office. "Why didn't you tell me?" Ella could barely stand still. Her flat-soled, round-toed Earth Shoes danced a little pattern against the beige industrial-strength carpet. "You've got a secret this delicious and you don't even think about sharing it? Shame on you, Pepper! Two guys, and you never told me about either one of them."

I had been up most of the night, listening to every creak in an old apartment building full of clanging pipes and groaning floorboards. I wasn't at my best.

I blinked at her in bleary-eyed surprise. Was everyone—living *and* dead—poking their collective noses in my love life?

"How—?" I untangled myself from Ella's maternal grasp. "Dan and Quinn? How do you—?"

She leaned in close. Like she was sharing a secret. She winked. "Waiting in your office."

"Both of them?" The prospect of Quinn and Dan in the same room together terrified me. I'm not sure why. It wasn't exactly like I needed to keep my relationship with Dan a secret from Quinn. Or my relationship with Quinn a secret from Dan. So far, I didn't have a relationship. With either one of them. The way things were going, it looked like I never would.

I made a move toward the door and actually might have made it that far if Ella hadn't taken hold of me again. "How long has this been going on?" she asked.

I shrugged off the question and her hand. "Oh, you know…" I said, and I hightailed it out of there.

My office door was closed and outside it, I pulled myself together. The good news was that in spite of my restless night and an imagination that bounced between *the guys in the black car were from the Prize Patrol* to *the guys in the black car had bags of cement in the trunk,* I hadn't just dragged on the first thing I found that morning. I was wearing black pants, a sweet little butter-yellow cami, and a black jacket.

Dan wouldn't notice.

Quinn would.

I took a deep breath and shifted my leather portfolio from one hand to the other, subconsciously registering the fact that a portfolio made me look professional and confident.

Quinn wouldn't care.

Dan would.

Right and left brain satisfied, I pushed open the door.

In black cashmere, Quinn Harrison looked like sin incarnate. In a charcoal suit, a crisp white shirt, and a silk tie in shades of teal that brought out the blue flecks in his eyes, sin wore the skin of an angel.

My heart skipped a beat.

Right before my gaze darted around the room.

In spite of what Ella said, Dan was nowhere to be seen. And believe me, in an office that small, if he was there, I would have seen him.

"Hi." Quinn was thumbing through the stack of papers on my desk and damn it, he didn't even look guilty about it. He gave me a quick but thorough once-over and a barely perceptible nod of approval. "You looking for someone?" he asked.

"No." Before I closed it, I checked behind the door, just in case Dan was back there somewhere. "Ella said there was someone here to see me."

"That would be me."

"And you look..." I was going to say "hot

enough to set off the smoke alarms" but that seemed kind of bold. Especially that early in the morning. "You're all dressed up. You must be going someplace special."

"Nope. Back on the job." He flicked the right side of his suitcoat back just enough for me to see that he was wearing a leather shoulder holster with a gun in it. "No more administrative leave. Everything got cleared up and in my favor, I'm happy to say. All's well that ends—"

"Well?"

"Well, sometimes all's well just because it ends."

"I'm glad." I was. I don't know what Quinn did to land himself in hot water but whatever it was, I suspected he had his reasons. Even if he would never share them.

I glanced at the papers—my papers—that he still held in his hand. "You looking for something?"

"Me? Nah." He set the papers back on the teetering stack of old newspaper clippings on my desk and stood. He was taller than I remembered. "I was wondering, though, why you stood me up last night."

I sidestepped around him and over to my desk chair, and believe me, as tempted as I was, I was careful not to brush against him. If we were going to fight about the fact that I'd canceled our dinner date—and from the thread of irritation that colored Quinn's words, I suspected we were—I couldn't afford to lose my concentration.

I set aside my portfolio and sat down. Quinn

perched himself on the edge of my desk, just a hair's breadth away from me.

"Technically, I didn't stand you up," I said, looking up at him because, like I said, he was tall. "I called you," I reminded Quinn. "I left you a voice mail. I told you I had an evening tour last night and—"

"Except that there was no tour scheduled for last night." One of the things Quinn had apparently been reading was the latest issue of the Garden View newsletter (complete with a listing of all our tours and lectures). "Want to try again?"

"Only if you think there's some reason I owe you an explanation."

He considered that for a moment or two before he shook his head. "Nope. There really isn't. Not if you didn't want to go to dinner."

"Except I did."

"Or if you think I'm a total loser."

"Which I don't."

"Or if you're telling me right here and now that you don't want to spend any time with me."

"But I do."

"Good. Because I want to spend time with you, too." Though we were in agreement, his smile was grim. "You've got to admit, it's only natural for me to be curious, then. Especially when you bail on me and spend your evening with Rudy Scarpetti."

I stared at him, my mouth open, and when he pinned me with a look, I knew how it felt to be on the wrong side of this boy in blue.

"How do you—?"

"What are you up to, anyway?"

By now, I had the story down pat. It didn't even feel like a lie.

"I'm writing a book." I had the nerve to look Quinn right in the eye. "About Gus Scarpetti. I told you all that back at the police museum."

"The way I remember it, you also told me you'd steer clear of these people. Hell, you promised! So why did you stroll into the homestead to interview the family?"

I didn't like the tone of Quinn's question so I matched my voice with just the edge of steel that hardened his. "Yeah. That's pretty much exactly what I did. I called and requested an interview and—"

"Ever wonder why Rudy Scarpetti's number is even in the phone book?"

He had me there. I shrugged. "So he can get phone calls?"

He rolled his eyes. "The number in the book is Rudy's public number. You know, the one he gives out at his country club and his church and his wife's women's groups."

"He's married?" I had never thought to ask about the Cootie's marital status because really, I didn't care. It was just that—

"He came on to you?"

Quinn wasn't one to mince words. I glanced away. "It wasn't blatant. He just said—"

"I can imagine." I wasn't sure if that was a compliment or not. "That didn't worry you?"

"Should it?" As much as I enjoyed the scent of Quinn's expensive aftershave and being this close to him, I stood and sidled around to the other side of the desk. "Are you telling me I should stay away from Rudy?"

"I'm telling you that these are dangerous people." Quinn stood, too, and turned to face me. "You have no idea what you're getting into."

"I'm not getting into anything," I told Quinn and reminded myself. "I'm just asking a few questions. And none of them is about anything that's happened in the last thirty years, so how dangerous can it be? I talked to Rudy about his father, about Gus. I asked him what he knew about Gus's murder and—"

"Pepper!" Quinn's voice cut me off. It was quiet, and it packed an emotional punch that hit me somewhere between my stomach and my heart. "Maybe you haven't been listening to me but I told you I'd like to see you again. That means I'd like to see you alive."

"But I didn't—"

"It doesn't matter. Not to these people. Rudy Scarpetti likes to put on a show. More than anything, he'd like a little respectability, a good image and a reputation like Mother Teresa's. He'd love to find some hack—no offense intended—to help perpetuate the myth. My guess is that's why he agreed to see you. He heard book. He thought publicity. And he figured he could convince you to make sure it was good publicity. Don't let the shiny exterior fool you. And don't think that contact with him can be casual or without consequences. Rudy's a criminal. His father was a criminal. And that big house was bought and paid for with blood money."

I knew Quinn was right. But that didn't relieve me from my obligation to Gus, did it?

"I promise not to do anything stupid." I held up two fingers, Boy-Scout style. "But there's more I need to know. Can you find out who killed Gus Scarpetti?"

"It happened thirty years ago. What difference does it make?"

"But my book—"

"Find someone else to write about."

It was as simple as that. At least to Quinn. Of course, he didn't know about the nine thousand dollars. Or about the dead don who was down but certainly not out. At least not out of my life.

He also didn't know that once I'd made up my mind about something, I wasn't easily talked down. I thought back to something Rudy had mentioned the night before and gave Quinn the little pout that used to drive Joel wild. Call me egotistical but I could tell it still worked its magic. Quinn's pupils widened and he took a step closer to me.

"I'm almost done with my research," I told him. "I've only got one more thing to check out. A retirement home. Rudy runs it for the guys who used to work for Gus."

"Not a chance."

So much for the magic of my pout.

"Oh, come on!" I might be down but I wasn't out, either. I moved close enough to finger Quinn's lapels. "All I need is a name and an address and something tells me you're just the guy who can get it for me."

"No."

"Quinn…" The front of my yellow cami grazed his white shirt. "What could it hurt? They're a bunch of old bad guys. And they're retired, which means that technically, they're not even bad guys anymore. All I want to do is ask them a couple questions about the old days."

"And you think you can turn on the charm and I'll give up the name of the place."

"You think this is charm?" One step closer and my breasts pressed against Quinn's chest. "You ain't seen nothing yet!"

"Then God help me!" Quinn laughed and fitted his hands around my waist. "Tell you what, if I hear anything that I think might help with your book—"

"No, thanks." I backstepped out of his reach. "I don't need you to decide what's right for my book and what isn't. Besides, what could you possibly hear? You said it yourself, it all happened thirty years ago." Another thought struck. "Unless you're investigating something now that has something to do with the Scarpettis."

"Brains and beauty." Quinn might have been handing out the praise but he didn't look happy about it. He dropped his hands and stepped back. "That's exactly what I've been trying to get through to you. They were dangerous people back in Gus Scarpetti's day and they're dangerous people now. Every single one of them. As a matter of fact, last night at Scarpetti's, you might have seen a certain business associate of Rudy's. Albert Vigniolli. Guy with a long, dark ponytail and a scar on his left cheek."

"Doesn't sound familiar." I lied because it was easier than admitting that just giving a name to Goon #2 made me break out in a cold sweat. I didn't ask what Quinn's interest was in the guy. Quinn was with Homicide. That pretty much told me all I needed to know.

Another piece of the puzzle clicked into place.

"That's how you knew where I was last night." I pointed a finger at him in an *aha* sort of way. "You're working a case."

Quinn didn't confirm or deny my suspicion. "Had a meeting with the FBI this morning," he said. "About a matter of mutual interest. They keep tabs on the Scarpetti place. And they keep track of who comes and goes."

"Then they're the ones who…"

"Followed you?" Quinn nodded, confirming something to himself. "I told them you were smart enough to pick up on it."

I swear, right then and there, I almost cried with relief. So they weren't exactly the Prize Patrol! Thinking that I'd been tailed by the feds was a lot more comforting than considering the alternative.

Even if I was inclined (which I wasn't) to tell Quinn that I'd imagined it was Goon #1 or Goon #2 behind the wheel of that black sedan, I didn't get the chance. His cell phone rang. He took the call, flipped the phone closed, and headed for the door.

"Got to go." He stepped out in the hallway and stopped. "By the way," he said. "You've got three unpaid traffic tickets you should take care of."

"Have you been checking me out?"

Quinn grinned. "Gonna do that. Later. I promise." As quickly as it came, his grin melted and his lips hardened into a thin line of determination. "You were listening, weren't you, Pepper? You were paying attention to everything I said?"

"Cross my heart." I did, and watching the way my finger skimmed across my breast, Quinn's eyes darkened.

"I'll call you," he promised. "And you'll stay out of trouble."

It wasn't a question so I didn't answer it. I watched him leave. No sooner was he past Ella's office than she was out in the hallway and headed my way.

"Oh my gosh!" She fanned her face with one hand. "You don't have to be premenopausal to enjoy that. Tell me all about him."

"After you tell me about Dan." No way had I missed him, but I leaned into my office and looked around again. "You said two guys. What happened to the other one?"

"You didn't give me a chance to explain. There

were two. First the other one. Then that one." She peered down the hallway the way Quinn had gone. "When are you going to tell me—"

"The other one. Dan. He must have stopped by to talk about his study. Did he leave a message or anything?"

"Dan? Was that his name? I don't think he said."

"Cute guy. My height. Shaggy hair. Glasses."

Her face puckered with confusion. "The hair, maybe. But no, no glasses. And cute…?" She wrinkled her nose. "I wouldn't call him cute at all. Not that I'm criticizing or anything. I mean, we can't judge other people by their looks. That's what I always tell the girls. But he does have that awful scar on his cheek."

Ella might have kept on talking. I'm not exactly sure. Whatever she said didn't penetrate the buzzing inside my head.

Albert Vigniolli? Goon #2? He'd been there?

I grabbed for Ella's arm and held on tight.

"What did he say?" I asked.

"Him? You mean…not this one." She looked after Quinn again. "You mean the other one?"

"Yeah. The big guy with the ponytail. Did he leave me a message?"

"He did. Only…well, it didn't make a whole lot of sense. Let's see if I can get this right…" She squeezed her eyes shut, thinking. "Oh, that's it!" She opened her eyes and smiled. "He said just to tell you that he'd stopped in and that even though he knows where you live, he didn't want to bother you at home. He said to tell you that he's been thinking about you. And that he'll see you very soon. He said when he does, he's bringing a big surprise."

Something told me it wasn't going to be the Prize Patrol.

Chapter 10

As it turned out, I didn't need Quinn's help after all.

I had my own personal Deep Throat.

Gus had hung around the Scarpetti compound long after I left, listening and (no doubt) reliving the old glory days. When he finally popped back to the cemetery the afternoon of the day both Quinn and Albert Vigniolli paid me a visit, I asked him about the project Rudy had mentioned in passing, the one Quinn refused to discuss. Lucky for me, Gus was ready, willing, and able to share.

Three days later we stood side by side on the walk in front of The Family Place, a retirement home with an exclusive list of residents and a strict policy of not accepting new applicants.

If anybody knew about Gus's death, it would be the men who lived there. Except for a couple who were dead, a couple more in prison, one who had retired to Florida, and another who was a permanent resident in the psych ward of a local hospital, the men inside that house were all that was left of what used to be Gus's inner circle. His crew. The made guys who made sure that the hits just kept on comin'.

I shook the thought aside and looked where Gus was looking, at the white three-story house. It was newly built but in Victorian style, a rambling structure complete with green shutters, a wraparound porch, and window boxes chock-full of purple and yellow pansies that bobbed in a stiff breeze.

All-American respectability in a good neighborhood. The house was situated on a bluff that overlooked Lake Erie. To one side of it, there was a park. On the other, a sweep of lawn and beyond that, an Art Deco mansion in the midst of a major revamping. There was a team of workers installing new windows. And a vaguely familiar-looking dark-colored car in the driveway.

"I gotta tell you, I'm real proud of Rudy." Gus's eyes sparkled. "Sure, he collects art glass. And he did make a pass at you. For that, I cannot forgive him. But I raised him right. He understands the value of family. Imagine him taking care of the guys like this."

"Unless the guys took care of you."

"Are you starting with that again?" Gus's top lip curled but he hardly spared me a look. He was still studying the house. It was an overcast day and a cold mist hung at the roofline and in the branches of the two huge oaks that framed the front porch. Beyond the house, I could see the lake. Whitecaps rolled in from Canada.

I was huddled in a chartreuse peacoat that I should have been able to put away weeks before. But, hey, it was Cleveland and only the end of April. I wrapped my arms around myself, shivering partly from the temperature and mostly because I'd been shivering since I'd heard about Goon #2's promise to pay me a visit.

So far, so good. No sign of Albert. And believe me, I'd been looking.

Over my shoulder any time I went out.

Under my bed and in the closets every time I stayed in.

I wasn't taking any chances.

Even in broad daylight, I glanced around. The sidewalk in both directions was empty. There wasn't much traffic on the street, either. Looked like Gus and I were the only ones dumb enough to be out on a day that raw.

"So what are you waiting for?" he asked me. "I want you to meet the fellas."

They were fellas, all right.

Goodfellas. Retired or not.

I told myself not to forget it.

Once we were inside the spacious entryway with its hardwood floors and thick Oriental carpets, I shrugged out of my coat. I handed it to the young man who introduced himself as Joe and said he looked after the needs of the residents of The Family Place. Joe pointed me down a long, airy hallway and toward the open double doors that led into the great room. I paused on the threshold, getting my bearings.

The room was furnished with a plush couch in muted shades of burgundy and mission-style tables that were sparkling clean. There were four leather recliners and reading lamps in front of a stone fireplace that was on one wall, and on the other three, floor-to-ceiling windows that looked out over a wide deck. At the center of the deck and facing the lake were broad wooden steps that led down to a strip of beach.

Prime real estate and a view to die for.

Something told me the irony was not lost on Rudy.

There were four men inside the room. Three of them were playing cards at a table on my left and the fourth was seated in front of a wide-screen plasma TV that was on too loud and turned to the History Channel. All Hitler, all the time. That day was no exception.

"That's No Shoes, Benny Marzano." Gus pointed toward the man in front of the TV and I saw that Benny was in a wheelchair. "He had a lot more hair the last time I saw him."

"And the others?" I asked the question under my breath, my teeth clenched, my lips barely moving. I knew how lucky I was to get past the front door of The Family Place. I didn't need to blow this chance by looking crazy. "Who are they?"

Gus peered into the room. "That's Johnny Vitale dealing," he said and I studied the man he pointed out. Though he was close to eighty, Johnny was still imposing. He had broad shoulders and hair the color of cold metal. He was wearing stretchy old man jeans and a gray T-shirt that showed off muscles that were still beefy, even if they weren't bulging. His face was heavily wrinkled and his hands shook when he dealt the cards.

The others…

My gaze went around the table as Gus narrated. "That's got to be the Pounder," he said, squinting toward the man who sat, stoop-shouldered, with his back to the door. "I'd know him anywhere. The other guy…" His gaze moved to the Pounder's left. "That there's the Weasel, Nick Trivilagetti. He looks lousy."

"He looks old. You'd look old, too, if you weren't dead."

"One of the advantages of dying young." Gus raised his chin and twirled his pinky ring. "I get to be this good-looking for all eternity."

I wasn't about to argue the point.

"So…" Johnny spoke up, never once glancing away from his cards. "You this Pepper Martin who called last week? This woman who said she was—"

"Writing a book. That's me." Even though no one was paying attention, I brandished my red leather portfolio as if it was all the proof they needed of my credentials. "I appreciate you seeing me on such short notice. It's nice to meet you. All of you."

"You think?" Pounder choked out the words along with a smoker's cough. He looked at the cards in his hand before he glanced over his shoulder at me. Except for a couple of stray curls, my hair was pulled back into a ponytail and for that day's meeting, I had chosen a brown pantsuit and a modest white blouse. It was apparently not modest enough. The Pounder looked at my chest and smiled. "Say, sweetheart, what's a nice girl like you doing in a place like this?"

At my side, Gus shook his head, disgusted. "Always the ladies' man."

Not with lines like that.

I kept the thought to myself. As inappropriate as it was, Pounder's comment gave me a perfect opening. I smiled right back and took another couple steps closer to the card table.

"What I'm doing is collecting information. About Gus Scarpetti."

"Who?" There was a commercial on and without the distraction of tanks and guns, Benny No Shoes had just noticed me. He squinted and looked from me to the card players. His voice was almost as loud as the television. "Who is she talking about?"

Johnny Vitale tossed five dollars into the pot at the center of the table. "The Pope." He spoke as loud as Benny did. "She wants to know about Don Scarpetti, *buonanima*."

"That means, 'God rest his soul,'" Gus whispered in my ear.

I slanted him a look that told him I didn't need any distractions and made a mental note to tell him that I also didn't need any help. Not about things like that. I'd spent the entire weekend boning up for that meeting. I knew at least that little bit of mobspeak.

The Weasel threw his cards down on the table. "Why would a girl care about Don Scarpetti?"

I didn't bother to explain about the book again. There was an empty chair at the table and I sat down. "He had a fascinating life," I said. "The story will make for a blockbusting book."

Pounder took another drag on the cigarette he had balanced between two nicotine-stained fingers. He laughed and coughed before he tossed down his cards, too, and Johnny scooped up the money from the table. "Yeah, blockbusting. That's us. 'Cept we're not blockbusting, we're ball busting!"

The others laughed and I smiled. Might as well go along with the pack.

"I'm sure your stories are very colorful."

"And you expect us…" Johnny's eyes were dark and as steady as a heat-seeking missile. His look went right through me. "You expect us to tell you all about Don Scarpetti's life."

"I…well…I…" Because I didn't know what else to do or how to keep these men from noticing that my hands were shaking, I flipped open my portfolio and took out a pen. I clicked it open, ready to take notes. "Actually, I know a whole lot about Gus's life. It's his death I'd like to learn more about."

"What's that?" Benny No Shoes must have picked up on something I said because he wheeled around and came closer. "You're writing about how Don Scarpetti died?"

"What can you tell me about it?"

"Nothing." My question was for Benny but the answer came from Johnny. "Ain't nothing to say."

"But who—?"

Johnny swept one large hand over the table, collecting the cards. "It was the FBI that had him hit.

It was the cops. It was some punk trying to make a name for himself. It sure the hell wasn't anybody in this room, so why are you bothering us?"

"Then what about Victor LaGanza?" After what Rudy had told me, it was a long shot, but it didn't hurt to double-check. "Do you think he had anything to do with it?"

Johnny glared at me. "It ain't smart to disrespect Mr. LaGanza," he said. He tapped the cards into a neat pile. "After all these years, what does it matter, anyway?"

"It don't matter. Not to you. You're not in this chair." Benny rolled nearer. "He's not in this chair," he said to me, raising his voice, convinced that if he couldn't hear me, I couldn't hear him, either. "He's not the one who got shot."

"You mean outside Lucia's?" I vaguely remembered something in the newspaper accounts of Gus's death, a mention of Benny Marzano and that he'd been wounded. I hadn't realized how serious it was. I never bothered to look into it. "You've been paralyzed since—"

"Thirty years." Benny was a beady-eyed man with yellow skin pulled tight across his face, so paper thin I could see the network of veins just below the surface. He was hunkered in gray sweatpants, a green turtleneck, and a polar fleece jacket. Even with all the layers and the plaid blanket draped over his shoulders, he shivered. "If I ever get my hands on the son of a bitch who—"

"It don't matter. Not anymore." Johnny's voice cut across Benny's.

"But it does." I twinkled at Johnny. "For my book. And for my book…" I turned in my seat so that I was facing Benny. "What do you remember about that night?"

Benny didn't have to think about it. Then again, I suppose the fact that he left Lucia's on his own two feet and hadn't used them since pretty much meant that night was firmly etched in his memory.

"We was done with dinner," Benny said, "and Don Scarpetti, he wanted to go over to Saluto's. You know, that bar what used to be over there on the corner near the church. We were headed that way—"

"Not to your car?" I don't know why it seemed important, I only knew I had to ask.

"Nah." Benny shook his head, and when the blanket around his shoulders drooped, he tugged it back in place. "It was close. We were gonna walk. We were waiting to cross the street when the car drove by."

"The one the shooter was in. Did you see who it was?"

"If he did, he would'a told the cops." Johnny shuffled the cards. His hands were big. His fingers were thick and in them, the cards looked small and fragile.

"What about the car, then?" I asked Benny. "What can you tell me about it?"

"It was green." Benny nodded. "Not new. You know, one of those kinds of cars the kids used to hot rod around in. I told the cops. They said they never found no car like it."

"They never looked." Johnny slapped the deck of cards onto the table and crossed his arms over his broad chest. The tone of his voice made it clear that the conversation was over. "The cops never cared about Don Scarpetti. And you shouldn't, either. What's done is done and nothing's going to bring the old don back. We don't need some little girl asking questions or digging up the past. We was told you were here to talk about—"

"How generous Rudy the Cootie is. How he keeps this place going. What an upstanding kind of guy he is." I should have known I wouldn't have gotten past the front door without Rudy's permission and under his rules. I flicked my portfolio closed, ready to call it a day.

Until I remembered what Gus had once said about bargaining chips.

Right now, the only thing I had going for me was all that homework I'd done all weekend long.

"For all your talk of respect and Gus Scarpetti, *buonanima*..." I used the same reverent tone Johnny had used when he spoke the word. "I would think you'd want to find out who burned him. Maybe that's the only way the old don will ever rest in peace."

Johnny's voice came out like a growl. "How dare you talk about the boss that way?"

"It's the whole karma thing, you know?" I shrugged like it was no big deal. "Let's face it, you guys might have been the enforcers, but Gus was the boss. He ran the show. It was his decision who got made. It was his decision who got whacked. He got points from all the Family businesses. You know, the shakedowns and the shylocking and the pump and dumps. He got a big taste from the bookmaking, too, and because of it all, he was a wealthy man, and he lived like a king. Makes you think of the old saying, doesn't it? *Col tempo la foglia di gelso diventa seta.*"

I gave them a moment to decipher my not-so-perfect Italian.

"Time and patience change the leaf to satin. That's what it means, right? But no time is going to change this reality, and if you think I'm gonna buy that, then you're a bunch of jamokes. You know it and I know it, Gus Scarpetti died like he lived. With blood on his hands."

Benny's face went ashen as opposed to Johnny's, which turned a shade that matched the wine-colored couch nearby. I didn't bother to look at the other two men. I didn't have to. The Pounder was busy hacking up a lung and the Weasel's voice split the air.

"You can't prove that," he said. "Nobody can."

He was wrong.

One person could. One very dead person.

I looked toward the couch where Gus was sitting and hoped he got the message. If I was going to find out anything from these four men, I needed to establish that I knew what I was talking about. I needed to prove that I wasn't a dilettante, a mobster wannabe looking to garner some vicarious thrills from the stories of a few of the old Mustache Petes.

I needed it all. And I needed it immediately.

Lucky for me, Gus realized it, too.

"Tell them…" He squeezed his eyes shut, thinking, and in one stomach-turning moment, I realized he wasn't trying to remember if he'd ever actually killed someone. He was trying to pick out which one he was willing to talk about.

When he looked my way again, his eyes were flat, remorseless. "Tell them you know about Tommy Two Toes."

"Tommy Two Toes." As mob nicknames went, this one was even more ridiculous than usual, and I would have laughed when I repeated it if not for the fact that the second the words were out of my mouth, the room went dead quiet.

Except for the TV. The narrator was still droning on about Axis war plans when Johnny hit the Off button on the remote.

Now the silence was complete. The quiet was ripped by the sound of Pounder's chair when he scraped back from the table and left the room. And the squeaking of the Weasel's sneakers against the floor when he beat feet, too.

"You can't pin what happened to Tommy on Don Scarpetti," Benny said, and it was hard to tell if the convulsive movement of his shoulders meant he was shrugging or shivering. "Must'a been close to forty years ago that Tommy got whacked. Ain't no way anybody cares no more. And you, writing about Don Scarpetti. You should know he can't ever be connected to that. Don Scarpetti, he didn't never—"

Johnny stood, effectively silencing Benny.

"This meeting is over," Johnny said.

"Just like that?" I couldn't believe my lousy luck. Even with the inside track, I couldn't get to first base with this bunch. "But I told you. I know about Tommy. Doesn't that prove that I've done my research and know what I'm talking about? Doesn't it get me anything?"

"I don't know what you're talking about," Johnny said. He looked toward Benny. "Nobody here knows what you're talking about."

And me? I knew a losing cause when I saw one.

At the same time I wondered what I'd said to hit such a nerve, I headed for the door, where Joe appeared as if by magic. He handed me my coat.

I guess all that research I'd done over the weekend gave me a kick like adrenaline and the sudden urge to prove that I wasn't a little girl and I wasn't a dabbler. After all, these guys and I had something in common. They once worked for the boss who was now my boss.

As for the Brooklyn accent…well, I'm not exactly sure where that came from, I only know I sounded mighty tough when I left with a parting shot.

"Thanks for nothing, Johnny," I told him. "And by the way, if you think those are nice, friendly neighbors moving in next door, you're a fuckin' mortadella."

I didn't bother to wait to see his reaction. Joe opened the front door for me and I raced outside. The damp air was colder than ever against my hot cheeks.

"What the hell was that all about?"

I might have asked Gus the same question but he beat me to it.

"You mean—"

"I mean shylocking. And pump and dumps. *Col tempo la foglia di gelso diventa seta.* And fuckin' mortadellas!" He pressed a hand to his heart. "Since when do girls talk like that? Since when do you know about such things?"

Honest, I couldn't help myself. I had to laugh. I didn't even try to explain. Not until we were in the car. Then on the way back to the cemetery, I gave Gus the lowdown on the research I'd done all weekend, a brief description of DVD technology, and a short history of the life and times of *The Sopranos*.

"I thought you said you recruited twelve people for this study?"

Dan had been thumbing through a file folder with my name on it. When he heard my voice, he looked over to where I stood in the doorway. He blinked, confused, then glanced around his empty office, as if it was the first time he realized we were the only ones there.

"I did say twelve, didn't I?" He hurried to the door to usher me inside. It was the typical hospital office with a tile floor, white walls, and standard-issue metal furniture. No photographs. No funny posters. The only thing that made the office look like it actually belonged to someone was the array of framed diplomas on the wall and a mirror where

I was pretty sure Dan never checked to see if his outfit passed fashion muster. If he did, he wouldn't have been wearing navy pants with a black shirt.

"The rest of my subjects for the study..." There was a metal credenza behind Dan's desk, and he motioned to it and to the neat stack of fat file folders on it. "They've been in and out all week," he said. "You're the final interview."

"Does that mean you saved the best for last?"

At least he knew flirting when he saw it. Dan blushed. Unfortunately, even flirting wasn't enough to distract him. He got right down to business, pulling papers out of my file.

"I've got this questionnaire for you to complete tonight. When you're done, we'll set up a time for your next visit. That's when we'll start the real testing."

Testing.

A word that had never agreed with me.

"Testing as in..."

"EKGs. EEGs. CAT scans and an MRI. You'll probably need to spend an entire afternoon here. I'd also like to conduct some of the classic ESP experiments. You know, just to make sure we have all our bases covered."

"You think I have ESP?"

Dan grinned. "Like I said, I'd like to cover all our bases."

"And our bases begin..." I glanced at the papers he still held in his hand. There must have been at least ten in the stack. This did not bode well for my plan of getting home early and crawling into bed. It was already after eight, the only time all week that Dan could see me. After my earlier visit with the retired wiseguys and an afternoon avoiding starting my research on tombstone symbolism for that article I was supposed to be writing, I was dead on my feet.

"You ready to get started?" Dan asked, and when I told him I was as ready as I would ever be, he invited me to sit in the chair behind the desk. "Sorry the accommodations aren't a little more luxurious, but you should have plenty of elbow room." He checked his watch. "I've got to pop over to the lab to check on the results of some of the other testing. I'll give you a few minutes so you can get started."

As soon as he was gone, I settled down to business. I dutifully filled in the blank lines on the top paper. My name. My address. My phone number. My health insurance information. It wasn't until I started in on the detailed information part of the questionnaire (*Please describe the circumstances that led to your head injury*) that I realized I wasn't alone. Spooky music or no spooky music, I was getting to be an expert in feeling a certain ghostly presence.

"You're not going to help me get through this, so why did you bother to come along?" I asked Gus.

"I dunno." I looked up to find him peering at the diplomas that lined the walls in sleek black frames. If the alphabet soup that followed Dan's name on each of them meant anything, he was one smart cookie. "Maybe I just don't like the idea of you seeing this guy here all by yourself. It's not the way a proper women behaves."

"First of all..." I scratched down the last few words of the story of the day I'd whacked my head on Gus's mausoleum. "Nobody worries about that kind of thing anymore. And besides, I'm here on business."

"He wants to shrink your head."

"Not exactly." I flipped the page to the next question.

What symptoms did you exhibit after your accident?

"Is passing out a symptom?" I asked Gus, and even before he could answer, I decided it was and detailed how I woke up and found myself in the ER.

"Still, the two of you alone..." Gus let the words hang.

I made a face. "Doesn't look like that's going to happen as long as you're around."

"You'll thank me for it later." He moved from the diplomas to the bookcase and when he walked past the mirror, I didn't see Gus's reflection. He tipped his head to read the titles on the bookshelf. "He has brains, this boy."

"Lots of them." I checked out the next question. *What unusual behaviors have you exhibited since your initial visit to the emergency room?*

"Think you qualify as an unusual behavior?" I asked Gus. Not that I intended to mention him. Ever. Instead, I talked about having trouble sleeping and about the ringing in my ears that started right after the accident and that I still occasionally heard. Ordinary stuff and nothing to worry about. Just as Doctor Cho had said all those weeks ago.

Which made me wonder how I even qualified for Dan's study.

I chewed the end of the pen, thinking it over. "It doesn't make a whole bunch of sense, does it? If everything's normal—"

"Then why were they so spooked—you should excuse the phraseology—when you mentioned Tommy? Exactly what I've been wondering."

But not what I was talking about. Because I knew it wouldn't do me any good to try and stick to my own agenda, I switched gears. It was easier to mull over the events of the afternoon than it was to try and fathom the workings of an Einstein like Dan, anyway. "The whole Tommy thing can't have anything to do with you. Tommy was dead ten years before you were. You're the one who had him clipped."

"You gotta stop watching them DMVs."

"DVDs," I corrected him. "And you're changing the subject."

Gus shrugged, making it clear that it was no bigger deal then than it had been forty years earlier. "Tommy was a rat. And it was strictly business. He got what he deserved."

"Then why *did* your associates seem to care so much?"

Gus pursed his lips, thinking. "They were surprised. That's all. You showed them that you're not just another pretty face. They didn't think a girl could be so smart."

Ridiculous to be pleased by such a small thing, I know, but it was as close to a compliment as I'd ever gotten from Gus. I smiled. "Am I smart?"

He winked. "You had me there to help you."

"Wish you could help me now." I flipped to the next page and the next question and paused with my pen poised over the paper.

Do you ever think that you are deluding yourself? Not facing the truth? Not dealing with reality?

"So how come you never told me about your old man?"

I was deep in thought, trying to figure out how to answer Dan's question when Gus's came at me out of the blue. I looked up, floored.

"You told Rudy," he said. "About your old man. You said he was in federal prison."

"Oh, that." I set down the pen and shook out my hand. "I never mentioned it because it doesn't matter."

"Matters to your father." Gus's smile was grim. He perched on the corner of Dan's desk. "Matters to you, too, I think."

"I'm dealing."

"That's good. Only if you ever...I dunno...want to talk about it..."

"I don't."

"That's good." He stood. "Sometimes it ain't easy for a kid...you know?"

"Good thing I'm not a kid." I glanced at the stack of papers still untouched. "And I'm not getting any younger."

I pulled the next page in front of me.

Do you ever hallucinate?

Okay, Dan had me there. Once upon a time that seemed like forever ago, I wouldn't have hesitated. Do I hallucinate? Ask me back then and I would have known the answer.

You betcha!

But there was that birthmark on Gus's hip that proved me wrong. And the inside information on The Family Place and Tommy Two Toes. Info I couldn't have dreamed up, no matter how vivid my hallucinations.

There was Gus standing in front of me, as real as the desk between us.

Did I hallucinate?

"No." I spoke out loud and wrote down the single word.

Do you talk to people other people can't see? Do you hear their voices?

"Shit." I tossed down the pen. "How can I even be in this stupid study when I have to start out lying to Dan?" I asked Gus and myself. I spun Dan's desk chair around, stalling for time, looking for a way out that was ethical without being too truthful. I glanced at the stack of file folders, the questionnaires completed by the other people in the study. "Do you suppose they're crazy, too?"

" 'Cept you're not."

"Something tells me Dan would disagree."

"Then he'd be wrong."

I poked the stack of folders with my pen. "You think they told the truth?"

"You think anybody does?"

I wasn't about to get philosophical. Especially when I'd just decided to hedge my bets and cheat. A little.

If I looked at what the other participants wrote, maybe I could come up with an answer that sounded at least a little believable.

My mind made up, I picked up a couple of the folders and flipped through them. That's when I heard the office doorknob turn. Dan was back.

As fast as I could, I tossed the folders back on the credenza and spun my chair around.

And that was too bad.

Because in the instant I'd looked through them, I saw something very interesting.

Sure the other folders were stuffed with papers. But those papers? They were blank.

Chapter 11

When I got home a couple hours later, I was still mulling over the mystery of those file folders stuffed with empty paper. I suppose I would have kept right on wondering what Dan was up to and why he'd lied about the other study participants except that the second I was inside my apartment and had the door closed behind me, I had bigger things to worry about.

An arm went around my neck and I got yanked back so hard and so fast, my feet left the floor.

"Some bitches don't know when to mind their own business," Albert Vigniolli grumbled in my ear.

After that...

Well, after that, the wondering and the worry were officially over. The panic kicked in.

I must have looked like a rag doll, thrashing and squirming, powerless with Albert's beefy arm around my neck, my feet dangling and my own arms flailing. I caused about as much damage as a rag doll would have caused, too. Which was exactly none.

I tried for an elbow to his ribs.

Albert laughed.

I did my best to get my foot up so I could bash him in the knee with the heel of my shoe.

Albert tightened his hold.

He had arms like steel bands and muscles on top of his muscles. Every one of those muscles clenched, slowly squeezing my neck. This was something Albert had obviously done before and he was plenty good at it. What fun would it be to cut off some-body's air supply quickly? This way, bit by bit, one heartbeat at a time, I knew exactly what I was missing.

What I was missing was oxygen.

My ears buzzed, and even though all the lights in my apartment were off, the scene in front of me got even darker. I tried like hell not to pass out. Not that I was looking forward to finding out what Albert was planning to do to me. But the idea of blacking out and not knowing was even worse.

Somewhere during all my gasping and strug-gling, Albert's foot hit the edge of the living room carpeting where it met the hardwood floor in the hallway. His shoe caught and he staggered back. For one precious second, his grip loosened, and at the same time I gulped in a breath that felt like fire in my throat, I slipped toward the floor. No way he was going to let that happen. He caught me around the waist, grasped, and lifted, spinning me around so that my breasts were pressed against a chest that felt like poured concrete.

My ribs were being crushed, my breasts were

squished, but lucky me, one of my knees ended up in exactly the right spot.

It was one of those silver platter opportunities and the only one I was going to get. I slammed my knee into Albert's balls.

"Son of a—" He yowled and let go and I hit the floor, butt first and full force. I didn't have the luxury of wallowing in the pain that shot up my tailbone and into my back. As long as Albert was still hopping around on one foot, dropping the f-bomb and clutching his hands to his groin, I had the advantage.

I rolled to my knees and scrambled for the hallway that led to my bedroom. Thanks to a former tenant who had a problem either with the neighborhood or with intimacy issues, there was a lock on the door and my cell phone was in the pocket of my peacoat. If I could get that far—

I didn't.

Still bellowing, Albert grabbed me, spun me around and let go. I slammed into the wall, headfirst, and like those characters in so many cartoons, I saw stars.

Except that there was nothing funny about the situation.

Pain racketed inside my head and something wet and hot trickled into my eyes. Rather than think about what it was and what it meant, I made a mental note.

Please describe the circumstances that led to your head injury.

I'd have a whole new paragraph to add to my answer on Dan's essay test.

If I lived that long.

As far as I could see (and with blood in my eyes and a strobe display going on inside my head, it wasn't far), I had one advantage. I lived there. Albert didn't. The lights were off. He didn't know that when he launched me into the wall, I landed about three inches shy of the table near the front door. The one where I dropped my purse and keys when I walked in. The one near where I leaned the big, black umbrella I took to Garden View with me on rainy days.

I struggled to my feet and groped along the wall, and when my fingers finally closed around the umbrella's wooden handle, I was filled with a sudden and insane courage. I spun to face my attacker, raising the business end of the umbrella.

"Bitch!" Albert swung one meaty fist and I ducked. The lamp on the table hit the floor and shattered.

I managed a thrust and before Albert knew what hit him, the metal point of the umbrella was nestled against his breastbone. I applied just enough pressure to get his attention.

"Out of here, scumbag." I poked him a little harder and Albert stepped back and toward the door.

"If I ever see your ugly face anywhere near here again..." I pressed again and again, he took a step back. "Well, let's just say that if I have to deal with you like this again, it's not going to be—"

He swung one arm, windmill style. My umbrella went flying. And one very pissed Albert came at me.

My only choice was to run, and at that moment, the bedroom wasn't an option. Not with two hundred and fifty pounds of muscle between me and the hallway. I headed for the living room and put the couch between me and Albert, fighting for breath and the inkling of an idea that might save me from a situation that was looking grimmer by the moment.

At the front of the apartment, the streetlight from the opposite curb threw squares of light through the two front windows. When Albert came hurtling in from the hallway, it was the first I got a look at him. It wasn't a pretty sight.

A vein bulged on his forehead and his face was dark and mottled. Against the palette of burgundy and purple, that scar on his cheek looked uglier than ever. His ponytail was mussed and his eyes... well, let's just say that the phrase *if looks could kill* came to mind.

It wasn't something I wanted to think about.

I backed away and Albert came around the couch and closed in on me.

"Looks like you don't take advice very good."

"Well." Even I'd learned that much from English 101. "I don't take advice well. And what advice, anyway? I was told—"

"You was told to mind your own business. And now..." He flicked his wrist. The blade of a long, skinny knife gleamed in the light of the streetlamp.

I took another step away from him. But like I said, the room was small; my back hit the wall. The knife blade glimmered and I stared at it, mesmerized.

I took a deep breath and held it. I don't know why. I guess I figured it would somehow keep it from hurting as much when Albert stuck that knife into me.

I was just about to find out when my front door shattered.

The lights flicked on and for a moment, I closed my eyes, blinded. When I opened them again, there was Quinn looking like a god and this time, it had nothing to do with his six-hundred-dollar suit, his Italian silk tie, or the fact that he was as hot and as tempting as sin.

It had everything to do with the gun in his hand.

"Back away, Vigniolli." Quinn cradled that gun like he knew how to use it. "Drop the knife and get down on the ground."

Albert wasn't very good at listening to directions. Before I could move and before Quinn could get a shot off, he lunged across the room and had me by the throat. "I'm leaving here," he said, stepping behind me and using me as a shield. "And she's coming with me."

Quinn didn't lower the gun. He sighted down the barrel, his eyes and his energies focused on Albert, assessing every twitch, anticipating every move. "Don't be stupid," he said. "You think I was dumb enough to show up here alone? I've got three black-and-whites waiting down on the street. That makes six patrol officers and my partner. How far do you think you'll get?"

"Far enough." Albert stepped toward the door, keeping me between him and the business end of Quinn's gun.

And what was I doing? For starters, I was busy being scared to death. At least until I saw Quinn. Yeah, things were still looking pretty bleak. But there was something about how steady his hands were as he held the gun, something about the intensity of his focus that made me think that—somehow—he was going to get me out of that mess.

Of course, the trick was how.

I was still wondering when Albert and I arrived at my front door.

"See you, cop," Albert said, and before I could figure out what he was up to, he had one hand at the small of my back and the other gripped around my neck. He wound up and launched me at Quinn.

Before either of us knew what hit us, Quinn and I were tangled together on the floor, listening to the sounds of Albert's departing footsteps.

"Shit!" Quinn was flat on his back. He pounded the floor with his fist. "I'm going to lose him again."

I was flat on top of Quinn. Considering that I'd been imagining that I'd finish out the evening at the bottom of Lake Erie, it was not a bad place to be.

I scooped my hair out of my eyes and raised myself up far enough to look into his face. "What do you mean, lose him? What about the patrol cars?"

He looked away.

"And those uniformed officers?" My voice was demanding and as shrill as every article I'd ever read in *Cosmo* said that it should never be. Especially when I was being demanding. "What about your partner? You know, the one who's waiting outside?"

Quinn sighed. When he moved to sit up, I had no choice but to slide off him. We sat on the floor side by side.

"I stopped on my way home from work," Quinn confessed.

"Which means—"

"No black-and-whites. No uniforms. No partner." He slammed his gun back in his shoulder holster.

"Shit."

"Yeah, you got that right."

He slipped an arm around my shoulders. "You okay?"

I wasn't, but things were starting to look up. I sniffled and snuggled into the warmth of Quinn's embrace. "I walked in the front door," I told him. "And he was here. Waiting for me."

"It's okay now. He's gone." He rubbed my back. "I'm afraid I did some damage to your front door. Sorry. But when I heard the commotion inside, I couldn't wait. We'll get the door fixed. We'll put on a deadbolt. In the morning."

"But what if he comes back before morning?"

"He won't. I swear."

Even in my weakened state, I knew Quinn could not make promises on behalf of overmuscled hit men. I went along with his story, anyway. After what he'd done in the saving-my-life department it was the least I could do for him and besides, believing him made me feel better. So did Quinn's fingers tracing lazy circles over my back.

"Come on." He hitched an arm around me and before I knew it, I was up and sitting on the couch and he was leaning over me. His hair was a mess and there was a button missing off the front of his shirt. He peered into my eyes. "Let's get you to the ER."

"No. No ER." He already had a hand around my arm to help me up, and I plucked his fingers away. "I don't need the ER. Unless..." I gently touched the spot on my forehead that hurt the most. It was right above my left eyebrow and when I moved my fingers away and looked at them, they were red and sticky. "Is it bad? Do I need stitches?"

Quinn's mouth pulled into an almost-grin. "No stitches. It's hardly even bleeding anymore. But we should make sure nothing is broken."

"Nothing is broken." Just to prove it, I flexed my arms and moved my legs. Nothing hurt. At least not more than it should have. "I'm fine," I told Quinn. "Just a little—"

"Shook up? Yeah, I can understand that." He got up and headed toward the kitchen. "Got any booze? And some ice cubes?"

"You want a drink?" It must have been some sort

of cop ritual, a way to celebrate not dying another day. "The bar down the street is open until—"

Quinn stuck his head out of the kitchen doorway. He rolled his eyes. "The booze and the ice are for you," he said, before he ducked back into the kitchen.

A couple minutes later he came out carrying one of my dishcloths wrapped around a sandwich bag full of ice cubes. He had a glass of wine in his other hand.

"Your bar stock leaves a lot to be desired." He handed me the wine, sat down, and gently pressed the ice to my eyebrow.

"Ouch!" I winced.

"Hold still. And drink up."

"I can't do both."

He sat back. "Okay then. Drink up," he instructed me. I downed the glass of wine and when I was finished, he slipped an arm around me. He wasn't being friendly, he was holding me in place. He tightened his grip and applied the ice pack.

"There. How does that feel?"

I leaned against his shoulder and closed my eyes. How did it feel? My eyebrow hurt like hell. The rest of me felt like heaven! Quinn's hand on my forehead. Quinn's body next to mine. That left only one question.

"What the hell are you doing here?" I asked him.

When I opened my eyes, his expression was grim.

"I told you to stay away from the Scarpettis."

"I—"

"I warned you, Pepper. And I shouldn't have had to warn you. You're the one writing the book. You know what these people are like. Just in case you didn't get the message, I told you they were dangerous. Do you believe me now?"

"I believed you then. It's just—"

"It's just that you decided you knew more than I did. That's why you were nosing around The Family Place this afternoon."

I wasn't surprised that he knew. Between the police, the FBI, and the Scarpetti crime family, I might as well post my daily schedule on the scoreboard down at Jacobs Field.

The realization soured my already touch-and-go mood. "So you showed up here to read me the riot act." I ducked away from the ice bag and Quinn's hand. "Am I supposed to be pissed or eternally grateful?"

His eyes lit. "I was hoping for grateful but not necessarily eternally."

"But you were betting on pissed."

"Yeah." He tossed the ice pack into my hands and got up. "But give me a little more credit than that, will you? I didn't show up here just to tell you to be careful. I've already told you that. You've already chosen not to listen. I'm not into games and you might as well know that right now. I'm not the type who's going to keep giving advice when I know you're not listening."

"Then what type are you?"

"I'm the type who stopped by on my way home

from the office to tell you that Benny Marzano is dead."

I heard what Quinn was saying. It was just a little hard to process the information. Just in case it had anything to do with brain freeze, I set down the ice pack.

"You've got it all wrong," I told him. "I saw Benny this afternoon. I talked to him. He was alive and kicking—" I cringed. "Okay, so he wasn't exactly kicking. He was alive when I left The Family Place."

"I don't doubt it for a minute. But he wasn't alive by the time his wheelchair went down the steps of the deck at the back of the house and he landed on the beach with about thirty broken bones and a whole bunch of internal bleeding." Quinn picked up what was left of my lamp and put the pieces back on the hall table. "Coroner says it looks like an accident."

I thought of the steep drop to the lake and the wide wooden steps that led down to the beach. I hadn't had time to take off my peacoat and inside it, I shivered.

"No way," I told Quinn. "Not a chance in the world. Benny wouldn't have been out there. It was too cold."

Quinn came back into the living room. "Nobody at The Family Place is talking. There's a big surprise."

"But he was their friend."

"He was their business associate. And if there's

one thing you need to learn about these people, it's that—"

"It all comes down to business. Yeah, I know." I shook my head, trying to order my thoughts. If Benny's tumble down the steps wasn't an accident...

My stomach flipped. Blame it on the wine. Or the couple rounds I'd danced with Albert. Blame it on the picture that formed in my head, the one of Benny's skinny body, broken and battered beneath the polar fleece, lying on the beach with those cold, gray waves lapping over it.

"Now do you believe me?" Quinn dropped onto the couch next to me. "Do you see how dangerous these people can be?"

"But nothing happened. Not when I was there. We talked. That's all. And Benny didn't say anything that would have gotten him..." I couldn't say it. I didn't have to. Quinn knew what I meant.

He twined his fingers through mine. "I'm not saying it has anything to do with you. How could it? But I did want to give you the heads-up. Just in case you had some kind of idea about going to see those guys again."

I think it was pretty safe to say that Albert's visit had disabused me of that thought.

"Thanks." I gave Quinn's hand a squeeze. "You're right. I was dumb to get involved in the first place."

"No more book?"

I thought of everything that had happened. Of everything that would have happened if Quinn

hadn't happened to happen by. Cheap & Chic slingbacks aside, was any of it really worth what Gus
was paying me?

Not if I ended up too dead to spend the money.

That's when I made up my mind. As of right there,
right then, I was officially off the case. "No more
book," I promised Quinn. "No more wiseguys. No
more Albert." I looked toward my shattered front
door and snuggled closer. "And what's that you
were saying about tomorrow morning?"

Quinn's eyes lit with interest. His voice dropped
along with his gaze until he was looking at my lips.
"It would be wrong of me to abandon you in your
hour of need. If you want me to stay..."

Instead of answering, I kissed him. It made more
sense than talking and it was what I'd been wanting to do since I met him, anyway. When Quinn
helped me out of my peacoat and wrapped his
arms around me, I knew it was what he'd been
wanting, too.

"He's not much of a kisser."

I heard the voice but to tell the truth, I figured it
was just some leftover echo, the result of my poor
little brain getting bashed by not-so-little Albert.
Besides, it couldn't be real because it was dead
wrong. Quinn was a very good kisser.

"And why you'd want to waste your time with a
cop, anyway..."

I jolted out of the warm and fuzzy haze that began and ended with Quinn's lips and Quinn's body
and Quinn's hand where it was unbuttoning my
white blouse.

Gus was standing behind the couch, watching us.

"Water." It was the first thing that came to mind and I blurted it out. Quinn was a nice guy and he wasn't about to argue. Especially since I'd been so recently waylaid. He patted my knee, got up, and headed for the kitchen.

"Out. Now." I glared at Gus. "Right now. There's no way in hell I'm going to let you stand there and—"

"So the boy can't kiss. This is my fault?" Gus shrugged. Without seeming to notice them, he stepped around a couple pieces of shattered glass and sat down on the couch next to me. "I'll just stay a while. That way, I can tell you what he's not doing right. I realize a girl of your age, you don't have much experience. But you should know this. So that when you meet the man who will someday become your husband—"

"Oh, no!" I leapt off the couch. "If you think I'm going to let you get your jollies at my expense—"

"Actually, I was hoping we'd both be getting something out of this." Quinn stood in the door-way, water glass in hand, his brows low over his eyes. He was staring at me. And me? Well, I was pointing at the empty couch. Or at least at what Quinn thought was an empty couch. That is, until I realized what I was doing and pulled my hand back to my side.

"I'm willing to chalk some of your behavior up to shock." Quinn handed me my glass of water. "But if there's something else going on here, Pepper, something you'd like to talk about…"

I took a long drink of water and shook my head.

"Good. But you should also know that if you're playing some kind of game...well, let's just say I'm not the kind of guy who appreciates that sort of bullshit."

I set the glass on the coffee table. "I'm not. I don't. It's just—"

"I don't think I like the way he talks to you." Gus got up and stood toe-to-toe with Quinn, who looked right through him to me. "He should treat you with respect."

"He does." I cursed when I realized I was talking to Gus again. "What I mean is, no. No games. I don't play games, either." My hormones had been leaping like salmon up a stream. Now they plunged into the icy depths and lay shattered on the rocky bottom. My shoulders slumped. "I'm not trying to mess with your head, Quinn. I'm just a little confused, that's all. It's been a long night."

"Fine." He headed for the door. "If you're not ready, I can understand that. If you're never going to be ready...Well, if you're never going to be ready, then I've been getting the wrong signals since day one. You'll understand if I'd like to know where I stand."

I glanced from Quinn to where Gus stood with his arms folded over his chest, watching the show. "This just isn't a good time," I told both of them.

"And let me guess..." Quinn stepped over bits of broken wood. "Next time won't be a good time, either."

"No!" I went after him. Call me needy. Call me

desperate. Maybe I was both. "It's just that right now—"

"Right now, you're not thinking with your head." This was Gus's voice but I ignored it. Instead, too angry at Gus for putting me in this predicament, I watched Quinn step into the hallway and walk away. The next second, though, he was back. "You got somewhere you can stay tonight?" he asked and before I could get the wrong impression, he added, "I mean somewhere here in the building? A friend you can stay with until you get somebody in here to fix this door?"

In the space of just a couple minutes, I'd gone from the next morning's project to somebody else's problem. I thought about Todd and Bob, the gay couple on the second floor who'd slept on my couch for a week earlier in the month when their heat wasn't working. They owed me. For the heat and for the fact that I'd put up with the two of them giggling on the couch like teenagers.

"I'll be fine," I told Quinn. "Not to worry."

"I'm not," he said, and this time when he left, he stayed gone.

My anger burst and I turned to fire it full force at Gus.

I would have done it, too. Except that he was nowhere to be found.

Chapter 12

There were only so many ways to say, "I quit," and on my way to the cemetery the next morning, I practiced every one of them. Just in case Gus still didn't get the message, I stopped at the bank and withdrew eight thousand dollars on the theory that nothing says *I'm packing it in* like cold, hard cash.

Why eight? The way I figured it, I was owed something. For my time. For my energy. For nearly getting my larynx crushed by Albert.

Not to mention coming off looking like a nutcase to Quinn and having my love life blown to pathetic bits by Gus's untimely arrival at my apartment.

Oh, yeah, I was more than ready to quit. And so angry, I could barely see straight.

Maybe that's why I couldn't find Gus anywhere.

It was one of those mornings that are all too rare in Cleveland. After the blustery gray misery of the day before, the sky had cleared. It was like crystal above my head, not a cloud in sight. It was still plenty chilly but once the sun was a little higher in the sky, I knew it would warm up fast. Until then, my sneakers left a trail in the dew that coated the grass around Gus's mausoleum.

Carefully, so that I didn't hit the bandage Todd and Bob had insisted on sticking on my forehead just above my left eyebrow, I pressed my nose to the glass mausoleum door.

No sign of Gus.

I retraced my steps and got back into my car. I drove past the angel statue where we'd had a confrontation of sorts early in our relationship of sorts. I checked out the picnic tables outside the monument to the dead president. I cruised Garden View from one end to the other and when I didn't see hide nor ghostly hair of him, I gave up and went to the office.

No doubt, I'd find him already there and waiting for me.

Except that he wasn't.

I was carrying around the eight thousand dollars in a brown paper lunch bag, and I dropped it into the bottom drawer of my desk and sat down, my chin propped on my fists, my insides simmering and ready to boil over.

Kind of hard to give notice when there was no one to give notice to.

And something told me Gus knew it.

Which only made me angrier.

"Oh! There you are."

The last person I wanted to talk to was Ella, but it was already too late for that. I'd made mistake Numero Uno and left my office door open and she spotted me and came inside. "Did you find the research materials I left for you?"

"Sure." I answered automatically, even though I didn't have a clue what she was talking about. "Er...thanks."

"No. Thank you." Ella dropped into the seat in front of my desk. That day she was a vision in peppermint-pink and white. Her rose quartz earrings shimmered. "You've given me real hope, Pepper. I see you hard at work like this and I know my own girls have a chance to make something of themselves, too. My fondest wish is that they turn out as well as you."

I hardly knew Ella's three daughters but I was hoping they'd do better for themselves.

I was, after all, the girl who had once had big dreams. Looking back on the whole mess now, I saw exactly where my mistakes began and ended. I could have been what Ella wanted her girls to grow up to be.

But I blew it.

All because I'd depended on Joel loving me enough to marry me, even after my life fell apart. All because I thought I'd always have Dad and Mom's money to shore me up. Not to mention their undivided attention and their unwavering support.

All because I'd never dreamed that someday I might have to take care of myself. I never knew I'd need it, so I'd never developed the self-confidence or the sense of self-worth that would make it possible for me to boldly go where I should have known I'd have to go all along—off on my own.

What had it gotten me?

My love life was a zero.

My career prospects were just as bad.

My head hurt.

And did I mention the part about talking to a ghost?

I sighed and looked at Ella only to find her with her brows low. She pointed at my forehead. "What happened?"

I gently touched the wound. "Eyebrow piercing," I told her, then remembered that I was supposed to be a beacon of hope and beacons did not come with body piercings. "I came to my senses at the last second. Decided not to go through with it. It should be back to normal in just a couple days."

"I'm glad." Ella leaned over the desk and patted my hand. "A pretty girl like you doesn't need piercings. It's one of the things I talked to the girls about just last night. Right after I told them the story about how you'd really taken control. About all the extra work you've been doing."

She lost me at "taken control" and I would have stayed hopelessly confused if not for the fact that as she talked, Ella looked at the stack of newspaper articles on my desk. It was the first I noticed that someone had been in my office.

The piles on my desk had been straightened. On top of them was a new pile. And a note. I recognized Ella's loopy writing as well as her trademark pink marker.

Why didn't you tell me about your interest in A. S.? Had these set aside for research—relationship

*between G.V. and the LCC. Let me know when
you're finished with them.*☺

"Oh, *that* extra work!" I tipped my head, hoping for a look at the stack of papers under Ella's note and some hint of what we were talking about. "You mean about AS and the lcd."

"LCC." Just to prove it, Ella pointed at her note. "That's local community churches. The relationship between Garden View and the—"

"Local community churches. I get that part. And AS?"

Ella laughed. "Augustino Scarpetti, of course. You are so much like my girls! You don't think I pay attention, but I do. Last time I was in here talking to you, I noticed that you had lots of extra research materials on your desk and that they were all about Mr. Scarpetti. I think it's wonderful that you're taking the initiative like this, Pepper. Trying to find out more about our residents even before you're asked. You're a real asset to Garden View."

"And you found information about Gus that I don't know about." Like it was a magnet and I was the helpless bit of metal caught in its pull, I looked at the new pile that had been added to my desk. Just as quickly, I warned myself to look away.

After all, I was quitting.

"Here are some photographs that I know you haven't seen." Ella set her note to me aside and pointed at the pile.

Which only proved how little she knew about me. I refused to get suckered. Instead of the pictures, I looked at a spot over her left shoulder.

"Photos from the church," Ella said. "That's why they weren't with the rest of the stuff about Mr. Scarpetti. I mean, not that anyone would have noticed. No one has looked through our information about him for years. But then I found out that you were doing your research. Like I just said. And I remembered that I'd put these in with the LCC stuff. Fascinating, aren't they? Funeral pictures always are."

Funeral pictures? Gus's funeral?

Against what little good judgment I appeared to have left, I took a look.

The picture at the top of the pile showed a crowd of mourners streaming out the front doors of a church. A casket led the procession. It was covered with enough flowers to make a Kentucky Derby winner proud.

Gus's funeral. Gus's casket.

I didn't care.

Just to prove it, I turned away and dragged the daily schedule in front of me. No tours scheduled for the day. No groups coming in. No—

"And did you see this one?" I heard Ella dig through the pile of photographs, but I stayed strong. I was quitting, and I had the eight thousand dollars to prove it.

"His family." I heard Ella's finger tap the photo. "I think that would be very important to your research. This is his wife—"

"Carmella?" I'd never seen a picture of the Widow Scarpetti and I admit it, my curiosity got the best of me. I looked to where Ella was pointing.

Too bad all the photo showed was a woman dressed head to toe in black, including a long, black veil that covered her face.

Not that I cared.

"Don't give up so easily." Ella must have noticed my sour expression, even if she did interpret it wrong. She clucked her sympathy. "Research isn't always fun and games. And you're not always successful finding what you're looking for the first time you look for it. Here's another picture of Mrs. Scarpetti and if you look really close..." She squinted and held the picture at arm's length. "You can see a little bit of her profile behind the veil. Look, she's got her sons with her, Rudy and Anthony."

"Gus only has one son." Sure, I was officially out of the private detective business. Almost. Still, as my final act in Gus's employment, I felt I had to set Ella straight. "Rudy the Cootie. That's his son. There is no—"

"Anthony." Ella slid the picture under my nose where I couldn't fail to see it.

This shot showed Carmella with a teenage boy on either arm. Even with a full head of wavy hair, I recognized Rudy right away. On the other side of Carmella...

I took a long look at a tall skinny boy with bad posture who was wearing a suit that looked like it was a couple sizes too big.

CARMELLA SCARPETTI, the caption said. WITH HER SONS, RUDY AND ANTHONY.

The words hit me like a punch from one of

Albert's meaty fists. I sat up and pulled the picture closer.

"Two sons." I would have slapped my forehead if my eyebrow didn't hurt. "Well, doesn't that just prove what a lousy detective I am!"

"Don't be so hard on yourself." From down the hall, I heard the phone ring at the main desk. Ella heard it, too, and always worried about Garden View's image and customer service, she cocked her head, listening to hear how long it would take Jennine to answer. When Jennine did and didn't come running, Ella was convinced it wasn't anything earth-shattering and that no one needed her immediately. She turned her attention back to me. "Like I said, these pictures have been put away for years. There's no way you could have known about Father Anthony."

"Father—?"

"Sure." Ella dug through the pictures. The one she pulled out showed the same skinny kid a few years later. Not so skinny anymore. And hardly a kid. He was dressed in black and wearing a Roman collar. "That's why these photographs were with my research and not with the Scarpetti materials. Father Anthony is the pastor at Blessed Rosary. You know, the church right down the street. He's quite a history buff. He used to be very active here at Garden View. Loved to attend our lectures and tours. Now that I think about it, we haven't seen him in a while. I wonder why."

Which was definitely not what I was wondering.

I was wondering why Gus had never bothered to mention Son #2.

Before I had a chance to formulate any sort of theory, Jennine poked her head into my office. "Somebody named Dan called," she said, waving a piece of pink paper at me like I could see the message she'd written on it. "He says he has time for you this morning if you can make it."

Ella gave me that mothering look that said she'd listen if I was willing to talk.

I wasn't. I mumbled something about an appointment and an early lunch hour and headed out of the office.

Sure, going to see Dan looked like an act of surrender. But that is so not true! We were going to have it out, me and Dan. About those empty files. About what he was up to. And why.

As for Gus...

Well, it looked like he'd been playing me for a patsy, too. Which meant that if I wanted information, I was going to have to find it somewhere else.

Was I changing my mind and getting back into the investigation?

Hell, no. All I was looking for was answers.

Just to prove it, when I walked out of the office, I left the brown paper lunch bag in my desk.

"You're kidding, right?" From behind his wire-rimmed glasses, Dan blinked at me. "You think the file folders I showed you last night are empty?"

"I didn't say empty." I took another step into his office but didn't go anywhere near the chair he had pulled away from the desk and waiting for me next to a machine that looked like the lie detectors I'd seen on cop shows on TV. It had cords and pads and electrodes attached to it on one end and on the other, a thing that looked like a mini copier complete with graph paper and an ink wand attached to it. "I said they were blank."

"Yes. Of course. I'm sorry. That is what you said." Dan came around from the other side of his desk. When he took my hand, I should have known he was up to no good. But hey, I'd had a bad few hours, what with Albert's visit, Quinn's questionable rescue, and the news about Anthony Scarpetti. I took Dan's action at face value.

I should have known better.

He gently piloted me toward the waiting chair.

"No." I brushed away his hand. "I said we needed to get this straight before I'll do any more testing. If you're pulling some kind of scam on me—"

"Does this look like a face that could scam anyone?" Dan pointed at his own face and I have to admit, his grin was so sweet and so honest, I knew he would never lie.

Which didn't mean I was convinced.

And Dan knew it.

He reached for my hand again. "I think I know what's going on here, Pepper."

"You do?"

"I do." He tugged me toward the chair and when I was close enough, he put a hand on each of my shoulders. Even then I refused to cave.

Or at least I refused to sit.

"You're downplaying the whole thing," he said, "and just so you know, that's a perfectly normal response. But I think it's time to face reality. Right here and now. That head injury of yours might be more serious than we thought in the first place."

"It is?" I didn't even realize my knees had collapsed until I was sitting. "You mean—"

"I mean..." Dan reached onto his desk and picked up the file folder with my name on it. "The answers to your questions tell me that something is going on."

"They do not!" I dismissed the notion instantly. I'd been careful not to let on. Not about Gus. Not about my investigation. There was no way Dan could know anything.

Was there?

He flipped through my file. "It's not what you say in here, it's what you don't say. When I asked about hallucinations—"

"No hallucinations. That's the absolute truth."

"Yet your answers..." He read over something inside my file and shook his head. "Listen to me." Dan pulled over the nearest chair and sat down. When he leaned forward, we were eye-to-eye. "I haven't seen you since you were here yesterday evening, right?"

I was reluctant to answer a question that obvious, but he kept on staring, so I nodded. "Right."

"And we haven't talked since then either, have we?"

"Right again."

"Then, up until you walked into my office and mentioned it to me, there was no way I could have known that you were worried about this empty file thing."

"That's right, but—"

"So there's no way I could have done anything to fix the problem because as far as I was concerned, there was no problem. You hadn't told me about it. I had nothing to hide."

I sat back and cocked my head, wondering what he was getting at.

"Pepper..." Dan grabbed for the rest of the files. They were the same ones I'd seen on his credenza the night before. He flipped through them, tipping the folders so I could see. Last night, the pages were blank. Today, they were—

"There's information." I sat up straight and glanced over the pages and pages of notes and charts and statistics. "In all of them."

"That's right." Dan closed the last file and set them all back down on his desk. "Now do you believe me?"

"I believe there's information in those files and it wasn't there last night."

"Do you really think so?" He gave me the same kind of understanding look I'd seen from Ella so recently. "Think about it, Pepper. Why would I go through that much trouble just to fool you?"

"You're saying—"

"That we need to get to the bottom of this. If you're not seeing things that are there and seeing things that aren't...." He reached for the first electrode attached to the machine at my right arm. "If you'll just hold still, we'll get this over with. Then we'll know for sure."

Of course we didn't know for sure. Not right away, anyway. And by the time I'd spent three hours being tested, poked, and prodded, Dan had changed his tune. We wouldn't know for sure, he said, until he had time to calculate and evaluate, measure and assess.

Until then...

Until then, I needed to keep busy. What with empty file folders that weren't and the half truths I'd been getting from my one and only client (who happened to be dead), it was the only way I could think to keep myself from dwelling on the fact that I really might be crazy.

Maybe what I decided to do instead proved I was past hope. I didn't question it, I just did it.

The priest who answered the door of the Blessed Rosary rectory introduced himself as Father David. He was barely older than me, an African American with a deep voice and a ready smile.

"Father Anthony is in the garden," Father David said. "He said if anyone came around to see him, I should send them back. But I don't think he was expecting you."

"I won't be long." I headed toward the back of the house where Father David looked when he mentioned "garden." "Just a couple minutes. I promise. I just need to talk to Father Anthony. I swear."

"No need for that!" Father David laughed. "Go ahead. It's nice and warm out there this afternoon."

Nice and warm weren't the words for it. The garden at the back of the rectory was a little piece of heaven on earth. There must have been a thousand daffodils in bloom along the brick wall that ringed the place, as well as a few early tulips and some purple flowers that were small and delicate and smelled wonderful. A stone path led around a tree that was just about to flower. In the center of the path was a bench and on it sat Anthony Scarpetti in a pool of sunshine.

"Father Anthony?" He sat very still, and I wasn't sure if he was awake or asleep, so I approached carefully. "Father, are you—"

"Still alive? I'm pretty sure." Father Anthony laughed and turned to face me. He didn't look much like the picture of the man I'd seen in the cemetery archives. That Anthony Scarpetti was young and vital, with a full head of curly, dark hair and eyes that burned with faith so strong that it was scary. This was a shadow of that man.

Father Anthony was wearing a baseball cap but I could tell there wasn't any hair under it. His skin was as white as chalk and mottled with blotches of red. He was dressed in jeans and a Notre Dame sweatshirt that gaped around his scrawny neck.

"I don't know you." Like every muscle ached, Father Anthony moved over. He patted the seat on the bench next to him. "What can I do for you?"

"I just..." I dropped down on the bench. "I didn't mean to disturb you. I just wanted to talk."

"Two ears, no waiting." Father Anthony pointed to either side of his head. "Listening isn't a vocation, but it is a big part of my job description. You should excuse my secular wording."

I smiled. "You sound a lot like your father."

Father Anthony tipped his head to one side. "You aren't old enough to have ever known my father."

"No. I'm not." I told myself I should have paid attention to the voice of logic inside my head that said I shouldn't have stopped to see Anthony until I knew exactly what I was going to say to him. Of course, I hadn't listened to my own advice. And now it was too late.

"I came to see you, Father, because of your father. That is, I've been doing some research about your father, Father, and…" I sighed. Father Anthony was watching me carefully, his dark eyes sparkling like the sun against the daffodils. I shrugged. "He's not resting in peace," I said.

Odds are, another man would have told me to get the hell out of his garden. Father Anthony nodded. "I suppose I knew that," he said. "Even after all this time, it's hard to imagine that Pop could find any sort of peace. But how do you…" He looked at me carefully. "You didn't know him. You said so yourself. You're too young."

I nodded. "I work over at Garden View. I give the tours. One of the places we stop is at your father's mausoleum."

"And you're looking to find out more about him."

"Something like that."

There was a book open on Father Anthony's lap. He closed it and set it down on the flagstone pathway at his feet. "You want to define that 'something?'"

I would have. Except that I wasn't in the mood to look like a nutcase.

I guess that was the reason I didn't explain myself more fully. It didn't explain why I said, "He's looking for closure."

Father Anthony sighed. "That makes two of us."

"But not in the same way, I bet."

He studied me, his dark eyes like pools against his washed-out skin. His fingernails were thick and yellow, and he scratched his ear. "Have you talked to him?"

I winced. "I'm not Catholic," I told him. "If you're looking for me to make a confession—"

Father Anthony laughed until he started to cough. It was a heavy, ugly cough and it took him a couple minutes to get settled again. He laid a hand on my arm.

"I'm not looking to give you absolution. I'm thinking maybe you're here to do that for me."

He was so darned sincere, I didn't have any choice but to set him straight. "I don't think so, Father. I mean, all I wanted to do was ask you a couple questions. But absolution..." I whistled low under my breath and shook my head. "That's definitely not in *my* job description!"

Anthony was not so easily put off. "I'll tell you what..." He shifted on the seat and I swear, I could just about hear his bones creak. He couldn't have been very old in that picture I saw of him at Gus's funeral. Which meant that now, Father Anthony was somewhere around fifty. He looked one hundred and fifty.

"You ask what you want to ask," Anthony said. "I'll make the decisions about absolution. Sound okay to you?"

"Sure." I put both my feet flat against the pavement and drew in a breath. "Did you know that Benny Marzano is dead?" I asked him.

He didn't look surprised. "Haven't heard that name in years. Benny No Shoes! He used to bring me Hershey bars when I was a little kid. He didn't have any kids of his own and..." The rest of the memory was lost in time and Anthony shook it away and looked at me. "I thought you came here to talk about my father."

"I did. You see..." I drew in a breath and let it out slowly. "I'm trying to find out who killed him."

Father Anthony sat quietly for so long, I thought maybe he'd fallen asleep. I was about to get up and walk away when he passed a hand over his eyes.

"I was eighteen years old when my father was killed," he said. "Seems like a lifetime ago. And though I was young and pretty naive...well, I was never stupid. I heard the way the kids talked behind my back at school. I saw what went on at our house. Even my brother, Rudy, never said much and by then, he was in the family business. But I knew. I'd figured it out a few years earlier. I knew exactly what my father did for a living."

"Did it scare you?"

"I never let myself think about it." He gave me a sidelong look, gauging my reaction. "That way, I had nothing to feel guilty about."

"I'm not in the mob, if that's what you're thinking."

"I didn't think you were. You should pardon the sexist comment but even these days, they wouldn't let a girl in the club."

"Then how—"

"I've been praying for years," Anthony said. "I knew that sooner or later, you'd show up to set things straight."

"Oh, no!" I jumped off the bench. "You're not going to lay that on me. I'm not some sort of engine of divine vengeance."

"I didn't say you were."

"But you said—"

"That I've been praying. For Pop. And for myself. Now you show up out of the blue. And you say you're here to find out what really happened. Are you sure you want to know?"

I walked to the place where the path intersected the one that led back to the rectory. If I'd been smart, I would have kept right on walking. Instead, I turned around and stalked back to where Anthony waited. "All I'm looking for is the truth."

"Then it's all I'll give you." This time, he didn't pat the bench. I sat down, anyway. "It's funny, isn't it, that he waited all this time to ask for anyone's help?" he said.

I didn't ask who *he* was. I didn't have to. At the same time I wondered if Father Anthony shouldn't be in Dan's crazy person study, I shifted uncomfortably on the bench. "It's because I hit my head," I said.

"Oh, I'm sure. I mean, I'm sure that's what precipitated things. But think about it. Why now?"

I shrugged. "Because there wasn't anybody he could ask before."

"Why else?"

"I've never been very good at this sort of philosophical bullsh—" I caught myself and had the good sense to blush. "Sorry, Father."

"No need." Father Anthony grinned, but the expression didn't last long. The next second, his eyes clouded with memory. "Let me tell you a story. When I was teenager, all I cared about were cars. I lived and breathed cars and I had a honey of a Firebird. Used to love to spend my Saturdays out in the garage working on it. That's where I was one day when I heard some men in the yard talking. I was a pretty quiet kid. They didn't realize I was there. I was just going to step out of the garage and say hello when I realized what they were talking about."

Even though he was sitting in the sunlight, Father Anthony chafed his hands over his arms. He looked at the dome of blue sky over our heads. "They were planning a murder. They never came out and said it in so many words, of course, but by that time, I was pretty good at reading between the lines. They were discussing a hit. And I was too embarrassed and too ashamed and, yes, too afraid, to tell anyone what I'd heard. That's because I didn't realize whose hit they were planning."

"Gus's murder?" I digested the enormity of the information. "But who—"

"That, I couldn't tell you." Anthony held up one hand. He must have known I was going to protest. "I'm not keeping secrets. I just can't tell you. I heard their voices, but I was too scared to look and see who was talking. If I'd said something to my father..."

"So you blame yourself for his death."

Anthony didn't confirm or deny this. He drew in a deep, labored breath and when he let it out again, it staggered on the edge of powerful emotion. "I've prayed for his soul. I've prayed for his salvation. I've prayed for my own forgiveness. Now you show up and maybe if you can find out who killed him..."

"Shit."

Father Anthony didn't seem to mind my profanity. He chuckled. "Shit as in—"

"Shit as in now I can't walk away." I folded my arms over my chest and plunked back against the wooden slats of the bench.

"You think that's all there is to it?"

"Isn't that enough?" Still, I wasn't satisfied. I

chewed over everything he'd told me. "Maybe you know more than you think you know," I suggested.

I don't think it was what Father Anthony wanted to talk about, but he gave in with grace. "I've thought of that," he said. "Believe me. I've spent years trying to analyze every second of that day."

"They must have been your father's friends. Otherwise they wouldn't have been at the house."

"That's true." Anthony nodded. "It made me question every single person who came to the funeral to offer their condolences."

"And it made you feel guilty."

"Guilty as hell."

"I can't offer absolution. Not for that."

"You still don't get it yet, do you?"

I guess my blank expression was all the answer he needed.

Father Anthony patted my hand. "I'm sick," he said. "But I guess you might have noticed. The doctors say I've got three months. Tops. Something tells me the fact that my father is suddenly looking for closure isn't a coincidence."

I felt as if I'd been sucker punched, and I guess I had. "He knew all along. And he never mentioned it. He didn't want me to know what a soft touch he is."

"He didn't want you to know how scared he is." Slowly, Anthony stood. He looked down at me. "Do you understand now? About the absolution?"

I understood, all right.

Damn it.

And I knew exactly what I had to do. I said my thanks and goodbyes to Father Anthony and headed back to the cemetery. I had to make a pickup and stop at the bank before it closed.

I had eight thousand dollars to put back into my account.

Chapter 13

I suppose I should have been relieved. I knew more than I knew when I left Garden View that morning. Way more than I'd known throughout my investigation. Okay, so I still didn't know who killed Gus. But I had insight into why, after all these years, he suddenly cared so much.

If what I suspected was true...

Well, if it was, I hated to admit it, but it broke my heart.

I couldn't stand waiting until the next day to find Gus and confront him. Not with the thought of Father Anthony's impending death weighing on me until I felt as if I had a rock in my stomach. After I dashed into the office for the brown lunch bag, then over to the bank just as they were getting ready to lock up for the evening, I went back to the cemetery.

It was nearly dark.

I drove over to Gus's mausoleum, but just like it had been early that morning, it was empty. I tried the angel statue again. And the office. There wasn't a soul around.

Not even a disembodied one.

Was I going to let that stop me?

I left my car outside the office and decided to do a quick turn around the sections that were closest to where I'd parked. Maybe if Gus didn't see my car, he wouldn't know I was coming.

Maybe not.

By the time I'd walked for what seemed like forever and was probably only a half hour or so, I still hadn't seen any sign of him.

And the sick, empty feeling inside of me just wouldn't go away.

I gave up somewhere between the section where the famous cookbook author was buried and the plot devoted to veterans of the Civil War, and I'd just turned to head back to the office when I was nearly blinded by a bright light.

Supernatural mumbo jumbo?

Only if Gus had developed a flair for the dramatic.

I put a hand in front of my eyes to help ward off the glare and squinted. As my eyes adjusted, I realized I was staring into the headlights of a car. It stopped ten feet or so in front of me and I tensed, not sure if I should stay or run.

The driver's door popped open.

"Pepper?"

I recognized Dan's voice, which was the only thing that kept me from ducking for cover behind the nearest headstone.

"Pepper? I've been looking all over for you."

He got out of the car, but he didn't turn off the

engine or the headlights. Against the bright light, Dan looked like a silhouette cut from black paper.

I guess I didn't know I had tears in my eyes until I realized I didn't want Dan to see them. I dashed my hand over my cheeks and coughed away the tightness that had built in my throat back at Blessed Rosary. "I'm here," I told Dan. I stepped closer to the two shafts of light. "How did you find me?"

Dan looked over his shoulder. Back toward the office. "I saw your car. The main gate is closed but I figured there had to be an entrance the staff uses after hours. I looked around until I found it. I tried the office but you weren't there. That's when I decided to drive around and find you."

"That's a lot of trouble to go through." I took another step toward the light. "What's up?"

"I've got news." When Dan waved something in the air, it was the first I realized he was carrying a file folder. Call me psychic; I was pretty sure it had my name on it. "I got some results back from those tests we did this afternoon."

"And they couldn't wait until tomorrow?"

I saw the quick flash of his smile. "I thought you'd like to know."

I suppose I did.

Which didn't explain why the rock in my stomach suddenly turned into a block of ice.

"What kind of results?"

I saw Dan look around. "Are you sure you want to discuss it here?"

"Who's going to hear us?" I didn't bother to point out that one somebody could. If he wasn't busy playing hide-and-seek. "If it's that important—"

"Well, I think it is." Dan hurried over to where I stood. He grabbed my arm and tugged me closer to the car so that we were standing full in the light. "Look. Right here." He flipped open the file and pointed to a scan of my brain. "I can't believe I didn't notice this the first time you came into the ER but then, I guess I didn't think it was possible."

To me, it looked like an oval with white glop in it. I told Dan as much.

"Yeah. Sure. I mean, it *is* a brain." He pointed. "But the occipital lobe—"

"Not that again." I sighed. I'd pretty much had it with his whole aberrant-behavior theory. I shrugged out of his grasp and started back toward the office and my car. "If that's the only thing you have to talk about, we could have done it some other time."

"But it's not."

Dan's words stopped me in my tracks.

"What I'm seeing here, Pepper, is a very high propensity for hallucinatory imaging."

I turned back to him, but I didn't budge from my spot near a headstone where a giant, crepe-draped urn sat atop a granite column. "And what exactly does that mean in English?"

"It means I think you're hallucinating."

"Yeah. I must be." I turned back around and kept walking. Better that than letting him see the way his

words slammed into me like a fist. I tossed my parting
shot. "I must be hallucinating. Because this goofy
conversation can't possibly be happening."

I heard Dan scramble to catch up to me. "Don't
you see what this means?"

"Nope." I didn't. I didn't want to. Call me crazy,
but—

But nothing. That's exactly what Dan was doing.

I stopped so fast he was already ahead of me
before he realized I wasn't at his side. He turned to
find me with my fists on my hips.

"Is that what you think? That I'm some sort of
nutcase?"

"I didn't say that." Dan hurried back to me. "I
just said—"

"That I see things. That I hear things."

"I didn't say you did. I said you had the propensity. That means you could."

And wasn't it exactly what I'd been hoping to
hear all this time?

I might as well have gotten clunked by that granite urn on the monument behind me. That's how
bowled over I was.

I thought back to the day when Gus had first appeared outside his mausoleum. Then, all I wanted
was to blow off his presence and convince myself
that he was nothing more than a brain blip.

I remembered the times I'd told him that this investigation was bogus and that he was, too. And I
wanted to believe it. More than anything.

After all, there was no such thing as ghosts and so, there could be no Gus.

Was that such a hard concept to get through my head?

Except then I found out about the birthmark on Gus's hip. Then I had the conversation with Father Anthony.

I'm not a soft touch. But on the off chance that what I suspected was true, there was no way I could write Gus off as a brain blip now.

No way in hell.

"I'm not crazy," I told Dan. "And I'm not listening. I do not, did not, and will not ever hallucinate."

"But you said—"

"No, I didn't say anything." I knew that was true. I'd been trying my best *not* to say anything— to anyone—for a long, long time. "I never said I was hallucinating because I'm not hallucinating. I never—"

"What about you talking to yourself?"

I was so shocked, it wouldn't have taken that urn to knock me over. A feather could have done the job. I stared at Dan in amazement. "And you're talking about what, exactly?" I asked him.

He glanced away and I swear, if the light was better, I would have seen a look somewhere between regret and anger wash over his face.

Dan? Angry?

I didn't think it was possible, but I reminded myself of the old saying about still waters running deep. And the bit my grandmother always added to the end of it: The devil lies at the bottom of them.

Instinctively, I took a step back. "What makes you think I talk to myself?"

He ran a hand through his hair. I'd always thought of the gesture as cute. Now I knew he was stalling.

"I've got to be honest with you." Dan stepped closer. "There's a mirror in my office. You might have noticed it. It hangs next to the bookcase. It's a...it's a two-way mirror."

The ice in my stomach melted, shooting frigid water through my body. The cold lasted only as long as it took me to process what he was saying. It heated up in a nanosecond and the ice turned to steam.

"You were watching me? While I was in your office filling out that questionnaire?" I thought of that night and remembered that Gus had been with me. "You son of a bitch."

"Now, Pepper..." Dan reached for me but I batted his hand away. "You weren't supposed to know. I shouldn't have even said anything but...well...I like you. And I don't think it's fair to start a relationship unless we can be completely honest with each other." He tried for that cute puppy dog look that always had a way of twisting around my heart.

Maybe it was the dark. Or maybe I'd finally seen the light. I wasn't buying it. When I glared at him, Dan backed off.

"It's part of the study," he said, the puppy dog cute replaced by sterile facts delivered just as clinically. "It provides me with a chance to observe my subjects without them knowing. A sort of check and balance."

"Check and balance, what? Check to see if you've found the right crazy person? Balance my sanity against what you think it should be?" I didn't exactly scream, but I did give a little shriek of exasperation. It reverberated against the headstones, echoing back at us like a spectral voice. "How dare you? How dare you spy on me?"

"I wasn't spying. I was observing."

"Oh, that makes me feel better." I turned and started back to the office.

"Pepper…" This time when Dan called to me, I didn't stop and I didn't look at him.

"Forget it, buster." I made a rude and unmistakable gesture over my shoulder. My footsteps slapped the pavement. My arms pumped at my sides. "And forget your stupid study. I'm out. Over. Finished. Don't call and don't write and don't think you're going to get a chance to look at my occipital lobe again because you're not."

When I heard him get into his car and close the door, I knew he was going to follow me. I left the road, darting onto the grass and between two tall headstones. From there, I headed off toward the center of the nearest section. By the time Dan turned the car around and cruised the road back to the office, I knew that like Gus, I'd be nowhere to be found.

I stood very still next to the statue of a grieving woman, refusing to move until he was long gone.

"Son of a bitch!" I tossed the word into the night and right about then, I wasn't sure which son of a bitch I was talking about. The one who tried to kill me. The one who walked out on me the night before. The one who thought I was a certifiable nutcase. Or the one whose presence pretty much confirmed the fact.

Then again, maybe it was the one who had broken our engagement.

Or the one sitting in federal lockup, the one whose greed and dishonesty had sent my life reeling out of control in the first place.

It all came down on top of me like a couple tons of bricks. I was pissed. And overwhelmed. I was exasperated. And so tired of trying to make sense of everything that was happening, I couldn't hold it together any longer. I plunked down on the grass and had a good cry.

My shoulders shook and my tears blinded me. I wanted to lash out, but I couldn't decide how or at whom, so I latched onto a clump of grass and pulled. I ended up with a divot in my fist, and I tossed it as hard as I could at the nearest tree.

Instantly, guilt filled me, head to toe. The grounds crew would find the destruction in the morning and think they had groundhogs to worry about.

"Like that's my problem?" I asked myself, and just to prove it wasn't, I pulled up another clump.

"How could I have been stupid enough to let all this happen in the first place?"

"Nobody ever said you was stupid."

I jumped to my feet and swigged back my tears. "Where the hell have you been?" I asked, swiveling to look all around me to find the ghost who belonged to the voice. Instead, all I saw was tombstones. "And what the hell do you think you're doing, scaring me like this?"

"Didn't mean to scare you." Gus stepped out from between two headstones. His white shirt glowed with reflected moonlight. He leaned forward and gave me a careful look. "What are you crying about?"

"I'm not crying." I swiped my hand over my cheeks. "Why would I be crying? Just because I sent Quinn away last night and then I found out that Dan is a dirtbag peeping tom and oh yeah, I almost got killed by good ol' Albert."

"And have you asked yourself why—"

"Oh, no!" I wasn't in the mood to be conciliatory. "No more questions. Not from you. Not from anybody. I'm tired of getting jerked around. I want some straight answers and I want them now."

Gus hesitated before he smoothed a hand over his tie. "It don't matter no more."

"Like hell."

"I said, it don't matter and you shouldn't argue with me about it, little girl." His voice rose to meet mine.

"And I said it matters plenty. How the hell am I supposed to solve this case when—"

"You're fired."

I was so stunned, it took a couple seconds for me to choke out, "What?"

"Fired. I said you're fired." Gus sniffed and pulled back his shoulders. "Don't need you no more."

"Like hell."

"You said that before."

"And I'll say it again. Like hell! You can't fire me."

"You should be glad it's not the old days. Then I wouldn't bother. I'd just have you clipped."

"Well, I hate to spoil your fun, but it's not the old days anymore. And if you ever had the chops...well, you sure don't have them now. You're not the don anymore, Gus. You don't have the authority. Nobody cares what you want or don't want. And that nobody includes me. I'm not quitting this case. Not now. Not ever."

"Have it your way. It don't make no difference. You're not going to see me no more."

And in the blink of an eye, Gus was gone.

I stood there for a couple minutes, peering into the darkness, sure that if I looked long and hard enough, I'd see him again.

I didn't.

I suppose I should have been grateful. Once and for all, I was rid of Gus and the stupid investigation that had taken over my life.

Of course, that didn't explain why I reeled, like the turf had been pulled out from under me. Or why I was so mad, I could have spit nails.

"Oh no, buster!" I called into the night. "You're not getting away from me that easily. You can't just up and walk away. I'm not finished with you yet."

No answer. No Gus.

"I'm not giving back the money!"

Even my appeal to his business sense didn't produce any results.

"All right, have it your way." I started back toward the office and my car. "Disappear. Who cares, anyway? You've been a pain in the ass since day one." I hiccuped around the tears that built in my voice and blocked my throat. "You want to spend the rest of eternity roaming around here all by yourself, that's fine with me. Just don't come asking for help again because you know what, Gus?" I raised my voice and at the spot where the grass met the road, I spun around, aiming my comments back toward the headstones, convinced that he was hiding among them.

"I'm not going to help. Not anymore. And once I'm gone…well, let me remind you that I'm the only one who can see you and I'm the only one who can hear you. Once I'm gone, you're out of options."

Even that wasn't enough to shake him loose.

"Okay. Fine." By now, I was yelling. I didn't much care. If Dan heard me…well, he already thought I was crazy. I crossed the road and ducked into the next section, weaving a path through the headstones. "Have it your way, Gus. But just so you know, I talked to Anthony."

"Anthony?" Like the breeze that rattled the branches of the tree above my head, I heard the name out of nowhere. The next second, Gus was right in front of me. I remembered the icy chill of our last contact and stopped myself just before I slammed into him.

"How do you know about Anthony?"

I pulled in a deep breath, hoping to calm myself and when it didn't work, I plunged right into the fight. "I saw him," I told Gus, raising my chin and daring him to challenge me. "I talked to him. Gus, I know Anthony is dying."

He aimed a look at me that must have intimidated plenty of wiseguys in its day. I was way beyond that. When I stood my ground, Gus cleared his throat.

"Anthony, he don't have nothing to do with this."

"It's not why you fired me?"

He scowled. "I fired you because I don't need you no more."

I snorted my opinion and poked one finger toward his midsection. "You fired me," I told him, "because you didn't want me to figure out why you're suddenly so anxious to go to that big spaghetti dinner in the sky. It doesn't exactly fit with your bad-guy image, does it? You didn't want me to know that underneath it all, you actually have a heart."

I knew I had him there and in my mind's eye, I saw him crumble like a stale saltine.

So much for my imagination. Instead of falling apart, Gus pulled himself up to his full height and pointed a finger right back at me. "I fired you because you work for me. I can fire you or not fire you. I can do anything I damn well want."

"Yeah, anything but be alive."

I regretted the words the moment they were past my lips. Not that it wasn't a great comeback. How often would I have the chance to throw a dead guy's mortality back at him? Still when Gus turned away from me, my conscience prickled.

He stepped toward a tall granite obelisk and I followed, refusing to let him walk away. I already felt like shit. If he left with my words still hanging in the air between us, I knew I'd never forgive myself.

"You fired me because you're a chicken, Gus," I threw the words at his back, my voice quieter now, and the tears that choked it more evident than ever. "You didn't want me to know it. You didn't want me to know that once Anthony is gone—"

When I heard him curse under his breath, I knew I'd pushed Gus beyond his limit. He spun around fast. But whatever I expected, it wasn't the pained expression that crossed his face. Or the emotion that clogged his voice. "I fired you..." His words wavered. His shoulders drooped. "I fired you because I never meant for you to get hurt," he said.

It took a moment for what he was saying to sink in. When it did, I realized there wasn't a sound around us except the far-off croaking of the spring peepers down by the pond at the center of the cemetery. That, and the rough noise of my own sobs. There was a huge marble slab nearby, a family marker, and I dropped down on it. It was still warm from the afternoon sun, but the heat didn't penetrate. I hugged my arms around myself.

"You mean Albert."

Gus shook his head in disgust. "I never would have allowed such a thing. Going after a woman..."

He mumbled something in Italian that I hadn't learned on *The Sopranos*. "You should know I never meant for nothing like that to happen."

It was as close as I'd ever get to an apology from Gus and I knew it. I also knew it meant I owed him something in return. All I had to offer was the truth.

I pulled in a breath that fluttered on the edge of my tears.

"When Anthony dies, you want to go with him."

"You think?" Gus reached into his pocket and pulled out his handkerchief. He held it out to me.

I brushed my hand across my eyes and sniffed. If there was ever a time I needed a hanky, it was now, and I would have liked nothing better than to grab it. But...

"It's not real, is it?" I asked Gus. "At least not for me."

He put the hanky away. "I suppose not. I just thought, you know, maybe..."

"Thanks, anyway." I sighed, the sound of it rippling in the air. There was nothing left to say and I got up and headed to the office. I didn't bother to look to see if Gus was coming with me. Spoken or unspoken, we had a truce of sorts. I knew he was right beside me.

"You think about why Albert tried to off you?"

I shook my head. "I haven't exactly had the chance."

"It must have something to do with your visit to The Family Place."

"And Benny's dead, too."

Maybe it came as no big surprise. Or maybe the dead have a line on such things. He nodded like he knew all along. "That makes me wonder, too. You know? Why get rid of Benny? Why now?"

"Benny was more talkative than the other guys. Maybe somebody was afraid that eventually, he was going to say too much."

"About what?" Gus threw his hands in the air. "You didn't talk about nothing that mattered. You asked about my murder, they said nothing."

"And then I mentioned Tommy Two Toes."

Gus dismissed the idea with a sneer. "He was a nobody."

"Then I don't know what I said to piss those guys off." We were close to the office now and before I stepped into the pool of light thrown by the security lamps on the side of the building, I looked around to make sure that Dan was gone.

When I was certain he was, I turned back to Gus. "You know, Anthony has been praying for you. All this time."

He pulled on his earlobe. "I figured it was his fault. All that praying, it's bound to lead to trouble."

"He thinks it's the reason I showed up."

"Like I said, trouble."

"Yeah." I unlocked my car, and when I opened the door and the light came on inside, I peered into the backseat. Just to make sure the coast was clear.

I turned and leaned against the car. "Am I still fired?" I asked Gus.

"You worried you're going to have to give all that money back?"

Somehow, I managed a smile. Still, I couldn't let things go like this. Before I got into the car, I looked Gus in the eye. "When Anthony goes," I told him, "you're going with him. I promise."

He didn't answer.

He just brought his thumb down on his index finger. Like he was shooting a gun.

Right before he winked and disappeared.

Chapter 14

I made a chart.

Gus's name was at the top of it. Below that, I wrote the names of anybody I could think of who might have had something to do with him being offed.

I know, I know...there were probably plenty of "anybodies" I didn't know anything about. That wasn't my problem. At least not then. I thought about the voices young Anthony Scarpetti had heard outside the garage that day, and wondered who they belonged to. I concentrated on the people I'd talked to and the ones I hadn't talked to who'd been mentioned by the people I'd talked to.

By the time I was done, I had what looked like a family tree. Rudy below Gus and below Rudy, the names of the guys at The Family Place including poor dead Benny and my friendly neighborhood hit man, Albert. Father Anthony and Victor La-Ganza had their own columns. So did Nick, the cook from Lucia's. The last column was headed with Carmella's name.

It looked impressive.

And got me absolutely nowhere.

I was staring at it when there was a knock on my office door.

"There you are!" Ella sailed in like a spring breeze. She looked like spring that day, too, a vision in yellow and orange. "I wanted to stop and talk to you earlier but I haven't had a minute to myself today. I had a meeting with Jim first thing this morning and after that, the folks from one of the local TV stations stopped by. They're planning ahead and talking about doing a segment on our Community Day in the summer. Isn't that terrific?"

I guess she didn't need an answer. She plunked down in the chair in front of my desk and kept right on going.

"This afternoon, we've got the trustees of the foundation stopping by." She fanned her face with one hand. "That's always stressful. And it's bound to run late. These meetings always do. That's why I figured I'd better find you now and remind you. Today's deadline day!"

I chewed the Pretty in Pink off my lips.

"Of course I remember." I smiled while I said it—no easy thing considering that my lower lip was still caught in my teeth. I thought back to my last conversation with Ella and how she thought I was the poster child for ambitious young women everywhere. I hated to disappoint her, but—

"I've got to get the next newsletter completely finished by tomorrow." Ella popped out of the chair. "I'm saving space on the front page for your headstone symbolism article."

My article.

The one I'd completely forgotten about.

I kept my smile firmly where it was and picked up the chart from my desk. "Almost done." I waved the paper at her and if it looked like a white flag of surrender...well, Ella didn't know that. From where she was standing, all she could see was a piece of paper covered with writing.

She gave me the thumbs-up and dashed back to the door. "I knew you wouldn't let me down. And don't get too carried away. A thousand words ought to do it."

A thousand words?

The grim reality sank in. I was hoping to spend the day getting my ducks in a row as far as my investigation went. What should I do next? Who should I talk to? Who could tell me something that I didn't already know? Considering that I knew very little, that didn't seem like it would be too tough.

All the while, inside my head, I heard the tick, tick, tick of the clock that was counting down Father Anthony's life. I knew there wasn't much time. If Anthony died and Gus was left behind...

Back in the day before I was a pushover without a very high propensity for hallucinatory imaging, I would have laughed at anyone who said they cared what happened to a guy who had already been dead for thirty years.

But that was then...

I didn't even realize I was sighing until I heard the sound ripple the quiet of my office.

Sure, Gus was a bad guy. There was no denying that or the fact that I found the whole wiseguy culture creepy, not to mention scary. But bad or not, there was another side to Gus. He didn't want me to know how frightened he was to think that Anthony might die and leave him behind. And Anthony had been praying for Gus all these years.

I hate to admit it, but something about it all tugged at my heartstrings.

It also made me feel responsible.

And responsible was not a feeling I liked.

The sooner I got my investigation over and done with, the sooner I could get on with my life. Such as it was.

Tick, tick, tick.

I turned down the volume of the sound in my head, punched the keys on my computer to connect to the Internet, and Googled "cemetery symbolism." I'd write the article and write it fast.

Then...

I took another look at my chart, picked up a pen, and circled one of the names.

It was time to track down Carmella.

I pulled my car into the driveway and doublechecked the address. Yep, I was in the right place.

If I needed proof, I guess that came when I got out of the car and saw the dark sedan parked across the street. I waved before I turned to examine the house.

This was no ostentatious mansion. There was no

picture-perfect landscaping. No goons at the front door.

Carmella's home was an unpretentious brick and aluminum-sided bungalow on a street full of similar houses in one of those middle-class suburbs where young couples like to start their families. The schools were decent and there were amenities galore nearby, including a small playground, a skateboarding park, and plenty of Big Box shopping.

There was a row of pink-and-white plastic flowers stuck into the dirt under the picture window to the left of the front door and just behind the flowers, a statue of the Virgin Mary.

It wasn't what I expected.

Not that I was passing judgment on Carmella or anything. I hadn't met the woman yet. I hadn't even talked to her. I wouldn't even be there if it weren't for Father Anthony, who called his mother on my behalf. But knowing that Carmella Scarpetti's name was—and had been since very soon after Gus died— Carmella Scarpetti LaGanza put a whole new spin on things.

"Come on! Don't stand out there. It looks like it's going to start raining any minute. Come on in!" The aluminum storm door swung open and a woman who looked like a cross between Mrs. Santa Claus and Sophia Loren waved me inside.

Carmella couldn't have been more than five feet tall. She had a head of thick white hair that was pulled into a ponytail and a figure that must once have been lush. Her skin was olive-colored and flawless, her nose was a little too big for her to ever be considered a real beauty. Her eyes were dark and reminded me of Anthony's in those pictures I'd seen of him from back in the days when he was healthy. They were animated and sparkling. She was wearing jeans, a pink sweatshirt that had BOCA RATON on it in turquoise lettering, and yellow flip-flops.

"You must be Pepper. I've been waiting for you." No sooner had I climbed the two steps to the cement-pad front porch than Carmella grabbed my hand and tugged me inside.

I found myself in a living room that was dominated by the gold velvet couch that took up most of one wall. It was covered with plastic. So were the shades on the porcelain Capo di Monte lamps on either side of the couch. Shepherd on one side. Shepherdess on the other. Both were embellished with lots of curlicues and gold paint. It matched the color of the flocked wallpaper. Across from the couch was a TV on a plastic stand. The rabbit ears on top of it were cockeyed.

Carmella led me through the living room and the attached dining room, where a table was covered with a lace cloth and a curio cabinet in the corner was filled with more frilly porcelain.

"You'll have to excuse the mess," she said, though where, exactly, "the mess" was supposed to be was beyond me. The place was as tidy as if a cleaning crew had just left. "We came back from Florida a few weeks early because of Benny Marzano's funeral. We've been down there since right after Christmas. We go every winter. I know you young folks don't understand but believe me, honey, when you're my age, you will. Can't take the cold and snow anymore."

When we got to the kitchen, she stepped back to let me walk through the doorway first. It was a room where one of those perfect sitcom moms from the fifties would have been right at home, immaculate and shining, from the pink countertops to the black-and-white ceramic tile on the floor.

"I made coffee." Carmella pointed to the pot on the countertop. "And cookies." She grabbed a plate heaped with chocolate chip cookies and held them in front of me. "You do eat cookies, don't you?"

It took a minute for me to catch my breath and while I did, I grabbed a cookie and sat down at the Formica-topped kitchen table. Carmella poured coffee into pink mugs with flamingos for handles and pushed a crystal sugar bowl in front of me. I didn't dare ask for sweetener.

She ladled three spoonfuls of sugar into her cup. "So...My Anthony called. He said you were a friend of his. He said you wanted to see me."

I was hoping to ease my way into what could be an uncomfortable conversation with a little more small talk. "How is Father Anthony?" I asked.

Carmella stirred her coffee. "Oh, you know." She tapped the spoon on the rim of the cup and set it down and when she looked my way, her eyes didn't sparkle anymore. "You always think of them as your kids. No matter how old they are. And kids, well, they shouldn't die before their parents. There's something wrong with that."

"He was enjoying his garden when I saw him."

Carmella smiled. "He loves his flowers! And that nice Father David, he makes sure everything is taken care of now that..." She took a drink of her coffee, and I knew it was a signal.

Time to change the subject.

"I don't know how much Father Anthony told you," I began, "but I'm writing a book."

"Yes." Carmella nodded and cleared her throat. "Yes, he did mention that. I'm sorry to tell you, honey, but I really don't think there's anything I can do to help."

"There probably isn't." I didn't know if it was true, but I figured it was the polite thing to say. "I just want to make sure all my bases are covered."

"Well, I feel like a celebrity!" Carmella twinkled. "What is it you want to know?"

When last I spoke to Anthony, I asked him not to tell his mother too much. After all, if she knew I was looking into Gus's death and if she or her current husband had had anything to do with it, I was pretty sure I wouldn't get as close as the front door. The flip side was that now I needed to explain myself.

"The book is about Gus," I said.

For a couple seconds, I don't think she was sure who I was talking about. Understanding dawned and her cheeks got pink. "Augustino. Oh my. No one's mentioned his name to me for a very long time."

"I don't mean to cause you any distress. It's just that—"

"Oh, honey..." She reached across the table and around the plate of cookies to squeeze my hand. "Don't you worry about making me feel bad. The past is the past. It was all a very long time ago."

"That's the problem. You see..." I took a sip of coffee, dragging my feet, hoping that somehow, that would help soften the blow. "I'm trying to find out who killed him."

If this was an episode of *Murder, She Wrote*, Carmella's face would have gone ashen and she would have leapt from her chair and declared that she'd done it and couldn't stand the guilt any longer.

But it wasn't.

And she didn't.

Instead, she gave me a tender smile. "Does it matter?"

"Not to anybody but me." I left out the part about how it mattered plenty to Gus. And apparently, to someone else, too. Otherwise Albert wouldn't have paid me a visit. "I just don't think my book will be complete if I haven't solved the mystery."

"And you think I can help you?"

"I heard that you were at Lucia's that night."

Carmella's snowy brows dropped low over her dark eyes. "Yes," she looked past me, through me. "I was there. I stopped by on my way home from Cathedral Latin, Anthony's school. That's where Augustino was supposed to meet me for a conference with his teacher. He never showed up. And I didn't have to wonder where he was. At Lucia's. Right where I thought he'd be. With his friends. Where he was every Thursday night."

"You were angry. You had it out with Gus in the restaurant, right in front of everybody."

Carmella's gaze snapped back to mine. "Back then, I was angry most days."

"You were drunk, too."

She picked up her spoon and gave her coffee another stir, even though it didn't need it. "I was drunk most days, too. At least back then. Been sober for nearly thirty years now."

"That's quite an accomplishment."

"It's worth it when you have children."

"But then..."

"Then?" There was no amusement in Carmella's laugh. She got up to pour herself more coffee. She didn't come back to the table but stood near the sink, her back to the counter. "When I was a young girl," she said, "I was very naive. My parents were from the Old Country and they treated me the way girls were treated there. I was a modern young lady or at least as modern as we thought we were back in the Stone Ages. I had my own ideas about what I wanted from life. I met Augustino and fell madly in love. He was so very good-looking!"

"Good-looking" isn't how I would describe Gus. But then, what is it they say about beauty and the eye of the beholder?

Carmella went on. "I'd heard rumors about him.

You know, people talking, saying that I was going to end up regretting it if I married him."

"And did you?"

"Not at first." Carmella came back to the table. She sat down, grabbed a cookie, and took a bite. "But it didn't take long. Don't put that in your book. If Rudy should read it, he would be upset. Big, tough Rudy and he still thinks his parents lived an ideal life. But think about it, Pepper. Think about what it's like living with a man whose whole life..." She twitched away whatever she was going to say.

"It doesn't take long before you realize...that thing of theirs..." She gave the words a sour twist. "Well, it's always going to be more important than anything to them. More important than wives. More important than children. I couldn't live that way. With men with guns at my door." She shivered.

"But you married Victor LaGanza!" Okay, so it wasn't any of my business. But it was kind of hard to keep my mouth shut. Especially when it was so obvious that Carmella was not practicing what she was preaching.

"Ah yes, Victor. Another handsome man!" She winked. "What is it you young girls say? A nice tight ass and good in bed? Don't look so shocked." She laughed. "I was young once, too. And Victor, he promised that he would keep his work separate from his home life. He did then and he does until this very day. You don't see his two boys from his first marriage in the business. Michael, he's a dentist, and Dominic is an architect. Very legit, those two. Not like my Rudy."

"Or like your Victor."

It was the perfect, logical argument but Carmella waved it away with one French-manicured hand. "When he's home, he's just Victor. And if the FBI chooses to park outside our home..." She looked toward the front of the house. "They must get bored. That's all I can say. There's never anything that happens here."

"But that's not how it was." I did my best to get the conversation back on track. "With Gus."

"It wasn't what I wanted," Carmella said. "It wasn't what I wanted for my boys."

"That's a pretty strong motive for murder."

"It is, isn't it?" She could have been angry. She laughed instead. "But I'm not the one who killed Augustino. I happen to have an alibi and I told the police all about it when they questioned me. You see, I was with Victor."

"With? As in—"

Carmella winked. "I told you I was young once, honey. With as in *with*. Yes. I remember it like it was yesterday. You see, it was our first time. Victor, he was a widower and he'd been after me for months. I would have nothing to do with him and I told him so. I believed in living my marriage vows. Until that night at Lucia's. That's when I knew for certain that nothing would ever be different for me and Augustino. That's when I knew it was over between us."

I had to admit, if it was true, it was a pretty solid alibi.

"The cops—"

"Yes, yes, they checked. They did their jobs. They went to the hotel where Victor and I stayed. They talked to everyone there. They found out that we were right where we said we were. Neither of us planned Augustino's death and neither of us participated in the shooting. While he was dying in the street, Victor and I were in bed together."

"Wow." I digested the information and wondered how—or if—I'd break the news to Gus. When Anthony first told me that his mother had agreed to see me, I thought Gus might like to come along. He refused and now I was glad. It wasn't the kind of thing a man wanted to hear from his wife.

Even a dead man.

In my mind's eye, I pictured another door slamming in my face. And still that clock in my head, teasing me with its tick, tick, tick.

I racked my brain. There must be some clue Carmella could offer me, some hint into her husband's death.

I glanced around the kitchen. There was a bookcase nearby filled with cookbooks. In front of them on the shelves were framed photographs. Anthony on his first communion day, looking like a cherub. Another picture of a woman with dark hair and a forbidding expression. And a third, a photograph of a young Carmella, all dolled up like it was Easter. She was standing with her two sons in front of a 60s vintage car. It was pink and black. Like the kitchen.

A jolt kick-started in my brain and I remembered what Benny had said back at The Family Place. "What about the car?" I asked Carmella. "The one the shooter was in? I've been told it was green, one of those souped-up racers. You know, something old that somebody fixed up."

"We never had a green car." Carmella sounded pretty sure of herself. "As for fixing up old cars, well, Anthony was always good at that, of course. But his car was black, I think. Green." She closed her eyes, thinking. "There was one. Anthony was very young at the time but I think he helped with the restoration. Have you talked to him about it?"

I hadn't. I hadn't thought of it.

Carmella tapped her fingertips against the table. "It belonged to that young man. What was his name? Lots of hair and bad teeth." She tapped some more, and just when it looked like she was about to give up, her expression cleared and she smiled.

"Tommy. That's who it was. Tommy Cavolo."

"Tommy Two Toes?"

"Yes. That's what they called him." Carmella finished her coffee. "He had a car just like that."

"And he died a full ten years before Gus did."

"Did he? I guess he couldn't have been driving the car when Augustino was killed, huh?"

I didn't bother to answer. "Do you know who got the car when Tommy was—" I didn't want to say what I almost blurted out. "After Tommy died?"

Carmella shrugged. "Can't say. Really, I didn't know anything about the boy except that he was what they called a *cugine,* you know, a young tough, itching to be made. He showed up at our home one day and started working for Augustino. That means someone recommended him. You understand about that, don't you? They don't take just anybody. You have to be a friend of a friend."

"And whose friend was Tommy?"

Another shrug. "All I know is that one day he was standing by my front door. Watching to see who came and who went. Keeping an eye out for Augustino and the rest of the boys. He stuck around for maybe six months, then he was gone. Did you say he died? I didn't know that."

"It's what I've heard."

"Maybe so. And I won't ask how. It's not something I want to know. And you..." Carmella gave me a careful look. "Are you sure you do?"

"I'm being very careful," I told her, leaving out any mention of Albert. "I'm not looking to get anyone into any trouble. All I want to do is write my book."

"But someone may not want to see that book get published."

"Not to worry." I finished my cookie and brushed the crumbs from my fingers. "The way things are going, there's no chance of that. I can't find anyone who knows anything about how Gus died."

"Gus." Carmella tipped her head, studying me. "Funny you should call him that. Hardly anyone did."

I got up and headed to the front door. "After all the research I've done, I feel like I know him."

Carmella grabbed my hand but didn't shake it. She gave it a pat. "Be thankful you never did," she said.

Her final words reverberated in my head. Even once the front door was closed behind me. Still considering them, I climbed back into my car.

Gus was there waiting for me.

"So how does she look?" he asked.

I turned the key in the ignition and carefully backed down the driveway. The last thing I needed was an accident report that involved the black sedan still parked across the street. I also couldn't risk looking like a crazy person, so I waited until I was all the way down the block before I said anything.

"If you wanted to see her," I told Gus, "you could have come inside with me."

He frowned. "Nah. Don't need to do that. I just wondered. That's all."

"You forgot to mention that she is married to Victor LaGanza now."

"Yeah. Well." Gus cleared his throat. "I told you she didn't know anything. She was nowhere near me the night I was killed."

He had mentioned that before. And I'd never wondered how he knew.

By now, I was out on a main street, and I turned into the next drive and parked in front of a health food store. "You knew. You knew about Victor all along."

"If you're asking if I knew where she was the

night I died…" Gus cracked his knuckles. "Yeah, I knew."

"But how?"

He looked out the passenger-side window. "She told me. About a year after I died. She must have been feeling guilty. Came into my mausoleum one day, crying and pouring her heart out." He turned to me. "I wonder what she'd say if she knew I was right there listening the whole time."

Chapter 15

How much did I really know about Tommy Two Toes Cavolo?

Short answer: Not much.

Longer answer: Not much, but the merry-go-round that was my investigation kept coming right back to him.

The big question, of course, was why.

I thought it over while I printed out my article on tombstone symbolism, and I thought about it some more when I delivered the article to Ella, listened to her rave about what a swell employee I was, and hightailed it back to my office before she could read what I'd written and come to the conclusion that "swell" was not the word to describe the information I'd cobbled together.

Gus was there waiting for me.

"You look worried."

"Do I?" I plunked down into my desk chair and propped my chin in my hands. "I'm not. Except about what Ella's going to say about that article. Actually, I'm just thinking. About Tommy Two Toes."

"You're nuts!" Gus settled in the chair in front of my desk. "And you're wasting your time. He's been dead longer than me. He couldn't have been the shooter."

"Then why do we keep tripping over him?"

Gus's shrug was elegant. "He was a mope."

"You had him killed."

"Did I?"

"Nobody else had the authority to order his hit."

Something very much like admiration glistened in Gus's eyes. "You're getting good at this."

I wasn't sure if that was a compliment and if it was, I wasn't sure I wanted to gloat about it. I concentrated on the problem at hand instead. "How did Tommy end up working for you, anyway?" I asked Gus. "Who recommended him?"

He pursed his lips. "Can't remember."

"It might be important."

"Trust me, honey, it wasn't then. It isn't now."

"Why did you kill him?"

Gus cocked his head and studied me. "Back when you lived in your big suburban house with your perfect suburban family, did you ever think you'd be talkin' about murder like it was just another day at the office?"

I didn't want to think about my big suburban house or the perfect family that wasn't so perfect so I just said, "Around here, murder *is* just another day at the office." I'd brought a salad for lunch, and though it was before noon, my stomach rumbled and I realized I'd been in such a hurry to leave the apartment that morning so I could get to the cemetery and continue my investigation, I hadn't eaten breakfast. I grabbed the salad out of the bag and popped the lid on the Cool Whip container I was using as a bowl. I drizzled on low-fat Ranch dressing and crunched into a pea pod. "Why'd you have him hit, Gus?"

He gave a barely perceptible sigh. "Tommy was a bigmouth. You know the type. Always trying to impress people. Always talking like he was some big man with a big future."

"So you cut his future short before he could do the same for you."

"Please!" Apparently, I offended Gus's idea of the right order of things. Disgusted, he got up and he would have done a turn around the room if there'd been enough room in the room to turn in. Instead, he paced to the door and back again. "I don't have . . . what do you call them? . . . issues. I don't have inferiority issues, if that's what you're saying. I was never worried that Two Toes was going to try and squeeze me out. He didn't have the brains, he didn't have the muscle, and he didn't have the balls, you should excuse my use of the word. He wasn't good at nothing except going on at the mouth. He was a *babbo*. You know, a dope."

"A *babbo* who merited a hit."

Gus sat back down. "He was talking. To the FBI."

"A snitch, huh?" I added a little more dressing to my salad. "How'd you find out?"

He tipped his head back, thinking. "It was Benny.

I'm pretty sure. He came to me one day. All upset. You've met Benny, you know how high-strung he is. Was." Gus corrected himself. "Benny, he had his sources, and one of them told him about Two Toes. Told him that the punk was downtown there at the federal building, talking to people he shouldn't have been talking to. He was gonna sell us out."

"Who did the hit?"

Gus's eyebrows rose. "You're gettin' mighty nosey."

"I'm getting mighty tired of trying to feel my way through this investigation like Helen Keller on a cloudy day!" I chomped a radish. "If you really want to leave when Anthony—"

"All right. All right." He clicked his tongue. "I had Johnny do the hit. I remember because his son was getting married that day and Debbie, his wife, she had one holy hell of a fit when he got to the church late. The woman could swear like a sailor. My ears are still ringing. But Johnny, he was good at that sort of thing and I trusted him. Wedding or no wedding, it had to be taken care of and taken care of fast. Before Tommy met with the feds again and said more than he should have. I knew Johnny was the man for the job. I knew it would be done clean. And I knew he wouldn't leave no evidence. He never disappointed me."

My chart was in the top drawer of my desk, and I pulled it out and drew a line between Benny and Johnny Vitale. Beneath them both, I added Tommy's name.

While I worked on my salad, I tapped the tip of

the pen against the paper, thinking. I was almost done with my lunch by the time another thought occurred to me.

"Why'd you hire him if he wasn't good for much of anything?" I asked Gus.

"Huh?" He'd been lost in thought, too, and he snapped out of it. "You mean Two Toes? Why did I hire Two Toes? We always had these young guys hanging around. Had a lot of stuff for them to do. Errands and things. And like I said, he came recommended. He must have. Otherwise we wouldn't have let him in the front door."

"Family connections?" I meant it in the traditional sense, though either definition fit.

"He didn't have no family." Gus was apparently thinking in the traditional sense, too. "Tommy was an orphan or something. It was one of the reasons I hired him on. Figured he wouldn't have any of them there divided loyalties. And hey, it was one hell of an advantage. No one missed him once he was gone."

I didn't bother to point out that Gus's attitude was cynical. Not to mention cold-hearted.

I finished up the last bite of my salad and tossed the Cool Whip container back in the bag I'd brought it in. I stuffed the whole thing in my bottom desk drawer, thinking out loud. "I wonder how we could find out more about Two Toes."

"Well, he's buried here."

I looked at Gus in wonder.

"What?" He was instantly defensive. "You never asked."

He was right. I never had. I'd never much cared. And maybe this avenue of my investigation would end up nowhere just like all the others had. But it was something to do and something was better than sitting there thinking. The fact that it was close to seventy outside and that the sun was shining might also have had an influence on my decision.

I grabbed my car keys out of my purse. "We're going to pay Tommy Two Toes a visit."

Tommy Cavolo was buried in what the folks in administration liked to call the "new" section of the cemetery. Considering that "new" covered everything from 1930 on, it was a little hard to understand the logic, but I suppose at one time, it made sense.

In that section, near the high stone wall that separated the cemetery from the neighborhood that surrounded it, most of the headstones were modest and flat to the ground. There were only a few standing headstones and no carved angels looking over the scene. No obelisks and only one fancy mausoleum as far as the eye could see.

It was the Garden View equivalent of general admission. The folks back there weren't rich or as famous as the ones who occupied the prime real estate near the main gate and because of that, the new area of the cemetery wasn't as active.

That didn't mean it was desolate. Or that it wasn't taken care of.

The grass was neat and from the scent that still

hung in the air, I could tell it had been cut earlier that day. I parked my car and Gus and I got out, and I noticed the wreaths and flowers that had been brought to some of the residents. Someone had hung a small wind chime from a tree near the road and it chinked and clinked in a sort-of song that was the only thing I could hear except for the sounds of traffic from the other side of the wall.

I checked the printout I'd accessed from the office computer against the numbers markers and got my bearings. If we headed to the right...

I stepped carefully over gravestone after gravestone, heading back toward the wall.

With any luck, that's where I'd find Tommy.

What I didn't expect to find was the bunch of wilting spring flowers laid on his grave.

"How long did you say this guy has been dead?" I asked Gus, though I didn't really need him to answer. Tommy's birth and death dates were carved into the modest gray granite stone.

"Nineteen forty-six. Nineteen sixty-eight." I didn't do the math, partly because I didn't need to and mostly because Tommy had died way too young and I didn't want to think about it.

"I thought you said he was an orphan with no family. Who do you suppose is still sending flowers?"

Gus shrugged. "Far as I know, nobody cared about the kid that much. Must be a mistake."

"Maybe." I glanced at the graves on either side of Tommy's. "This guy died back in the thirties.

And the woman on the other side of Tommy conked out in the forties. I can't imagine someone would still be bringing flowers to them."

"And I can't imagine that anybody would ever bring flowers to Tommy. He wasn't the flower type, you know?"

"A woman." I don't know why I decided I was right, I only knew I was. "A woman is the only one who would think flowers. She's the only one who would still care."

"He could have had a *comare*, but even a girlfriend or a mistress doesn't hold on. Not all this time."

"Always the romantic, huh?" I didn't suppose Gus knew sarcasm when he heard it so I didn't wait for him to reply. I stepped back to consider Tommy's grave from another angle and think about what the flowers meant and as I did, I heard a car out on the road. I turned just as a white van slowed down and parked opposite from where we stood.

The driver got out. He was a pencil-thin guy with a scraggly ponytail and a wispy goatee. He was wearing dirty jeans and a Pink Floyd T-shirt and carrying a bunch of white carnations.

What were the chances he was bringing the flowers to Tommy?

I was inclined to say slim and none—any right-thinking person would—but for what seemed like the first time in this investigation, my timing was good. He headed right toward me.

"How you doing?" The delivery man gave me a look that said he thought it was pretty weird to find me standing by myself there at Tommy's grave. He probably would have thought it was weirder if he realized that when he walked up, he stepped between Gus and me. "You the one that sends these flowers?"

"I was hoping you could tell me who does."

He shrugged and bent to remove the wilted bunch. "All I do is bring 'em," he said. "Every week. Take the old ones away. Bring the new ones."

I glanced over at the van. There was no name written on the side of it. "Who do you work for?"

"Something wrong with the flowers?"

"No, there's nothing wrong with the flowers. They're beautiful. Maybe I'd like to send some."

"Waste of money, if you ask me." The delivery man dropped the bunch of carnations down on the stone. "I've been doing this for what feels like forever. Must cost somebody a frickin' fortune."

"And who did you say you worked for?"

"Sully's." He poked a thumb over his shoulder, though as far as I knew there was no florist anywhere nearby. "You know, down by the freeway."

"And do you suppose somebody there knows who sends the flowers?"

He shrugged. It wasn't so much an I-don't-know gesture as it was an I-don't-care one.

I didn't pursue it. What was the point?

I waited until the delivery man was back in the van and had driven away, then started toward my car.

"Come on," I told Gus. "Time for a road trip."

* * *

The manager of the flower shop wasn't as helpful as I hoped. Oh, he tried. He was chatty and charming in a gay sort of way and would have loved (or so he claimed) to give me the information I was looking for.

But he'd only bought the business eighteen months earlier, and according to his records, the money that paid for Tommy's flowers was left in a lump sum with the previous owner a couple years before that. It was a lot of money, he did share that little fact with me, enough to keep Tommy in fresh flowers for years to come. He also admitted that he was pretty smart. Rather than keep the money squirreled away as the previous owner had done, he'd put it in an interest-bearing account and was making a good chunk of change off it. The whole thing was completely on the up-and-up, he assured me. He sent the flowers every week. He deducted the amount from the total for each sale. As far as he was concerned, what happened to the rest of the money was completely up to him.

As for that previous owner...well, it turned out that he was a resident of Garden View, too. Whatever he once might have been able to tell me about the person who ordered the flowers, he no longer could.

By the time I got back to the cemetery, I was tired and discouraged. It was after five and even though the front gate was open and would be until sunset, I'd come at Garden View from the other side. Rather than negotiate the maze of city streets that surrounded the cemetery, I took the easy way and drove in through the staff gate.

It was the way Dan said he'd come in the night I told him to get lost, and in spite of the fact that I knew I was over and done with both him and his stupid study, I couldn't help thinking about the whole thing.

Maybe my brain had been too busy processing everything I'd learned about Tommy Two Toes and Anthony and Carmella with her flamingoes and her yellow flip-flops.

I'd never bothered to question anything Dan had said that night.

Now, a thought struck out of the blue, and I jammed on my brakes.

"How do you suppose he knew?" I didn't even realize I was talking out loud until I glanced toward Gus and saw that he was looking at me like I was crazy. I filled him in on my thought process. Such as it was.

"Dan the Brain Man. The other night. He said he knew I was here at the cemetery because he saw my car parked over near the office. But Dan's never seen me except at the hospital or when we've met somewhere. How do you suppose he knows what kind of car I drive?"

"Son of a bitch has been following you. I never did trust those shaggy-hair types."

It seemed out of synch with Dan's character. Maybe that's why the thought made me think of stalkers. And serial killers.

Automatically, I checked my rearview mirror and when I did, I breathed a little easier. There was no one around.

I told myself to get a grip, let up on the brakes, and continued toward the office. I'd been on that particular road a dozen times since I'd started my job at Garden View, but it was the first I'd realized that it took me right past Tommy's grave.

I don't know what possessed me. I got out for one more look.

In the late afternoon light, the bouquet of white carnations gleamed against the gray granite. The way the delivery man had dropped them, Tommy's name was covered.

Call me a softie. It just didn't seem right. Tommy the orphan who'd opened his mouth once too often and paid the ultimate price. The thought of his name being hidden much like his life was seemed like adding insult to injury.

I picked up the flowers and moved them to the side of the stone.

It was the first I realized there was a symbol carved in the granite just below Tommy's name. I hadn't seen it earlier because of the iris and tulip bouquet.

I bent to brush away some grass clippings that were scattered over the carving.

"It's a broken ring." I wish I could have said what significance the symbol had but let's face it, I hadn't exactly devoted a whole lot of time to my newsletter article. But I did know one thing: I'd seen the symbol listed on the Web site I'd consulted for my research. "And look, there are letters underneath it." I knelt and brushed away more grass. The carving of the ring was no more than four inches high and beneath it were letters that were even smaller. "D.V.M." I read the letters out loud and looked over my shoulder at Gus. "Mean anything to you?"

"Nah." He shook his head. "And that there broken ring...It ain't nothing I've seen before."

I hadn't seen it before, either, or if I had, I hadn't paid any attention. I squeezed my eyes shut. I could picture the Web page where I found much of my information and the listing of symbols, nice and neat and alphabetical. "A broken column is a sign of decay and mortality," I said, proud of myself for remembering even that much. "A broken ring..." Something flared inside my brain and I hopped to my feet, grinning.

"The ring stands for a family circle," I said. "It's broken because one of the members has been lost." I wrinkled my nose. "I thought you said Tommy was an orphan."

"I'm sure of it. I told you. An orphan. Or a foster kid or something."

"But, Gus..." I looked from the carnations to the carving. I wondered about the letters D.V.M. and what they might tell us not only about Tommy but about the people or person who missed him.

"Gus, somebody really cared about this kid. They still do."

Okay, so it might have been a little obvious, but I thought it was a pretty brilliant deduction. I actually might have had a chance to feel smug about it except that at that very moment, a bullet whizzed by my head.

Chapter 16

"Get down!"

I didn't need Gus's warning. And I didn't need to freeze up like a strawberry daiquiri when he jumped forward and tried to push me out of the way. I dropped like a rock, flat on my face.

"See anything?" It would have been easier to talk if I didn't have a mouth full of grass clippings. I turned my head to spit them out and waited for Gus to answer. No nose to the ground for him. He was invisible and didn't have a thing to worry about. From the corner of my eye, I saw the tips of his shoes.

"Son of a bitch." I heard him grumble before he moved a few steps in the other direction. "Wherever he is, I can't see him. Come on. You gotta make a run for it."

"Run?" How was I supposed to do that when my knees were rubbery and my heart was pounding so hard, I expected it to smash out of my chest? "I can't run."

"You can't stay here. A shooter never tries only

once. Not a professional. Believe me, I know these things."

He did, and I didn't doubt him for one second.

Which didn't make my legs any better able to support me.

Gummy legs or not, though, I knew I had no choice. I swallowed down my terror, took a deep breath, and pushed myself up on my elbows. "I can't." I collapsed again just as quickly, my voice clogged with tears and grass clippings, my arms crossed over my head.

"You've got to." Suddenly, Gus was down on the grass with me, looking right into my eyes. "If you stay here, you're gonna end up dead like me."

"But—"

"Ain't no buts. Not about this. You're a sitting duck. Come on, kid. You gotta run. You got no other choice."

Technically I did. I could lie there whimpering and the next time the shooter took aim, maybe he'd find his mark. It was a frightening thought, sure, but it was only a little less frightening than thinking about running while he was taking potshots at me and I was wondering when and where the next bullet would hit.

I squeezed my eyes shut, my brain cycling through all the things I could have/should have/would have done if only I'd known that I was destined to die too young.

I could have called my mom over the weekend like I'd been planning before I got wrapped up in my investigation and convinced myself I'd do it another time.

I should have written to my dad like I'd been saying I was going to do ever since he was sent to the Big House.

I would have called Joel Panhorst. If I knew I was going to buy the farm that day, honest, I would have picked up the phone and called the creep. Not that I was feeling emotional when it came to Joel. Heaven forbid! But it sure would have been gratifying to let him know that sometime—somehow—between then and the day he walked out on me because he was worried about what his country club friends would say when he married a girl whose father was in the federal pen, I'd realized that getting rid of him was the best thing that ever happened to me.

After all, how pathetic would it have been to have PEPPER PANHORST on my tombstone?

"You're not going to let them find you here like they found me bleeding in the street." Gus's voice reverberated like thunder, breaking into my morbid thoughts. "You're not giving up."

Maybe if he had added that last bit like it was a question, I would have decided that yes, giving up was exactly what I was thinking about doing.

But Gus didn't ask. He took it for granted. Like he took everything for granted.

The fact that what he took for granted was that I had a smidgen of courage in me somehow made the situation seem a little less hopeless. I raised my head and chanced another look around. As far as I could tell, the shot came from the section of the

cemetery directly across from us and my car was
between us and there. If I made a run for the Mustang, I'd not only be a chump but a way-too-easy
target. About ten feet to my right was a giant sycamore and right about then, it was looking like my
best bet for cover. Beyond that was one of the few
standing monuments there in the new section. If I
could make it to the sycamore and from the sycamore to the monument...

Well, hell, I didn't know what I'd do if I got that
far. I only knew that it was better than dying there
on top of Tommy Two Toes.

My mind made up—even if I wasn't sure my legs
would support me—I hopped to my feet and ran. I
was almost behind the broad trunk of the sycamore when another bullet smacked right into it.

"Shit." I braced my back against the tree. "He's
a good shot."

"And he's being careful, too. I don't see him
anywhere." His eyes narrowed, Gus stood in the
open and scanned the area. "He's probably in those
bushes over there." He pointed but I didn't dare
look. "What are you going to do?"

I was hoping maybe he'd have a suggestion. Bar-
ring that, I guess what I was going to do was run.
Instead of discussing it and definitely before I could
stop and think about the consequences, I did just
that.

I got all the way over to the standing monument
without another shot being fired.

Still, I knew I wasn't out of the woods. Especially
when Gus pointed again.

"There! I saw something move over there. He's following you and you can be sure that he's got you in his sights."

"That makes me feel a whole bunch better." I peeked around the corner of the monument, looking for another spot where I could hunker down. The only one I could see right off the bat was a tall, skinny headstone closer to the road. Between me and it was nothing but...well, nothing but nothing.

"This isn't going to work," I told Gus at the same time I pushed off from my hiding place and took off like a bat out of hell.

I had seen enough old *MacGyver* episodes to know not to travel in a straight line. I swerved left and feinted right. I dodged and darted and when another bullet zoomed by an inch from my ear, I bent over to make myself a smaller target and ran as fast as a bent-over person can. When I got to the shelter of the monument, Gus was already waiting for me.

His face was twisted with anger. His cheeks were dusky. "There are two of them," he said. "And one of them is Albert."

Didn't it figure?

I fought to catch my breath and wished that when I got into my car back at Sully's Flowers, I hadn't slipped my cell phone out of my pocket and left it next to me on the front seat. I pressed a hand to my heart and felt it beating with the rhythm of a high school marching band drum line.

"Can you see them?" I asked Gus.

"That Albert, he's graceful like a moving van. He's tromping through the shrubbery over there. He's carrying a .357 and I'd bet a dime to a donut he couldn't hit the side of a barn with it. Not from this distance. He's muscle, not a shooter. No, it's the other one you need to worry about. Light-haired guy wearing sunglasses."

It didn't sound like anyone I'd run into in the course of my investigation, but just the fact that Albert was involved told me one thing. "Rudy's got to be behind this."

"No way." Gus shook his head. "Not his style."

"What? Killing isn't part of the family business anymore?"

I could tell Gus was itching to aim a sneer in my direction. Instead, he kept his eye on Albert and his friend. "We wouldn't kill women."

"Ella will be thrilled to know that her sixties-sisterhood-equal-rights bullshit worked."

"You call this progress?" Gus ducked behind the monument with me. "Look, kid, this next bit is going to be a little tricky. You've got maybe thirty feet. Across to the road, then over to the next section. There's a couple statues over there. Angels, I think."

I thought so, too. They were part of my angel tour.

"Once you're there, you're home free. There are a few mausoleums. A couple big monuments. How close are we to the office?"

Not close enough.

I refused to think about it.

"There might still be somebody over in the chapel," I said instead, because even though I knew it was unlikely that one of our minimum-wage part-time employees would stay around that late, it seemed like a better plan than thinking about how I was surrounded by three hundred acres of nothing but dead people. "If it's still open, I can get inside and lock the door behind me."

"Good." Gus stepped back, but just as I was about to sidestep my way around him, he hesitated. "Look…" He straightened his tie. "I want you to know that I'd run interference for you if—"

"Yeah. I know. Thanks," I said, and bolted for the nearest angel.

Just as I got there, a bullet smacked into her wing and flakes of marble rained down on my head. I darted behind her but even then, I didn't stop. I ran to the next angel and from there, I ducked behind a tall, oval monument with a carving of a man's face at the center of it. By the time I made it from there to the statue of a woman seated with a book open on her lap, I was feeling invincible. A few more headstones, a couple hundred more feet, and I was home free.

Maybe.

I put my head down and ran. Hell bent for leather as they say in those historical romances my mother loved to read and I loved to mock. I didn't know what it meant but at that moment, I sure understood how it felt. Like my lungs were on fire. Like my heart was going to burst. The calf muscles in my right leg cramped and I staggered but I didn't stop. Not even when a shot rang out when I was near the monument to folks called WILLIS and another plunked into the turf at my feet as I was rounding one side of a pink granite mausoleum and heading to the other side.

Now, the chapel was directly in front of me and I refused to think about anything but making it that far. I raced there and plastered myself behind one of the massive granite columns that flanked the brass front doors.

I was right about the part-timer assigned to the building. He was long gone and the doors were locked. But the building was big and it was surrounded with unusual plants that tourists came from miles around to see. There were plenty of places to hide. There was also a back door that few people knew about. It led directly to a stairway and from there, into the receiving vault, the place they used to store the bodies when the ground was too frozen to dig graves. Always the planner, Ella left an extra key under the mat in front of that door. Just in case anybody ever got locked out. If I could get my hands on that key...

It wasn't much in the hope department but it was all I had, and I hung onto it for dear life.

Literally.

My back against the chapel wall, my eyes scanning the area in front of me for any sign of movement, I slunk around to the other side of the building. I actually might have made it if I hadn't slid around a corner and run right into Albert.

"Hey, bitch, thanks for the exercise." Albert was

breathing hard. So was I. He grinned at me over the barrel of a big, nasty-looking gun. "Worked just like we planned it."

"We—?" There was no sign of the other shooter. That didn't make the grim reality any less grim or less real. Albert and the other guy, they knew I'd run. They knew which direction I'd go. They knew I had no choice but to head for the chapel, and they'd herded me there where my body could be tucked under a bush or behind a bench or rolled down the hill behind us and right into the pond where nobody would find it until the gasses built inside me and I bloated like a blowfish and floated to the surface.

And I fell for it.

I didn't have the time to second-guess my strategy. It was too late for that. It was too late to be mad at myself, too. "This is nuts." Like I had to tell Albert? He knew it. That's why a slow smile brightened his plug-ugly face.

"No cops here this time." He poked his gun toward his right and I knew that he wanted me to step that way. To my left. Toward the hill. Yep, I was headed into the pond.

I held back. "How do you know? How do you know I didn't dial 911?"

"Nice try." He reached into his pocket and pulled out a phone. When he held it up for me to see, I recognized it as mine. "Bet this is the last time you'll leave your phone in the car." Albert laughed. It wasn't a pretty sound. "On second thought, I don't need to bet. This is your last time.

For everything." Again, he waved me toward my left. Like he was positioning me in just the right spot.

I didn't have to think for what. I didn't move. If he wanted the shooter to get a nice, clean shot, he was going to have to pick me up and put me in place.

"The least you can do is tell me what this is all about." Sure, I was stalling. But I was also curious. If I was going to die, it seemed a shame to die without the answers I was looking for. "Who put you up to this?"

"What makes you think anyone did?"

"Come on, Albert. You're not smart enough to do anything on your own. Somebody's giving the orders. Somebody wants me out of the way. Why? What does all this have to do with Tommy Two Toes?"

He didn't answer. But he did look over my shoulder and raise one hand. Like he was giving a signal.

I knew it was coming but, I swear, I didn't have time to react. I heard the clear crack of a rifle shot and all I could do was brace myself for the impact.

After that...

Well, after that, everything that happened happened so fast, I wasn't sure if it was real or if I was already dead and inhabiting some sort of parallel universe designed to tease me with the possibility of all that might have been.

Gus stepped up behind Albert and tapped him on his shoulder and Albert turned, startled. He made a gurgling, choking sound and when he turned back to me, all it took was one look at his face for me to realize the impossible.

Albert saw Gus.

Albert's face was white. His mouth was open. He made a croaking sound from deep in his throat.

And then he did what anybody would have done when faced with a man who was dead and buried.

Albert turned and ran.

The wrong way.

I heard a dull plunk and a spray of liquid jetted out of Albert's chest. Against the evening sky, the color reminded me of wine. Something hot and sticky splattered against my cheeks and my shirt. Albert crumpled at my feet.

Gus urged me to run. "Come on!" He started toward the other side of the chapel.

"But Gus…" I was frozen in place, staring at Albert's body and the spots of red like polka dots on my shirt. "How…?"

Gus waved me around the back of the chapel. "Don't worry about that now. He's not going to wait before he tries again. Come on!"

He was right and I knew it. But I wasn't about to let him waffle when it came to an explanation. As soon as we were safely on the other side of the chapel, I started in on him.

"He saw you, Gus. Albert saw you. How—"

"Don't you get it?" Gus peeked around the corner of the chapel. Apparently, the coast was clear. At least for a moment. "The way I understand it, this is how it works. At least for everyone except you. If a person is close to death, he can see the other side. You know, ghosts and things."

"And that's why—"

"I figured it was worth a try. Worked pretty good, didn't it?"

It had. But it wasn't the end of our problems. Albert might be dead but there was another hit man out there somewhere.

I didn't have to wait long to find out where. Gus didn't hear him coming and I didn't, either. But the next thing I knew, the light-haired man rounded the corner. He didn't come close. He didn't have to. He was carrying a high-powered rifle and, cool and steady, he lifted it to his shoulder and took aim.

I didn't wait around to see any more. I dropped and rolled, allowing the momentum and the weight of my body to take me down the hill toward the pond. My shoulder smacked into a tree root and my flesh ripped. My hair snagged on twigs and branches and got yanked by the roots. My legs tangled, my knees hit the rough edges of stones, my teeth knocked together.

I kept rolling, and landed in the muck right where the pond water lapped against the shore.

Just in time to see the hit man spin to get a bead on me.

As he did, something came flying at him from the other side of the chapel.

At least I think that's what I saw.

I scooped the hair out of my eyes and shook my head, sure that my brain was playing cruel tricks on me.

The *something* was a person. A man, I thought, but it was kind of hard to tell. That's how fast he moved.

It was like a scene straight out of a Jet Li movie. The mystery man knocked the rifle off the hit man's shoulder. At the same time, he did a round-house kick and caught the hit man square in the chest. Mr. Light-Hair-and-Sunglasses staggered but didn't fall. He took a poke at Mr. Mystery, who ducked under his fist, got in a right hook that snapped the hit man's head back and knocked off his sunglasses. He finished the slick moves with an expertly delivered karate chop.

Even from where I lay in the mud, I saw the whites of the hit man's eyes when they rolled back in his head. Right before he passed out.

By now, I was sitting up, my breath tight and painful, my astonishment, I thought, complete.

Except that astonishment turned to amazement and amazement morphed straight to flabbergasted when the mystery man skittered down the hillside and hurried over to me.

It was Dan.

He knelt down in the mud and reached for my arm, searching for a pulse. His hold was firm. His voice was even. "Are you okay?"

Was I?

I guess the fact that I started to laugh proved I

was. Or maybe it just proved that I had finally gone over the edge where I'd been dangling since the day I met Gus. I couldn't stop.

"It's all right." Dan rubbed my back. Just like Quinn had done that day back at my apartment when I ran into the Albert welcoming committee. "You're just a little shocky, that's all. You'll be fine."

I swiped my hands over my cheeks. When I was done, they were wetter and stickier than ever. Mud. Blood. Tears. It was an ugly mix and I didn't even care. I latched on to Dan, sure that when I made the move, he'd disappear in a *poof* that proved this was all just a figment of my warped imagination.

"What are you doing here?" I asked him. I looked over to where the hit man lay beaten and battered. "How—"

"I came to see you. At your office. You weren't there but then I heard the shot. There's no mistaking the sound of an AK-47. I knew somebody was in trouble, I just didn't know it was you."

From a distance, I heard the wail of police sirens. "I called." Dan said it almost apologetically. "I didn't have much of a choice. I knew you'd need some help and I can't..." He hopped to his feet. "I can't stick around. You wait here. They'll find you. They'll take care of everything."

"But Dan..." If I'd thought about it, I would have convinced myself that my legs wouldn't support me. I didn't care. I had to get to Dan before he got away. I struggled to my feet, grabbed his arm, and refused to let go. "You're the Brain Man. How could you...How would you know...How did you do that?"

The light was failing but still, I caught the flash of Dan's grin. "There's a lot you don't know about me," he said. Right before he kissed me quick and disappeared into the evening shadows.

Chapter 17

*"Imagine you getting caught in the crossfire be-*tween two hoodlums!" Ella's voice wavered between out-and-out terror and motherly concern. "Thank goodness the police showed up before anything really serious happened to you. You're so lucky!"

Lucky?

Yeah, I guess I was.

Maybe I was in shock, too. That would explain why I felt like I was floating, like I was watching a scene happening to someone else.

Ella was on call that week for cemetery emergencies and she was already home when she heard from the Garden View security service that something was up and she had to get back as soon as possible. She was dressed in blue jeans, sneakers, and a tie-dyed shirt. It was red and green and blue, and the colors swam in front of my eyes, twirling and swirling into a blur.

When she held out a different shirt to me, I accepted it automatically. We were in my office and for the time being—at least until the cops who were milling around outside and trampling the plants near the chapel showed up to have at me again with a barrage of questions like the ones they'd asked me when they arrived—there was no one else around. I stripped off my shirt and slipped into the T-shirt. It said MONTICELLO JUNIOR HIGH SPRING FIELD DAY on it in big green letters and it was too tight in the chest and too big at the hips.

Still, it sure beat my own shirt. Or at least what was left of it. I hadn't even realized how bad I must have looked until I dropped the shirt on the floor and I saw that it was torn at the neck, muddy in the back, and stained just about everywhere with dark red dots.

Blood.

Albert's blood.

My stomach flipped. My head spun.

"Sit down. Quick." Ella rolled my desk chair up behind me and as soon as it hit the backs of my legs, I collapsed into it.

"Put your head between your knees if you have to." She pushed down on the back of my neck and have to or not, my head went down.

"Breathe deep."

I tried. Not easy considering that I was twisted like a pretzel.

"Relax, and let all that tension melt away. Let it out. Let it go. Be one with a peaceful universe. There you go. Better?"

I fought against the pressure of Ella's hand to sit upright, and when I was finally able to, I gulped in a breath. "Better. Yes. Really." I *was* better once I could breathe. "I just—" My shirt was still on the floor and I chanced another glance at it. My stomach wobbled. My ears buzzed. "I guess I'm just a little overwhelmed."

"I'll bet." Ella dug through the trash can next to my desk. She found the plastic grocery bag I'd used that morning to carry my breakfast to the office and she dug out the empty raspberry yogurt carton and the lifted-from-McDonald's plastic spoon. Gingerly, she picked up my shirt and dropped it inside the bag.

"Evidence," she said. "At least that's what I think the cops will say. They'll probably want to take your shirt to the lab and test it or something. You know, like they do on *CSI*. But that doesn't mean you have to wear it and it doesn't mean you have to look at it. Sorry about the T-shirt." She looked me over and frowned. "One of the girls left it here the last time they stopped after school to see me. It was the only thing I could find for you to wear."

Ella tossed the plastic bag—and the shirt inside—over near the door. She brushed her hands together, dragged my guest chair from the other side of the desk, and sat down, knees-to-knees with me. "You want to talk about it?" she asked.

I didn't. But I knew Ella wouldn't settle for that. Besides, I owed her. For the T-shirt and because she was genuinely worried about me. "Not much to say. It was late and I came in through the side gate. I stopped for a minute at Tommy's—" This wasn't the time to explain that part of the equation.

I didn't know where to start and besides, if I told the truth, Ella would think I was delirious and take me to the ER like she'd already threatened to do.

"I stopped for a minute," I said, picking up the narrative as seamlessly as I could. "That's when the shooting started. I didn't know what was happening." Not entirely a lie. "So I ran."

"Good thing you did. The police lieutenant I talked to said that man, the one who got killed . . . he said that man had ties to organized crime. Imagine!"

I could.

"And the other guy?" I'd been eager to find out what happened to the light-haired man in the sunglasses ever since the cops showed up and brought me over to my office. In true cop form, they weren't talking. This was the first I had a chance to ask. Or at least the first I had a chance to ask someone who might actually answer my questions.

Ella patted my hand. "Don't think about it. It's over. You're right, according to the police, that horrible man was going to shoot you. I'll bet he knew that you saw him kill that other man and he wanted to silence you. Good thing he tripped and fell. He was out cold when the cops found him. They have him in custody and he's not going anywhere. And just in case you're thinking about it, you're not, either. You're coming home with me tonight. No arguments! Even as we speak, the girls are cleaning their room for you to use. Believe me, that in itself is a major accomplishment, and after I talked them into it, there's no way you can say no."

"I appreciate it. Really. But I've got things to do and—"

Relieved to hear me talking about what she assumed was everyday stuff and convinced that it proved that after everything, I was still the same old Pepper, Ella laughed.

"You are too good to be true," she said. "Thinking about work. Even at a time like this."

If only she knew that I wasn't thinking about the work she thought I was thinking about. I was thinking about Tommy Cavolo. I was thinking that I'd better find out how he figured in Gus's murder and why so many years later, somebody didn't want me to find out the truth.

Before that same somebody sent somebody else to try and kill me again.

"I know what you need. A nice, hot cup of tea." Ella popped out of her chair. "You'll be fine by yourself for a minute. I'll be right down the hall in my office getting the tea for you, and the police are outside." She promised she'd be right back and left.

"You okay, kid?"

I figured Gus was around somewhere. Luckily, he'd kept his mouth shut until Ella was gone and the door was closed behind her. I didn't think I could have dealt with the two of them. Not at the same time. Not that night.

I shrugged in answer to his question. The T-shirt tugged over my chest. "I dunno," I told him because at that point, it didn't seem to make any sense not to be honest about the whole thing. "I know I wouldn't be all right if it wasn't for you. And Dan!"

I'd been so busy being dazed and confused, I'd blocked Dan's sudden appearance from my mind. It came back at me like a cold Lake Erie wave, slapping me in the face. I looked at Gus in wonder. "What do you think that was all about?"

"You mean how he kissed you?"

It wasn't what I was talking about it, but once Gus mentioned it...

A flicker of heat sparked inside me.

Not something I wanted to think about with Gus watching me closely.

"I wasn't talking about the kiss," I told him and reminded myself. "I was talking about Dan and the whole Jackie Chan thing. Was that weird or what?"

"Some guys will do anything to impress a woman."

"I don't think that's what it was all about."

"You gonna talk to him about it?"

"Maybe. One of these days."

"And that cop of yours?"

"Quinn is not *my* cop." I didn't add that I was glad he wasn't among the army of cops who had arrived, sirens blaring and lights flashing. He was probably at Pietro's sharing the candlelight and dinner that was supposed to be mine with another one of his conquests. I suppose, after the way we'd said goodbye, it was just as well. The middle of a mob hit was not the right way to say hello again.

I twitched away the thought. My T-shirt strained. "For now, we have more important things to worry about."

"You mean Tommy."

I wheeled my desk chair back into place and hit the space bar on my keyboard. My computer screen flicked on. "What were those letters again?" I asked Gus. "The ones under the carving of the broken ring on Tommy's headstone?"

"D.V.M." He supplied the information and it was a good thing. My brain was fried.

"D.V.M." I repeated them to myself, connected to the Internet, and Googled.

Unfortunately, when Ella's mind was made up, it didn't take her long to get a job done.

My computer was old and slow, and Ella was back in my office, steaming cup of tea in one hand and organic shortbread cookies she claimed would make me feel better in the other, before I had a chance to find out much of anything.

Then the cops showed up to interview me again. Between them, Ella's constant mothering, and the noisy, question-crammed reception I got from her three daughters, I was exhausted. By that point, I was also beyond caring about Tommy Two Toes, DVMs, or anything else except that I was safe and alive and once I had a long, hot shower, there wasn't a trace of Albert's blood anywhere on me.

It was the next morning before I had a chance to try my luck with the Internet another time.

Then again, maybe *luck* wasn't exactly the right word.

"Do you have any idea how many doctors of veterinary medicine there are in the world?" I grumbled the question, not exactly at Gus, who was standing behind me, but at the universe in general. Just for good measure, I made a face at my computer screen and what seemed like the millionth page of vets, veterinary organizations, and magazines devoted to the practice of animal medicine that I'd seen in the last fifteen minutes. "I think we can be pretty sure those letters on Tommy's tombstone don't mean he was a vet."

"He was an animal." It was a lame joke and I didn't acknowledge it. "There's got to be a better way than with that...what do you call it?"

"The Internet." I clicked on Next and another page full of useless information loaded. "DVM stands for doctor of veterinary medicine..." I scrubbed my hands over my face. After a good night's sleep, another shower, and a quick trip home for a fresh change of clothes, I felt better. But apparently, my brain had yet to get the message. "None of it makes any sense," I groaned.

"Maybe that's not all it stands for." Being careful not to make contact, Gus leaned over my shoulder and pointed at the screen. "DVM. What do you call that?"

"Letters?" I rolled my eyes.

"I know they're letters. No, I mean when you use just the letters like that. What do you call that?"

"You mean an abbreviation?" I hated it when he was right. I needed to narrow my search, and Gus knew that without even knowing what an Internet search was. I did just that, adding the word "abbreviation" and making sure I put quotation marks around it. No use wasting my time with more useless junk.

"Again. Vets." I scanned the first page and my shoulders slumped but I refused to give in so quickly. I looked over the rest of the page and found tempting hints that there might be life—or at least information—beyond veterinary medicine.

"Distributed virtual memory. Digital voltmeter." I tried the next page.

"Deo volento. Whatever that means and whatever the hell language it is." I whined but kept reading and scrolled down the page a little farther. "D.V.M. Genealogical terms."

It was the first thing that had made me smile for nearly twenty-four hours. (Well, except for lying in bed and thinking about that kiss from Dan.) I clicked on the page and waited semipatiently for it to load.

When it did, I poked the screen with one finger.

"Paydirt," I said. "DVM. It's Latin and it stands for *decessit vita matris*. That means died while mother was living." I sat back, satisfied. "Told you it was a woman sending those flowers."

* * *

"No Thomas Cavolo."

The woman at City Hall was so sure of herself, she almost had me convinced.

Almost.

"There's got to be." My comment stopped her as she was about to walk away from the counter where she was filling out forms, consulting her computer, and helping folks get copies of birth certificates. "If there's no Thomas, try Tommy. Try—"

"Look..." She glared at me over the rims of her glasses, and I guess I couldn't blame her. We'd been at it for nearly half an hour and the folks in back of me in line were getting impatient. So was the clerk. She drummed her fingers against the countertop, her inch-long nails clicking her frustration. "I tried Thomas. I tried Tommy. I tried the letter T just in case it's Tomaso or some other foreign name that translates into Tommy. It doesn't work. There isn't a Thomas Cavolo. Like I told you before, there isn't even one single Cavolo in the birth certificate system."

"But there's got to be. I know he died. So he had to be born, right?"

"Right." I would have been a little more encouraged that she agreed with me if not for the fact that even as she did, she waved the next person in line forward. "Only it doesn't mean he was born in Cleveland and Cleveland birth certificates are the only ones I have."

"And if he wasn't born here?"

Her glare dissolved into an expression that was more like oh-you-poor-thing-how-stupid-can-you-be. "Could'a been anywhere," she said. "Anywhere in the whole, wide world."

"But he died here. He's buried here. I know he existed. I've seen his grave."

She shrugged. Clearly it was a sign that she was finished with me. "So try the obits."

Sounds easy enough.

And maybe if I was a real private investigator like I was pretending to be, it would have been a piece of cake.

But who knew that the Cleveland Public Library maintained what they called a necrology file? It took me a couple days to find out that was the place I needed to look for what they called "historical" obituaries.

"*Thomas Cavolo.*" I read the name out loud to Gus, who was sitting in my guest chair. I breathed a sigh of relief, pleased that days of research had finally yielded something of value. "*Age 22, died unexpectedly.* That's putting it mildly." I scanned the rest of the obit. "*Beloved son of Lester and Linda Mercer.*" I glanced at Gus uncertainly. "Ever heard of them?" I didn't wait for him to answer and I didn't ask myself what the chances were that they were still around.

I grabbed the phone and the phone book and ten minutes later, I had not only found Lester and Linda, I'd somehow talked myself into a face-to-face meeting with them. By five-thirty that evening, I was standing on their front porch.

The Mercers lived in what I'd charitably call a

modest house in a neighborhood just this side of the Cleveland city limits. There was a twelve-year-old Chevy up on cinder blocks on their front lawn and from what I could see, the postage-stamp-sized backyard offered a panoramic view of a steel mill that had been abandoned years before.

The mill might be gone, but no way could it be forgotten. The stench of chemicals still clung to everything from the boarded-up house next door to the convenience store across the street where I was forced to park in a lot strewn with broken bottles because there were no spots anywhere else.

I shifted from foot to foot and tried the doorbell. I didn't hear a sound from inside the house and I waited a few more minutes. When no one answered, I knocked.

The door opened a crack and a skeleton-thin woman with a long nose stuck her head out just far enough to get a look at me.

"You must be the girl that called." Linda Mercer was no bigger than Carmella, maybe five feet tall. Her hair was a color somewhere between mousy brown and mousier gray. Her eyes were pale, like her skin. Her nose twitched like she was nervous and she refused to meet my eyes. "I got to apologize. When you called, I thought I could help you but...well..." She made a move to close the door.

Now that I was this close, I wasn't about to let the trail go cold. I stuck my foot between the door and the jamb.

"You told me on the phone that you knew who

I was talking about. You said you knew Tommy Cavolo."

Linda licked her lips and threw a quick glance over her shoulder and all I can say is that her instincts must have been better than mine. Then again, she'd probably had years to hone them.

Before I even knew he was anywhere nearby, Lester appeared in the doorway.

He was a big man. Maybe sixty years old and at least a hundred pounds overweight. He was wearing brown polyester pants that sagged over the bulge of his beer gut, and a sleeveless, wife-beater undershirt. He smelled like stale cigarettes and beer. He needed a shave. And a bath.

Something told me that wasn't the reason Linda held her breath when he came up behind her.

"You heard what my wife said." Lester's voice was rusty, like he'd breathed in too much steel mill residue. "Must be some kind of mistake. We don't know who you're talking about. Go away. Or I'm gonna sic the dog on you."

Considering that I could see into the window and right into Mercer's living room and that the dog in question was a rotund Chihuahua who was sound asleep on the couch, I wasn't very worried.

I tried for the reasonable tone of voice that always worked on the old people who took my tours. "I'm sorry to inconvenience you and I promise not to take up too much of your time. I'm just looking for information. About Tommy Cavolo. I'm sure you knew him."

"You're wrong." Lester tugged on his wife's arm.

"But your names are in his obituary."

"Must be a mistake."

"But it said you were his loving parents. Is that a mistake, too?" When her husband gave her another rough tug, Linda backed away from the door and followed him wordlessly.

But not before she glanced at the store across the street.

Chapter 18

It was hard to be inconspicuous in a store where the clerk was inside a booth made of bullet-proof glass and the other patrons were (in no particular order) one teenaged mother with a squealing baby in her arms and another on the way, a homeless guy with Bob Marley hair who was talking to himself while he whisked containers of ramen off the shelf and stuffed them in his pockets, and two young punks who whistled when I walked in, cruised the aisle where I was pretending to look at the canned soup, and told me that I was (in their words) the sweetest piece of ass they'd seen in as long as they could remember.

By the time Linda Mercer showed up with four bucks clutched in one bony hand and a request to the kid behind the glass for a pack of Winstons, I was so relieved, I smiled like she was my long-lost aunt.

She, on the other hand, acted like I wasn't there.

I was teed off and frankly, more than a little disappointed. I thought that telling look back at the house actually meant something. Like Linda and I were sharing a secret. Now, Winstons in one hand, gaze firmly on the pitted linoleum, she walked by me without a word or a glance and right out the back door.

Okay, so it took me a while. But I finally got the message.

Or at least I hoped I did.

I waited what seemed the right amount of time, paid for a can of tomato soup that I promptly handed over to Bob Marley, and followed Linda outside.

I found myself in a back alley and I had to look around twice before I saw Linda. That's how well she blended with the drab surroundings. I might not have seen her at all if I hadn't heard the click, click of a lighter and followed the sound of a long, anxious intake of breath. I saw a stream of smoke rise from between a garbage can and what looked like it used to be a doghouse before it rotted into a pile of soggy wood. There she was, wedged there where no one could see her, darting anxious looks out at the street.

Like maybe she was expecting company.

"We got to be quick." She didn't explain why and I didn't ask. One meeting with Lester was all it took to figure out that he was a no-good bastard. "I wouldn't of even come except..." She took in another lungful of nicotine.

"Except that his obituary says that you were Tommy's loving mother." She didn't have to elaborate. I knew my mention of the obituary back at the house is what finally made her cave and I played the sympathy card again for all it was worth. "Are you the one who sends flowers to Tommy's grave every week?"

Linda laughed. Her teeth were crooked and yellow. "Do I look like I got the money to send flowers?" She shook her head and maybe she was emphasizing her point. Maybe she was just wishing she could have sent those flowers. "Even if I did have the money, Lester, he'd find a way to spend it. On something other than sending flowers to that boy."

"But you did know Tommy?"

I held my breath, partly because I was waiting for her answer. Mostly because she blew out another puff of smoke and I didn't want to take the chance of inhaling any of it.

"Raised him," she said. "And you know what? He was nothing but trouble from the day I brought him home."

"You didn't say 'from the day he was born.' You weren't his biological mother, were you?"

It was the first time she actually looked me in the eye. "Why do you care?"

I knew it was bound to come to that, and on the way over there, I'd come up with a story that was plausible, even if it wasn't true. It was all about my burning interest in genealogy and how Tommy was the final branch on a family tree that was oh-so important to my gray-haired granny.

Funny, looking into Linda's lifeless eyes, I decided nothing short of the truth was good enough for her.

"I need to know how Tommy might have been mixed up in Gus Scarpetti's death," I told her.

She dropped the butt of her cigarette on the ground and stubbed it out with the toe of her worn sneaker. "Tommy died back in the sixties and that Scarpetti fella, I remember seeing him on the news. He died way later. Around the same time Lester was laid off from the paper plant."

"But there was some connection between Tommy and Gus. Something more than the fact that Tommy was a foot soldier in the Scarpetti Family."

"A connection? Yeah, I guess you could say that." She looked me up and down. "If you know what's good for you, you'll be satisfied with that and leave it alone."

"I can't. Besides, it's already too late for that. I've poked my nose in one too many places. Somebody's trying to kill me and the only thing I can figure is that it has something to do with Tommy. If I can find out the truth, maybe I can get these people off my back."

"Think so?" Her lips thinned into an expression that wasn't exactly a smile.

And I wasn't exactly going to back down. Not when I was this close.

I stepped nearer, sensing that Linda might share her story if she felt safe. "I've got to find out. And you're the only one who can tell me. I know that Tommy died before his mother did. If you're not her..."

"He was a foster kid. Even had a different name

from ours. Nobody was ever supposed to know where he came from."

"But you did. And it wasn't from Children's Services or any formal agency like that, was it?"

She aimed a look at the convenience store as if she could see through it to the shabby house across the street. "I had plans for the money we was paid. Thought maybe we'd take a vacation sometime. You know, Florida or Vegas. Like regular folks do. Even thought maybe we'd have a couple kids of our own. But Lester, he said I couldn't make those decisions, me being only a woman. Turned out it didn't much matter. He spent the money before I ever could think what to do with it."

"Then someone paid you to take Tommy?"

Linda's hands were small and nervous. They flittered over her face and through her thinning hair. "You're young and things are different now. You don't know what it was like in the old days. A girl who was single and pregnant...well, it would have been a big scandal if anybody found out. They sent her away. To New York. When he was born, she was supposed to put him up for adoption."

"Only she gave Tommy to you."

Linda propped another cigarette between her lips. It took her six flicks of her lighter to get it fired up. "We met at that home. That's what they called it. A home for unwed mothers. Guess we needed to be locked away where nobody could see us and get embarrassed."

"And your own baby?"

Linda looked at the blacktop. "Died. No sooner than he was born. That's what gave us the idea. She told everybody her baby was adopted and that the whole thing was over and done, but really, I took Tommy. Hell, my own family, they already kicked me out on account of I was pregnant and they said I was a slut. I figured I might as well end up with a baby. I was already with Lester by that time and she asked us to move to Cleveland so she could be close to the baby and visit. She even bought us our house. Believe it or not, back then, this was a real nice neighborhood. Didn't need no bars on the windows then."

It was getting dark and when Linda took another drag on her cigarette, the tip of it flared red. "That boy was hell on wheels." Even so, she smiled. "Nothin' but trouble, but I suppose that was to be expected with where he came from and all. Lester, he never did want nothing to do with him. He would have dumped Tommy in a minute if the money didn't keep coming in. She paid for Tommy's school and his doctor visits. She gave us money for food and clothes."

"And Lester spent that, too, right?"

She didn't answer. She didn't have to.

I stepped closer to Linda without getting too close to the garbage can. "Tommy had a tough life," I said. "Maybe this is your chance to make it up to him. You know, to put an end to the secrets and the lies."

"We promised we'd never say nothin' to nobody about who Tommy was or where he came from."

"Sure. But that was a long time ago," I reminded her. "And it doesn't matter to anyone anymore. Except me. No one will care if you tell me. And Linda, you'll be doing me a huge favor. I'm being followed by the FBI. I'm being shot at by hit men. I need to figure out what's going on and right now, you're the only one who can help."

Linda's scrawny shoulders rose and fell. She took another look out toward the street.

I tried again. "I know you cared about him, Linda. He took the place of your own little boy and you raised him just like you would have raised your own baby. Even though Tommy was a bad boy, I know you wish things could have been different. Otherwise you wouldn't have listed yourself in his obituary as his loving mother. You did that for yourself. To help ease the hurt. And you did it for Tommy. You did it because even though you didn't give birth to him, he was your son and you loved him."

She looked away from me and when a streetlight flickered on at the curb, I saw that her eyes were misty. "Lester, he never reads the paper. He didn't know nothing about that obituary."

I could have kicked myself for mentioning it back at the house. "I'm sorry, I—"

She brushed off my apology. "Don't matter no more. Besides, Lester, he was drunker than a skunk when you came to the door. If he says anything about it, I'll tell him he heard wrong."

I knew that for her, lying to Lester would be a major accomplishment. It might be dangerous, too. "Look, Linda, if you need anything—"

She laughed. At least I thought it was a laugh. It was kind of hard to tell since she coughed and gagged at the same time. When I moved forward to help, she put up one hand to stop me. "Too late to help me," she said. "But I got to tell you, I do appreciate you asking. Nobody has cared about me. Not for a very long time. I suppose…"

Her scraggy shoulders went back and she lifted her chin. "I suppose the least I can do in return is tell you what you want to know."

And with that, Linda leaned closer and whispered a name in my ear.

When I talked to him, he sounded tired and weak. Still, Anthony came through for me. I'd never been a religious person, but I promised myself I'd make a donation to Blessed Rosary soon. It was the least I could do to thank Anthony for his help. I never would have gotten as far as the front door without a call from him on my behalf.

Of course, now that I was there, I wondered if I was doing the right thing. If I was, maybe I could find some hint that would lead me to the answers Gus needed to finally rest in peace.

And if I wasn't?

Well, if I wasn't, I knew word would go around to all the wrong people. And very soon, another hit man would be headed my way.

Like it or not, there was only one way to find out.

I gulped down a breath for courage and knocked on the door.

When it opened, the last person I expected to see was Johnny the Rat Vitale.

"Oh!" Not exactly the coolest opening statement, especially considering that the last time I saw Johnny, I'd been pretending a bravado that I hadn't had a chance to resurrect. "Mr. Vitale. I'm here to see—"

"Yeah. I know. I told Anthony it wasn't a good idea but he wouldn't listen. And me?" He laughed but not like it was funny. More like he was disgusted by his own failings. "Even I'm not tough enough to argue with a priest. That's not the way I was raised." He stepped back to allow me inside a pleasant room painted green and white and accented with touches of pink. "Father Anthony didn't say what you wanted but I'll tell you one thing, it won't do you no good to try and talk to her. She's a little out of it today."

"A little out of it" was a kind way to describe it. The woman I'd been searching for was seated at a table tucked into the sunny bow of a bay window. There was a bird feeder outside and she was staring at the cardinals and chickadees diving in for seed. She didn't blink or move or smile. She didn't look at me or acknowledge me. Not even when I sat down in the chair opposite hers.

What on earth had made me think that this might actually work?

I glanced at Johnny, who was standing in the doorway with his arms crossed over his broad chest and an I-told-you-so look on his craggy face.

And decided I'd be damned if I was going to admit I was beat that early in the game.

I slapped a cheery smile on my face, added the little lilt to my voice that the tourists at the cemetery loved, and slid my chair over so that I was in her line of vision. "Hi, Marie. Remember me? My name is Pepper. I stopped by a few weeks ago to see your nephew, Rudy."

Like the last time I saw her, Gus's sister was impeccably dressed, this time in white slacks and a lacy sweater of the same, icy color. This time just like last time, she wore a string of pearls and this time—just like last time—when she looked my way, her expression was deadpan and her eyes were blank.

"Did he come with you?" she asked. Just like last time.

Only this time, I knew who she was talking about.

A spark of hope flared. I might actually be able to get through to her. I leaned closer. "You mean Tommy."

No sooner did I speak the name than Johnny abandoned his post near the door. He hurried over and stood behind Marie, his hands protectively on her shoulders.

I ignored him. I could afford to. I knew the secret. The magic name that just might unlock Marie's psyche. I used it for all it was worth.

"No, Tommy couldn't come today," I told her. "But I saw the flowers you sent him. The white carnations. And the irises and tulips. They were red and purple. Really beautiful."

"He likes tulips." A tentative smile played around Marie's lips and over her shoulder, she reached for one of Johnny's hands. "He always liked tulips. Just like you did." She turned and smiled up at Johnny. "He was so much like you in so many ways."

It took a second for what she was saying to sink in and when it did, my mouth fell open. I hadn't seen Gus since the night before when Linda told me who Tommy's mother was. I hadn't had a chance to tell him about Marie or to ask him to speculate about who the boy's father might have been. But, knowing that it was Johnny...

My stomach swooped and a ball of emotion clogged my throat. The expression on Johnny's face told me to back off and shut up, but I couldn't. The words were out of me before I could stop them. "Gus had you do the hit. He didn't know he was ordering his nephew's murder. He had no idea he was asking you to kill your own son."

Johnny's eyes sparked lightning. There was another empty chair at the table and he scraped it over next to mine and dropped into it. He leaned too close for comfort and glared at me. "How the hell do you know about that? No one knew about the hit. No one but me and Don Scarpetti." He looked at Marie, who had returned to her own world, her gaze fixed on the table in front of her.

"It was business. And business..." Johnny shrugged.

He suddenly looked old and far more vulnerable than the poker-playing tough guy I'd met back at The Family Place. Call me an opportunist but I knew that at least for the moment, I had the upper hand. I went for the jugular.

"Revenge is a pretty good motive for murder," I said.

Johnny's voice was as steady as the hand he slashed through the air. "I was loyal to the don. More loyal than to my son. More loyal than to anyone. Even her." He didn't have to look at Marie for me to know that's who he was talking about. He passed a hand over his eyes.

"I was married, see. And Marie, she was eighteen and as pretty as any woman I'd ever seen. When she found out she was pregnant...well, her parents reacted like any parents would. They sent her away to have the baby and when she came back, we all pretended like nothing ever happened. Eventually she married and had daughters. Raised them herself, too, when her husband was killed in a traffic accident. And when she came to me years later and told me this punk named Cavolo needed a job...honest to God, I never questioned it. I never thought..."

"But eventually you knew. You knew before you killed Tommy."

"Yeah. I knew. And it didn't make no difference. The don got what the don wanted."

"And then he got what he deserved."

Johnny didn't respond. Did I really expect him to? He might cop to a forty-year-old murder of a nobody like Tommy Two Toes but if I thought he was going to admit to having Gus whacked, I was as loony as Marie.

I looked her way. "Did she know?" I asked. "About Gus. About how he ordered—"

"You leave her out of this!" Johnny moved pretty quick for an old guy. He was on his feet in an instant, glaring down at me, his hands curled into fists at his side. "Don't you ever accuse her of anything. If you do—"

His anger choked him, and it was just as well. I was pretty sure I knew what he was going to say. I didn't need him to spell it out.

I also didn't need to see the writing on the wall. This writing said *Albert* in twelve-foot-high flashing neon letters.

I jumped to my feet, too, and though I was no match for Johnny, I stood toe-to-toe with him. "You're the one who's been after me all this time! You didn't want me to find out about Tommy. You don't give a damn what people say about you, but you didn't want anyone to ever know that Marie was his mother. You've been protecting her all this time. You still are."

He didn't confirm or deny my suspicions. "You shouldn't stick your nose where it doesn't belong," he said. "If you're smart, you won't forget it."

"But why?" Frustrated, I threw my hands in the air, whirled around, and paced to the other side of the room. I came back the other way, my mind working furiously. "What difference does it make if the whole world knows that Marie was Tommy's mother? Tommy's been dead for forty years and in case you haven't noticed, out-of-wedlock babies are a big ho-hum these days. Why do you care that much about Marie's reputation, especially since Marie is too far gone to even know what's happening? Unless—"

As if he was watching the wheels turn inside my head, Johnny stepped toward me just as the truth of the thing hit me like a ton of bricks.

"It was Marie." I looked at the smartly dressed old woman with the porcelain skin and the empty eyes and tried to picture the way she'd looked thirty years earlier. She'd been young and vital then and I knew from looking at her that Johnny's memory was spot-on; she had been beautiful. She was also a woman grieving for the child she'd never had a chance to raise. A mother who had to stand by and watch as her lover took her son's life.

"Marie's the one who ordered Gus's hit."

That'll teach me for thinking out loud.

Johnny came at me, his hands reaching for my throat, curled and ready to squeeze the life out of me.

He would have done it, too.

If Marie didn't stop him. "Johnny, you quit that! Right now." The old woman rose to her feet and pounded the table with one fist. "It's not her fault."

"But she knows!" Johnny spun to face Marie. "She knows and she's gonna—"

"No. She isn't." When Marie looked at me, her eyes were as clear as if a switch had been turned inside her head. She smiled. "That's not why she's doing this, Johnny. She's doing this to give Augustino peace."

Johnny wasn't buying it and frankly, I wasn't, either. How could Marie possibly know about Gus and his search for the eternal happily ever after?

"Don Scarpetti is dead." Johnny's voice was heavy with disbelief. "How can you—"

She reached for him and I guess even hit men with murder in their hearts have a soft spot for the women they love. It wasn't easy for him to turn away from me but Johnny did. He went to stand at Marie's side.

"Someday when you're like me, then you'll understand," she told Johnny. "For now...promise me, Johnny. Promise me you won't hurt this girl. If it wasn't for her..." Her smile was as soft as twilight and when her gaze moved up, somewhere over my right shoulder, I figured we'd lost her again.

Until I looked that way, too, and saw a wisp of white behind me. It looked like a cloud but it got bigger and bigger and the center of it glowed. Like there was a light on inside there somewhere. When Gus stepped out of the cloud, Marie smiled.

"I didn't think I'd ever see you again."

Johnny thought Marie was talking to thin air. But I knew better. I watched Gus walk up to his sister and fold her into a hug.

Why she didn't turn into a popsicle, I couldn't say. I only knew that when Johnny saw Marie's arms go around nothing, he turned to me.

"I told you. I told you not to listen to anything she says. Her mind is gone. She's talking nonsense."

"Shut up, Johnny." I moved closer to the table, and when Gus and Marie sat down, I did, too. I wanted to hear what they were going to say to each other.

"Augustino!" When Marie saw her brother looking well, she smiled. "I can't tell you how many times I've tried to talk to you. You never answered."

"It wasn't time then." Gus didn't look mad and I can only guess that Anthony had something to do with that. Anthony and all the years he'd spent praying on his father's behalf. "I didn't know it was you," he told her. "I never imagined. I suspected LaGanza. I even thought it might be the cops. But my little sister..."

"I gave the order. You should know that. Johnny...." She looked toward her lover, who was watching the scene, slack jawed and confused. Regret, searing and painful, simmered in Marie's eyes. "Johnny tried to talk me out of it. But I wouldn't listen. Tommy was my son, Augustino. My only son. And I was crazy with grief. I wanted you to pay for what you did to him."

Gus shook his head. "I never knew. You should have said—"

"What?" Marie's laugh was high-pitched and sad. "What difference would it have made? Business is business. Isn't that what you always said? Tommy was bad for business. He had to die."

"Just like Benny." I figured I might as well join in the conversation. So what if Johnny thought I was crazy, too? I turned to him.

"You knew Benny had a tendency to run off at the mouth. You were afraid that one of these days, he was going to say too much. He knew about Tommy, and you knew that Tommy would lead me to Marie. You couldn't risk anyone finding out that she was the mastermind behind the hit."

"And the shooter?" Gus asked his sister.

She brushed aside the question. "Some mope from Chicago. I imported him for the job and I paid him well. Even had him use Tommy's old car. You know, like poetic justice. You can't hold it against the man who killed you. But me..." A sigh wracked her fragile body.

"I was angry and hurt, Augustino. I couldn't think straight. Now, I'm a prisoner in this body and all I can do is think. Augustino..." She took Gus's hand. "Forgive me," she said. "Please."

He didn't answer. He didn't have to. When he smiled at his sister, she had the only answer she needed.

And after all those years, Anthony had the answer to his prayers.

Chapter 19

Marie saw Gus and I knew that could mean only one thing: she would be dead soon. But even I didn't think it would be as soon as Gus and I returned to the cemetery.

Gus asked me to drop him off at his mausoleum, and just as we got out of the car, a light as bright as two suns and as white as snow lit the sky to the east of us. I didn't have to ask what it meant. I'd heard about enough near-death experiences to know.

It took me a moment, though, to realize that the light was close. Too close to be hovering over the Scarpetti compound out in the suburbs.

As a matter of fact, it was right over Blessed Rosary church.

I guess I should have been sad and in a way, I was. I hardly knew Anthony Scarpetti, but one thing was for certain, he was a good person. When he walked into that light, he was sure to go a happy man.

I smiled and when I looked at Gus, I realized he was smiling, too. He raised a hand as if he was going to pat me on the shoulder, then decided it wasn't such a good idea. He kept his distance and tipped his head back to let the light shine on his face, and I looked up, too.

"Thanks, kid." His voice sounded like the rustle of a breeze.

"Sure. I—" I turned and Gus was gone.

"Gus?" I looked around, but there was no sign of him. And didn't it just figure that he'd decide to get cute on me now? I stalked over to his mausoleum and pressed my nose to the glass.

"Hey!" I tapped on the door. "Come on, Gus. Don't disappear on me while we're wrapping up the case. I'm feeling pretty proud of myself. I really earned that nine thousand bucks. The least you can do is sit here and listen to me rehash the whole thing, just to prove what a genius I am!"

No answer.

I was annoyed but I also knew that at a time like that, even a don needed his privacy. We'd talk about the case the next day. I started back to the car.

That's when I heard another car glide by out on the street. From the powerful sound of the motor, I knew it was a big car. The windows must have been down and the stereo was cranked.

As clear as day, I heard the music. Sinatra singing "My Way."

And suddenly, I remembered what Gus had said all those weeks ago. About the way he'd head to the Other Side when it was his time.

I froze in place, one foot on a flat headstone, the other on the turf. A tear slipped down my cheek and I admit it, I didn't even try to wipe it away.

Instead, I walked to my car, and when I got there, I turned to Gus's mausoleum one last time.

"Goodbye, Gus," I said, and drove toward the office. Maybe I'd give my mom a call. And if I had time before five o'clock rolled around and I headed home, I figured I'd drop my dad a line.

As much as I hated to admit it, I knew I was going to miss Gus, but by the time I got back to the office, I'd pretty much convinced myself that everything that had happened was for the best. The Scarpetti family (immediate and business) was finally at peace and, hey, so was I.

No more Gus.

No more ghost.

No more investigation.

I have to say, though I hadn't realized how much the whole thing had weighed on me, I was suddenly as light as a feather. I could finally get back to my own life.

I was jazzed. Which explains why I was so taken aback when I opened my office door and found a woman sitting on my desk waiting for me.

She was in her twenties. Pretty in an old-fashioned sort of way. She had short-cropped blond hair (a little darker at the roots) and she was wearing a black top and a pink cardigan with the letter D written on it in rhinestones.

Oh, and one of those poodle skirts.

The kind women wore back in the fifties.

When she saw me, she grinned and waved. She snapped her gum.

"Hiya, honey," she said. "Gus sent me."

Investigate the Hottest New Mysteries!

Sign up for the FREE HarperCollins monthly mystery newsletter,

The Scene of the Crime,

and get to know your favorite authors, win free books, and be the first to learn about the best new mysteries going on sale.

To register, simply go to www.HarperCollins.com, visit our mystery channel page, and at the bottom of the page, enter your email address where it states "Sign up for our mystery newsletter." Then you can tap into monthly Hot Reads, check out our award nominees, sneak a peek at upcoming titles, and discover the best whodunits each and every month.

Get to know the magnificent mystery authors of HarperCollins and sign up today!